DEAD END

C.P. RIDER
ALEX PITONES

VC GROUP, LLC

For Maria Guadalupe Hernandez Pitones, beloved mother-in-law and grandmother

Want to Keep up with Dead End?

To find out how to sign up for new release notifications and bonus content not available anywhere else, follow the link at the back of this book.

1

It was three fifteen in the morning and I was lying in a musty motel bed, sneak-reading the last pages of my book by the light of a burner phone, when the ghost popped into the corner of my vision.

What are you doing here? I mouthed the words so my dad wouldn't hear.

The ghost slouched against the table where Dad and I had eaten dinner and stared at me. Then he looked at the bathroom door. Then me again.

Not only do I see ghosts; I speak to them, too. The fact that this isn't even close to the strangest thing about me goes a long way toward explaining the weirdness that is my life.

I set my book and phone aside, and threw back the covers. *All right. I'm coming.*

The ghost's first name was Aedan. I didn't know his last name. He was around my age, nearly a foot taller than my 5 foot 3, and built like a baseball player—muscular, but slim. Aedan and I were color opposites. I had brown-olive skin, dark brown hair and eyes, and he—was a ghost. So, mostly colorless and a little fuzzy around the edges. Even as a ghost, he was hot. Long hair, nice smile, and eyes that stared into a person's soul.

He grinned at me and my heart did a flip-flop in my chest.

I glanced at the next bed, where Dad and my dog Toby were sprawled out, both snoring. Toby usually slept with me, but he'd abandoned my bed an hour ago when it became clear I wasn't putting down my book anytime soon.

Aedan passed through the closed bathroom door. I followed him into the closet-sized room, after stealing a last glance at Dad to be sure he was asleep. He was.

The bathroom, much like the rest of the motel room, stank of bleach, smoke, and mildew. The windows and walls were yellowed from nicotine, and there were traces of dried blood in the tile grout. Honestly, I was kind of shocked there weren't more ghosts in the room.

"My dad could have seen you," I whispered.

Aedan shrugged.

With another glance at the closed door, I turned the hot water tap on the sink to full blast until the mirror fogged up. Ghosts don't speak, so the only way he could communicate was by writing on a steamy mirror. We spent a lot of time in the bathroom together, although Aedan never approached me in there when I was showering or—anything else. He wasn't a perv.

What's shaking, babe?

I rolled my eyes as he silently laughed at his own stupid joke. "Not funny, ghost boy."

Zero. That's how many people knew that I was born with the ability to make the earth quake—other than my dad—until Aedan. I told myself it was safe to tell him because he was a ghost, but the truth was, I'd have confided in him even if he were a living person. Something about Aedan made me feel like I could trust him.

Ghost MAN. He wrote the words close together with small letters as if trying to squeeze as much as he could on the small mirror.

"Ghost *child*. And you were asking for it."

The old motel mattress creaked with movement from outside the bathroom door, and I shot a quick glance over my shoulder. Dad could just be turning over in his sleep.

Not wanting to take the chance, I turned back to tell Aedan it was time to go. Instead, I locked onto his latest mirror message.

Missed U.

My cheeks warmed, and I combed my fingers through my hair. "I missed you, too, but you can't stay here."

This was the hard part about getting attached to ghosts. Eventually, you had to let them go.

Want 2 stay w/U.

My heart did another little joy-jump. In my seventeen years of life, Aedan was the closest thing to a boyfriend I'd ever had. A spirit that I couldn't see clearly, couldn't touch, definitely couldn't kiss. But he'd listen to me talk, sometimes for hours while Dad was out looking for work, and I'd gotten attached to him.

"I don't want you to go, but there's a whole other world waiting for you. You don't want to get stuck on this plane forever."

Behind the door, Dad's cell phone went off and there were a few more creaks, followed by footsteps and slippers scuffing across the floor and fading out as the outside door opened and closed.

I turned back to find that the mirror had cleared while I was distracted. I ran the tap, fogged it up again.

Don't U like me?

"You know I do."

I like U. A lot.

He reached for me, and if I tried hard, I could almost feel him stroke my hair, my cheek, my lips.

No one sees me like you do. He wrote every word out, even though he had to write small to fit it on the mirror. The extra effort made me think he meant it.

"Because of my ability. There are others who could see you." I gave a sideways glance to the door. I could hear Dad moving around. It was making me nervous. "My dad, for instance."

As if on cue, he knocked on the bathroom door. "Loops, you in there? Hurry up. We gotta move. *Now.*"

Electricity sparked and the sink handle spun, sending hot water shooting out of the faucet. This steamed up not only the area in front of the mirror, but the entire small room.

"What was *that*? Some kind of static electricity? I've never seen a ghost do that before." I stared hard at the black scorch mark on the sink.

You see me. Not ability. You.

You see me. He wasn't being literal; he was saying I understood him. I whispered back, "Yes. You see me, too, don't you?"

Yes.

Aedan took a step closer. His body gave off no heat, but the room got hotter anyway. I felt my heartbeat in my throat, and my fingers went all tingly.

"Aedan?"

With hands that had no substance, he cupped my face. Leaned in and brushed weightless lips over mine. The contact buzzed through me—it felt like my cell phone in my pocket when it rang on vibrate mode. I wanted so badly for him to be alive that my mind was playing cruel tricks on me. Making me feel the sensation of his nonexistent touch. The warmth and pressure of his mouth on mine.

"*Maria Guadalupe Flores Thompson*, get out here." My dad hit the door with his fist and I jumped away from Aedan. "We don't have much time—half hour, tops."

"Coming." I took a step toward the door. Hesitated. "I'm sorry, Aedan, I have to—"

I was talking to myself. My ghost boyfriend was already gone.

WHEN I WALKED out of the bathroom, Dad was shoving clothing, his and mine, into suitcases, a frantic grimace on his handsome face. Lately, he looked older than his thirty-seven years.

"Grab your chewy, Toby. Loops, grab your stuff. Time to go."

My dog wagged his tail, stood at attention. We'd adopted the scruffy terrier from a rescue a year ago, when he was two years old and we weren't changing addresses every six weeks.

Two weeks now, if Dad's current behavior was any indication.

I flopped back on my bed. "It's three thirty in the morning. We never run away from home this early."

"The Thompson family is trying something new. Fleeing at the

4

first blink of sunrise rather than the jowly yawn of midnight." He flashed me his straight-toothed, wrinkle-eyed smile, the one that made all the diner waitresses fill up his coffee cup before he needed it.

It seemed more strained than usual. He was acting the way parents did when things were bad, but they didn't want to let on exactly how bad they were.

I shot up on my bed, my spine straight and stiff. "How close are they?"

"Close." His smile slipped. "We need to put Tucson in our rearview. Now."

"Maybe I can help slow them down. I can use my ability to—"

"*No*." The word came out short and crisp, like a dead branch snapping underfoot. "No," he repeated, as if I didn't hear him the first time.

"It won't be like before. I promise I won't hurt anyone."

He didn't respond, but he didn't have to. Dad had a way of making me feel guilty without saying a thing.

"I didn't mean to do it," I mumbled. "I was trying to create a diversion to help us."

"I know, but this ability of yours." He sighed. "Honey, it's best if you don't use it."

He didn't trust me not to lose control of myself again. Honestly, I couldn't blame him. I didn't even trust myself half the time.

"Please don't look at me like that."

"I'm not blaming you. It's fine. I get it, okay?" I didn't like it, but I got it.

Dad raked his hands through his dark blond hair. "Look, you know I've got a friend or two left on the force back in California, people who don't believe that BS story about us being wanted by the feds. Whenever something odd rolls into town, they give me a call."

He zipped up my suitcase, then his. "Turns out some private science organization brought in one of those heavy trucks with seismic equipment—the kind that measures earthquakes. My source said it was odd enough to warrant a call. Especially since the town hasn't had a real shaker in two years."

Translation: The town hadn't had an earthquake since *I* left.

"You think it's Kilshaw."

5

"Yeah. And if the Kilshaw Agency has access to that kind of equipment in other places and you were to do ... your thing, they might find us even faster." One more rake through the hair, this time capped with a sigh that went on so long I thought he might run out of air. "The evidence would suggest the agency thinks we're back home, but my gut tells me it's a diversion."

Dad's gut was never wrong. If he thought it was a diversion, it was.

I popped off the bed, grabbed my suitcase. "I'm ready. Let's go."

2

"Did the ghost want anything?" Dad rested his wrist on the top of the steering wheel and stared at the open road stretched out in front of us.

"Ghost?"

"The kid who keeps showing up."

"Oh, him." I stared down at my freshly painted nails. A shimmery gray—my next to last bottle of polish. "No, he didn't." *Does a kiss count?*

"Guess he was just hanging out." Dad glanced at me sideways. "Probably wanted some company."

"Yeah, maybe. He seemed lonely." I'd discovered many ghosts were, and Aedan had always looked a little sad to me.

"Tell him he should hitch a ride with us. Maybe he's a rich ghost who could kick in some gas money."

He was joking, of course. Our truck didn't need gas. Dad had filled up when we pulled into town. He always did that it when it got any lower than three-quarters of a tank. After all, we never knew when we were going to have to drive really far, really fast.

"Did you finish your book? I saw you were up late draining the battery on my phone. I need to get you a flashlight."

"Don't bother. I'd probably still use your phone." I scrunched my nose at him when he pretended to pinch me. "Yeah, I finished it. I read the epilogue while I was waiting for you in the truck."

"Another scary one?"

"Not horror this time. Urban fantasy." I held up the paperback with its leather-clad, raven-haired, sword-wielding heroine on the cover. "Funny, scary, with a kick-butt heroine."

"She's like you."

Hardly. The only thing kick-butt about me was my book collection, and most of that was in my room back home. Or maybe it was more accurate to say, in my room *at my old house*, because it wasn't likely we'd be able to return to it. More and more, *home* felt like a luxury Dad and I couldn't afford.

"It's chilly." I shivered and tugged Toby close. His tiny, sausage-shaped body was warm and snuggly.

Dad flipped on the heater.

It was the early morning sort of dark out, the Arizona sky purpled with streaks of gold and violet and pink. I peered through the windshield of our old Ford and tried to recall the last time I'd been up this early.

Swim team. Right before freshman year.

I'd gotten up before dawn to practice my butterfly. It wasn't my best stroke, and it was the last day of tryouts, so I'd decided to jump the pool fence and get some extra practice.

I dove in and swam the length of the pool twenty times, but I could not find my rhythm. My dolphin kick looked more like the lethargic fin flaps of a beached porpoise, and I couldn't seem to coordinate my arms and legs.

This went on for another hour, but I ended up with the same result as when I started. I just could not nail that kick. There's no way I'd make the team without it. I'd be cut for sure.

My frustration mounted. It was stupid—even worse, it was dangerous—but I'd wanted to make the swim team so badly that I ignored the signs that *things were about to go sideways*, as Dad liked to say.

When the ground beneath the pool made a rumbling sound, I ignored it.

When the bottom of the pool erupted in hairline cracks, I ignored it.

But when the pool cratered open, water circling the crack like a cartoon whirlpool, I could not ignore it anymore. I gripped the cement lip and tried to climb out, but it was slippery, the current was strong, and I'd already been swimming for a long time. I was tired.

So tired.

I looked back at the water swirling around the ever-widening crack. Fist-sized chunks of cement bobbed in the frothy surface, then disappeared. A pool hook and my beach towel followed them down, both having shaken loose from the lifeguard chair with the force of the quaking. Now, I couldn't see anything but dark water. It eddied and churned hypnotically, calling to me.

Just let go, it said. *Everything will be all right.*

Who was I kidding? I wasn't ever going back to school. I was way too big a risk around other people. I'd never be a normal kid doing normal kid things. If I got angry, I'd be more than "that weird girl" with her nose stuck in a book, as I'd been called in middle school. I'd be "that dangerous monster" who made fissures and cracks and holes in the earth whenever my emotions got the best of me.

The stupid, lying thoughts were a swarm of angry bees, buzzing and stinging into my brain. I loosened my grip on the edge, distracted by the turbulence of the twisting water, the grinding gnash of the disintegrating pool, and my own treacherous mind.

And then suddenly, I wasn't distracted. In fact, I was utterly focused on the temptation to simply let myself go, let the hole in the pool suck me into the earth, let the pain that my existence caused not only me, but the person I loved most in the world, simply disappear.

"*Maria Guadalupe Flores Thompson, get your ass out of that pool.*" The flat horror in Dad's voice sank into my soul. How had he known I was here? What was he doing here?

"Don't you dare let go." His face was like a ghost's. He'd seen the moment I'd considered letting the water take me away. I was certain of it.

I felt embarrassed and ashamed. Worse than the time he'd accidentally walked in on me going to the bathroom. Worse than when he'd taken me bra shopping. So much worse than when he'd held up a package of tampons at WalMart and yelled, "Are these good for you, Loops? They're on sale."

Dad had gone through so much to keep me safe, and he'd nearly watched me throw it all away in a weak, stupid moment. As I heaved myself out of that pool, I vowed that I would never let him down like that again.

And I hadn't.

Not like that, anyway.

Toby jumped on my lap and yipped, rescuing me from painful memories. Guess he needed the window so he could bark at all the exciting desert nothingness we were speeding past.

I boosted him up and placed his paws on the door. One was white, the other brown. His fur was wiry, about ten different shades of silver, brown, and white, and he had the look of a dog much older than he was.

Distinguished, I said when someone commented on it, not old.

To accent his dignified appearance, Toby wore a different bow tie every day. I made them myself with bits of fabric and elastic, and we kept them in a plastic bag in his doggy backpack. He liked the ties, stood at attention at the foot of the bed every morning waiting for me to put a fresh one on his collar.

"Did you write on your dog blog today?"

"No." I scratched Toby's ears and his tail wagged. "Nothing new to blog about. '*Hey everybody, it's day five thousand-million-billion of fleeing for our lives. Oh, and my mom let me look out the window.*'"

"Lupita."

"It's okay." It wasn't, but what was I supposed to say? It wasn't Dad's fault the Kilshaw Agency was after me. It was my stupid ability's fault.

A minute of awkward silence stretched into two, then three. Dad finally broke it.

"Norfolk."

I smiled. Time for a round of *Guess Toby's Breed*. This was a game we'd played since adopting him and it never got old.

"Cairn terrier," I said.

"Possibly, but I'd like to suggest Doberman as a breed you have yet to consider."

"Noted, although I was thinking more along the lines of Rottweiler. Mixed with Yorkie."

"Norfolk *and* Yorkie," Dad countered.

"*Pfft.* Maybe a smidge of Yorkie, but no Norfolk. Look at this guy. He's so Scottish he should be wearing a kilt. Definitely Cairn."

Dad laughed. "You've got me there."

A little farther down the road, I switched on the truck's radio. I had zero expectations of finding anything worth listening to this far out of the city. After a few moments of heavy static, I could hear what sounded like a news story coming through. I slowly raised the volume, leaning close to the speaker to decipher what was being said.

"*...ten more carcasses found. Law enforcement states that they are doing everything they can to find the perpetrators, human or animal. Zoology experts have been consulted to look into what sort of native Arizonian animal could shear a full-grown cow in half...*"

Dad twisted the station selector knob. "There has to be something else on."

He landed on a country station playing an old Garth Brooks song. *The Dance.* His hand shook a little as it hovered over the radio. My Mexican American mom had loved mariachi music while my Texas-born dad preferred classic rock, but the one music they could always agree on was country. Dad liked George Strait. Mom had bought all Garth's albums—the last one a few days before she died.

He turned up the volume.

I rummaged in my backpack for my iPod cord—the truck was too old to use wireless—but I didn't offer to change the music. Not yet.

I missed her, too.

When the song was over, I smooched Toby's scruffy head. "Where are we going, Dad?"

"A café." He gave me his handsome grin again. There was something wrong with that smile. Something I didn't trust.

Icy fingers stroked the bones of my spine. "Dad?"

"Here." He flipped down his visor and tossed me a white plastic card. It was the size and texture of a credit card, but there were no numbers on it, only a name in raised letters edged in gold.

"The One Way Café?" I handed it back. "Where's that?"

His smile drooped. "If we're lucky, where it was when your mom and I saw it last. Right smack in the middle of nowhere."

"Is that why we came to Arizona? To see this café you and Mom used to go to?"

"No. I hadn't intended... I'd hoped..." He cleared his throat, straightened his shoulders. "Loops, I'm taking you to your grand-fathers."

Before she died, my mom had told me stories about her fathers, Grandpa Hollister and Abuelo Emilio. About how much they had loved her, how sad she had been to leave them, and how she hoped they would be able to meet me someday.

Even though I was excited to finally see them, I couldn't help but be suspicious of the timing. "Why?"

"Thought you wanted to meet them. Aren't you always asking about your grandpas?"

Nice deflection, Dad. How dumb did he think I was? "I thought they lived in Europe or something. Mom said they lived too far for us to visit."

"They live on the other side of the café."

"In *Arizona*? That's only one state away from California *where we've lived since forever*. Why have we waited this long to visit them?"

Dad let out another long sigh. "It's complicated."

3

THE ONE WAY CAFÉ WAS A ROUND-EDGED RECTANGLE OFF THE highway in the middle of nothing. No mountains, no valleys, nothing remotely resembling a town. It was painted with grime and dust, so that what was once a bright red exterior now looked dark and wet, like congealing blood.

"You're being dramatic," Dad said, when I told him. "It's those fantasy books you read."

"*Urban* fantasy, and what does it look like to you?"

The grim look from before returned. "Safety."

That was an odd thing to say and I started to tell him so, but he was already out of the truck, one hand shading his eyes as he stared at the dirty gray ribbon of highway behind us.

Dad never talked about his ability. He once told me that, compared with what my mother and I could do, it was hardly impressive at all. But it had gotten us out of some tough spots, and was the only reason the people from the Kilshaw Agency hadn't caught up with us yet.

"Can you see them?"

"Yes."

"How close are they?"

"Thirty miles. Too close." His voice cracked, and my heart started beating faster.

"Dad?"

"Get your things. Toby's too." He strode onto the highway, ten feet from the back bumper of the truck, hiking boots scuffing against the grainy asphalt. Shaded his eyes again. His special vision worked better on long flat stretches, which was why we'd kept to the desert when we started running. At least, that's what I'd thought before he mentioned my grandfathers. Now I wasn't sure why he'd brought us out this way.

I glanced at the abandoned diner. "Are my grandfathers meeting us here?"

"They don't know you're coming." He jogged to me, grabbed my suitcase. "Honey, they don't actually know…" He looked to the right and jumped a little. "Twenty miles now. Come on."

We picked around loose bushes and yellowed brush and dragged our luggage to the front door. I made a circle on the dusty window with my fingers and peeked inside. Red vinyl stools edged in rusted chrome lined a long counter. Six matching vinyl booths rested beneath six windows, similarly coated with sticky dust. The only thing missing was one of those old-timey jukeboxes.

And people, of course.

"This looks like it would have been a cool place. You know, sixty or seventy years ago. Are you sure this is the right spot? I don't see a sign."

"Loops." Behind me, I heard my suitcase drop. Heard Dad's intake of breath. Heard my panicked heart pounding in my ears.

"I'll come for you as soon as I can."

I spun around. Dad held Toby under one arm, and reached for me with the other. Hugged me tight. So tight I couldn't breathe. Then he kissed the top of my head, whispered, "I love you, Loops," and opened the door of the abandoned café. He gently set Toby on the cracked and filthy linoleum floor.

"He doesn't like to get his paws dirty." There were tears running down my cheeks, but I couldn't figure out why. It was as if my eyes knew something the rest of me didn't.

"Scoot, Toby." Dad tossed my suitcase and backpack through the door, slung Toby's backpack on top of it. Toby wagged his tail and barked at his belongings, probably reminding me to change his tie.

"Make sure you hold onto him," Dad said.

"But where's your luggage?"

"I ... I can't go with you guys."

Black spots danced in front of my eyes. "I don't understand. What's happening?"

"It's all right. Just go inside, honey. Shut the door."

"Come with us."

He shook his head. "I meant what I said. I can't. I'll follow when I can, but, for now, this is the safest place in the world—safest place for you."

"So ... what? You're just going to leave Toby and me in this abandoned café in the middle of nowhere?"

"Your mother wanted you here."

"What are you talking about? Mom is gone. And now you're leaving, too." Tears poured down my face, and now I knew why. "You say you're coming back, but you really aren't, are you?"

Red splashed across his cheeks like an instant sunburn and tears welled in his eyes. "I will do everything in my power to get to you, but I don't know if I can. Someday you'll understand. I hope."

"No. No, I won't understand." An explosion of desperate panic burst inside me. I crossed my arms over my chest and hugged myself ... as miles below the earth something rumbled. It came up through the soles of my sneakers and rattled my bones.

Dad planted his feet and held out his arms as if to brace himself. "Don't lose control, Maria Guadalupe." He only called me by my given name when he was dead serious. "Relax, honey. Breathe. Just breathe."

Relax? He was abandoning me in the middle of nowhere and he wanted me to *relax*?

Dad peered at the highway. "They're close. You have to go inside now."

"No." The rumbling beneath me continued to build until the truck swayed back and forth and the framework of the old café creaked.

"Loops." He swung around, his gaze settling on my expression. He froze. Sweat broke out on his forehead and upper lip. It looked like golden beads on his white skin in the brilliant morning sunlight.

"You can't just leave me here."

He opened his mouth, closed it. Cursed and kicked a rock so hard it skipped through the dried grass and onto the buttery smooth sand, sending concentric circles rippling as if it were the still surface of a lake.

"Please, don't go, Dad. *Please.*"

"I have no choice. Not anymore."

"Why?" Tears clogged my throat. "Why would you abandon me?"

"Because *I'm not strong enough to protect you!*"

I fell back a step. "Dad?"

"It was selfish. *I* was selfish." He fisted his hands at his sides. "I kept you too long. Before she died, your mom told me to take you to your grandpas right away so it wouldn't be so hard, but I couldn't let you go. I'd just lost my wife. I couldn't lose my little girl, too."

He sniffed, his eyes clouding with moisture. "It's late, but I have to do this for her now. For you." His voice came out in a croak. "*Please.* Please go inside. It's the last thing I want to do, but it's the only way to keep you safe."

I stared into the darkened interior of the abandoned café. The sun streaked in through the open doorway revealing dust motes like snowflakes, floating on the hot desert breeze. I shivered.

"Once you're inside, lock the door. I'm going to lead them away from here."

Toby plopped down on his furry behind, gave me his panting, tongue-lolling grin. I dragged myself up the crumbling steps. Looked back at my dad as he climbed inside his truck, my throat so tight I could hardly swallow.

"Don't forget to hold onto Toby and *lock the door.* Tell me you'll do it. *Say it,*" he yelled to me through the open passenger window.

"I-I'll lock the door."

"Hold Toby tight. Keep a hand on your things and they'll go with you."

Go with me? Where was I going? He was the one leaving, not me. So many questions rocketed through my head. I didn't ask them. I didn't say anything. Just stared at him. It was as if all the air had been let out of me.

"I love you, Loops. More than you could ever imagine."

With a last look down the road behind us, he ducked his head back inside his truck and drove away.

4

HE WAS GONE.

The old truck left nothing but a cloud of exhaust behind as it faded into a pinpoint dot on the horizon.

"Dad," I whispered, so hurt I could hardly form the word. Still, I did as he said and yanked open the door, joining my dog inside the dusty old café.

The grimy tile floor cracked, and fissures ran up the dirty plaster walls, rattling the stacks of old food crates, tables, chairs, and demolished booths. The ground shook hard enough to bring me to my knees, but it was a few minutes too late. Dad had already taken care of that.

Toby whined and rubbed his furry body against me. I wanted to reassure him, but I was fresh out of everything-is-going-to-be-all-rights, so instead, I pressed myself to the back panel of a dirty booth and drew him close against me.

A piece of the ceiling smashed to the floor a few feet away. Toby barked. I didn't flinch. This was my rage; this was my despair. This was the monster in me.

I was the monster.

Toby threw his head back and howled. That meant trouble. He had an almost preternatural way of knowing when the Kilshaw Agency was close. Between Dad's super vision and my dog's early warning system, we'd been able to stay ahead of them—until now.

A black SUV screeched to a halt outside the café, kicking dust into tall plumes of dry tan smoke. The passenger door flew open and I hunkered down, hugged Toby to me, and whispered, "Shh," and prayed he'd listen for once.

He whined, but stopped his howling, even after I released him. I was reaching out to lock the door, when I heard a voice, muffled through the thick door glass. "No way. I'm sure this is it. This is the café."

I drew my hand back and tried to hide, but there was nowhere to go. Debris blocked every exit but the one in front of me.

"Fine, I'll take a look." A guy in black sunglasses strode through the billowing dust clouds and headed straight for me. He appeared to be eighteen or nineteen, twenty at the most, and his slim, muscular body was covered from neck to boots in a tight black jumpsuit. His skin was two shades darker than mine, the deep brown of an October leaf, and his silver hair was pulled into a ponytail.

He propped his shades up onto his head, his pale gaze sliding over the abandoned café from one end to the other, then zeroing in on the center. On the grimy front door.

On me.

I edged closer to the door, to the lock.

He held up a hand. "Don't. Not yet."

The ground jerked, sending Mr. Sunglasses stumbling to the right. I hadn't meant to do it, but I wasn't sorry.

"Nice one." He grinned.

"I don't like this, Toby." My dog whined. He didn't like it, either.

Another black SUV skidded into the dirt in front of the café. Kilshaw's agents were piling out of both vehicles before it had even stopped—some older, most young, one female who looked younger than me. All were dressed alike.

The group stomped through the dead grass around the abandoned diner, kicking up loose rocks and dirt. One of them gestured to me with her smart phone and said something to the silver ponytail guy.

While they were busy, I reached for the lock, tried to twist it. It wouldn't budge.

"Yeah, I see her." Silver ponytail jogged up and dropped to his haunches in front of the door, only the filthy glass separating us.

He was good-looking from far away. Up close, he was insanely hot. High cheekbones, wide-set jaw, long black eyelashes surrounding sparkling silver eyes. I wondered if he wore mascara, but I thought it was probably natural because his eyebrows were also dark, not silver like the rest of his hair.

And I could not shake the feeling that I'd seen him before.

"Hey, you don't have to be afraid. We won't hurt you."

I gave him a look that told him exactly how much I believed *that*, and tried the lock again.

"Smart." He laughed.

Behind him, the woman with the phone spoke into it. "Yes sir, it's definitely her. We felt the tremors ten miles away. She's holed up with her dog in some dilapidated café." Pause. "Not a problem. Thompson is long gone. Yes sir, it does seem out of character. We'll be cautious, sir. Sterling is talking her into…" Her voice faded as she walked away.

"Why did your dad leave?" He leaned against the glass. "Wait. Do you have a café card, Maria Guadalupe? Is that why you're here?"

I stared at him with my lips pressed together.

He glanced over his shoulder at the others, who were watching but didn't seem inclined to come closer. "They think you're dangerous, you know."

"They're right." I meant it. I would not go down easily—I had a dog to protect and a life I planned to keep living.

The ground simmered in a series of low, steady quakes.

"Maria Guadalupe. Lupita. Loops."

"Maria is fine," I snapped, not wanting to hear Dad's nickname for me from my enemy's mouth.

"Maria." He tipped his head to one side, offered me a killer white smile that made my frightened heart thump even harder than it already was. I'd seen that smile before…

"Who *are* you?" I asked.

"A friend." He held up both hands, palms facing me. "I get it. Why would you believe me?" His smile fell and, for a second, his eyes looked intensely sad. "Believe it or not, I'm trying to help you."

One of the older uniformed men—he looked around Dad's age—glanced at his heavy black watch. "Quit ogling the girl and pull her out of there. If we leave now, we can still track down the dad. Two-for-one deal. Kilshaw will probably double our bonuses."

The silver-haired guy replied to his friend without turning around. "Don't hold your breath, Montez."

The man sighed. "Come on, Aedan. Let's wrap this up and go home."

Aedan?

The face shape was a little off, the features sharper, and there was a lot more color to him, but this was my ghost boyfriend, all right. Now that I could see it, I couldn't unsee it.

Bile burned at the back of my throat.

"Maria…"

"*Liar.*" A ripping sound, like that of close thunder, tore the air, and a fissure opened in the earth under the tires of the first SUV. The nose of the car sank into the crevice, lifting the back tires off the ground.

His head whipped around to the SUV, then back to me. "Damn. This is not how I wanted you to find out."

"*Ass.*"

"Maria, come on." Aedan stared at me through the glass. "It's not what you think."

"Really?" My voice came out edged in heat. "Because I think you were astral projecting yourself into my life—in disguise—pretending to be a ghost to keep tabs on me for your evil boss."

He scrunched up his nose. "Wow. Well, yeah, okay, that was pretty close. How do you know about astral projection, anyway?"

"I read a lot of fantasy. And enough fiction that I recognize it when I hear it. Usually." My breath was coming out in short, harsh puffs of air. "I can't believe you told them where I was. Oh my God, you have no idea what you've done."

"It's not… I tried…" He jerked his hands through his hair. "Maria, I had to give them something. Look, can we discuss this later?"

"*Later?*" The earth rumbled and a crack appeared in the dirt under

Aedan's feet. He hopped up the concrete steps and fell against the door to avoid sinking into the opening.

"Whoa." His eyes went wide. "Impressive. Like that kiss this morning."

I wanted to choke him.

However, I was smarter than that, so instead, I smiled sweetly and cracked open the door a little, motioning him closer. "That *was* a nice kiss."

"*Maria*." Aedan scooted so close, my lips nearly grazed his ear. His skin was warm and smelled like soap and desert heat. "Please believe I'd never hurt you."

"I do, Aedan." I tilted my head closer to his. "You know, there are benefits to being corporeal." I said the last in a low, silky tone I hadn't realized I possessed. I had no clue where it had come from. It's not as if I'd ever talked to a guy this way. Or any guy in any way, really. Except for Aedan, when I thought he was a ghost.

The smile he gave me was movie star quality, wide and pearly. "What benefits do you mean?"

"For one thing, it's much easier to do *this*." I balled my fist and punched Aedan square in the mouth the way Dad had taught me. His head whipped back, and he toppled on his butt on the step.

"Ouch, jeez. You punch like Rocky." Blood oozed down his chin from his cut lip. "That hurt."

"Now you know how I feel."

"Maria, I really do like you. That wasn't a lie."

I shoved the door shut and fumbled with the lock again. Toby whined as the other Kilshaw agent, the one Aedan called Montez, approached.

"You've had enough time, Sterling. Unless you'd like to get popped in the mouth again?"

Aedan glared at the other man.

"We need to take her down before she does any more damage. *Move*." Montez pulled an over-sized gun out of his pocket. It was unlike any weapon I'd ever seen outside of a cartoon.

Aedan scowled. "Back off, Montez."

"Look around you." The other agents had gathered around a hole the second SUV's back tires had sunk into. "The ground is unstable. She has to be stopped." He raised the gun, pointed it at me. My heart jumped around in my chest like a hyperactive dog.

"I hate you, Aedan Sterling." As last words go, not very original, but I meant every syllable.

"Don't hate me. Please. *Montez, put that thing away.*"

"All that stuff I told you about my life, my mom, my ability…" My chest tightened until it hurt. The ground trembled again. "You used it against me."

In the distance, the agents back-peddled away from the SUV as it sank lower in the sand. The diner windows rattled, and the floor cracked some more.

Aedan shook his head. "No, I didn't."

"Everything you told me about your mom dying, that was a lie to gain my trust so you could lead them to me."

"What I told you was true." His bloodied mouth flattened into an annoyed scowl. "I've never told anyone about my mom."

"Shut your lying mouth, Aedan, if that *is* your real name."

"It is. I—"

"*Move*, Sterling," Montez yelled.

The ground was shaking so hard I was having trouble staying on my knees. I desperately wished I had better control of my ability. I wished I had *some* control. I'd have made the earth swallow Aedan and the rest of them whole.

"Maria, listen to me." Aedan's expression went from annoyed to worried to desperate.

"No." I pulled Toby close, shielding him with my arms as best I could.

"He's going to do it. He's going to shoot. Montez takes his orders from the top, and if he thinks I'm compromised, he'll shoot me, too. Plus, he's always been kind of a dick." Aedan tapped the glass by the door handle. "Maria, *lock the door*. Do it *now*."

"I've been trying! It won't—"

"I'm not screwing around here. He's going to shoot. *Lock the door*."

I scrabbled for the rusted deadbolt above the keyhole. Stupid thing still wouldn't turn. I stood, put all my weight on it, twisted it so hard I thought my thumb was going to break off.

"Hurry," Aedan whispered.

Montez called out, "She's trying to barricade herself inside to prepare for another attack. Everyone here has seen what she's capable of. I don't have to warn you. *Positions*."

He pulled the trigger on the cartoon gun. The force that flew out of it hit the windows like a bomb blast—or at least, what I thought a bomb blast would feel like. Strong, heated power. I went down to my knees again, but kept my fingers on the lock.

"What is that?"

"Sound wave. Disorienting as hell, but not deadly unless he cranks it up to high. Keep trying." Aedan whispered this to me, then shouted at Montez. "*Cut the shit.* You almost blasted half my ass off."

"If you don't want it blasted all the way off, get it out of the way." The gun went off again, this time to the right of me. Every window in the old café fractured.

"*Montez*," Aedan yelled, but the other man wasn't paying attention. He was too busy issuing orders to the uniformed people behind him.

"All right now, move in."

"Cover your face, Maria. Now."

I did and Aedan punched through the spiderwebbed glass in the window. He stuck a bloodied fist and part of his arm through the hole he'd made, and grabbed hold of my hand. Silver threads of electricity shot out of his hand and the lock finally began to move beneath my fingers.

"What was *that*?" It felt like walking across new carpet and touching something metal—times ten. "You did it before when you were a ghost—when you astral-projected into my motel room, I mean."

"My ability."

"You never told me you had one."

"I know."

"Jerk." I yanked my hand out of his and went back to working at the lock.

"This isn't necessary," Aedan said to the other agents. "She's not going anywhere."

"No, but if we don't stop her, she'll kill us all with that ability of hers," one of the agents commented. "We know what she's capable of. Most of us were there the day she destroyed that highway."

My hands shook and my eyes filled with tears. I hadn't meant to hurt anyone.

"Don't listen to him. He doesn't know you," Aedan whispered. "You'd never hurt an innocent person on purpose. Hold onto your things, to Toby. If you don't, he'll be left behind."

"What are you talking—"

"No time. Just do it."

I reached for my things and tucked them under me, then I gripped Toby's collar with the hand not uselessly working at the lock, trying to protect him while at the same time anticipating the death I knew was hurtling toward us. My chest tightened. My head felt disconnected from my body. My fingers were numb.

"You can do this. Try *harder*," Aedan said through gritted teeth.

I stared at his handsome face, even more handsome in person, and hated him because he'd meant the world to me and ended up being yet another disappointment. "Go to hell."

Montez leveled the gun. Stared straight into my eyes.

Aedan sighed. He stood and faced Montez, fingertips sparking. "Be safe, Maria."

I pinched my eyes shut, gave the lock one last hard twist, and braced myself for impact.

5

A CHOIR OF ANGELS, NO, WAIT—*ELVIS PRESLEY*—WAS SINGING MY NAME. Was this Heaven? Instead of Saint Peter, had God hired Elvis to do roll call?

The singing got louder. Clearer. I realized he wasn't singing my name, but the name of his latest "flame." An old song.

I opened my eyes. The café was gone—well, not *gone*, but I was no longer stuck in that dusty abandoned death trap. This café was pristine. Cleaner than any restaurant I'd ever seen. Even the old-fashioned jukebox glistened like brand new.

Where was I? Was I dead? If so, at least Toby was with me and not with the Kilshaw group. But then, if he was with me, that meant he was dead, too.

"I'm so sorry, Toby." I hugged my little dog, sniffled into his fur. "I wasn't much of a rescue dog parent. I saved you only to get us both put to sleep."

A friendly voice interrupted my sad conversation. "*Put to sleep?*"

I gave Toby a smooch on the head—an affection he returned with a swipe of his tongue on my cheek—and glanced up at the owner of the voice.

The man had sunburned white skin, graying brown hair, and a pink bulbous nose that took up half of his face. He pulled on the knees of his overalls as he bent forward to peer down at me from his seat at the counter. A trucker hat with a pest control logo stitched across the front lay on the chrome edged, red vinyl stool beside him.

"Put to sleep. Killed," I clarified.

"Goodness. You aren't dead, miss. You're as alive as I am. Unless we're all dead and this is a hallucination playing out in our brains as the last sparks of life energy fizzle out." He tapped his index finger on his chin. "That's always a possibility, I reckon, but not likely. Here, now, I'd better get Laverne to help before I get you all confused." He cupped thick, age-stiffened hands around his mouth and projected his voice without yelling. "Hey, Laverne? Looks like you got a couple new customers."

I tried to stand but went straight back down on my butt, nearly landing on Toby.

"Give it a second, kiddo. Takes a minute for your body to catch up with your mind." He broke off a piece of the bacon on his plate and offered it to my dog, who gobbled it down. "Name's Bert. Laverne's in the back. She'll be right out. Who are you?"

"Loop—Maria. My name is Maria."

Bert slapped his knee. "Like the Elvis song I just played. Isn't that a coincidence?"

Not particularly, since Elvis was singing about Marie, not Maria, but I nodded because the man seemed nice and also because I had other things to worry about.

"You look like you might be staying for a spell." He nodded toward Toby's and my bags. "You got people here in Dead End?" He set the trucker hat on top of his head, gently, the way Dad did when he didn't want a line in his hair.

"Dead End?"

"Yep. You're in Dead End now. End of the world, it is. At least, this one. Or maybe it's the beginning." He scratched his ear, dislodging his hat. "I sometimes lose track. Do you have any people, then?"

No. I didn't have anyone. My mom was dead, and my own father had just abandoned me.

Then I remembered.

It was worth a shot. What else were Toby and I going to do?

"I think my grandpas live here."

LAVERNE TURNED out to be a large woman in a vintage-style red server uniform with a black and white checked apron and thick-soled black shoes. When describing her as large, I didn't mean she was over-weight. Only enormously tall, at least six and a half feet, and as thick and solid as the trunk of a sequoia tree.

After Bert called her for the third time, she had emerged from the kitchen, tying a fresh apron around her waist. Her smile was kind, her brown eyes long lashed and pretty, her brown skin unwrinkled, even though she appeared to be at the latter end of middle age.

"Heaven's sake, Bert, quit your hollering. I was in the freezer and you know I couldn't hear a banshee scream when I'm in there. Next time, haul your carcass off that stool and come fetch me."

"Sorry, Laverne." Bert looked sheepish. "This here's Maria and her friend, Toby. Showed up about a minute or so ago. Says she's got kin here."

Laverne shut one eye and peered down at me. "Kin, huh?"

I nodded. "My grandpas. At least, I think they live here."

"Names?"

"Emilio and Hollister McCain-Flores." I knew that much. Mom had told me about her dads. She'd loved them very much.

"They do," Laverne said.

"You know, Maria here reminds me a little of your niece. The one who works the night shift," Bert said.

I was still sprawled on top of my stuff, on the floor, disoriented. I'd looked behind me, trying to find the door I'd come through, but it was gone. Patrons entered this café from a side door.

"You do look like my Lucinda. Bit younger." Laverne seized me by the back of my shirt and tossed me into a red vinyl booth. It wasn't a mean sort of toss; it had the feel of a little-too-rough hug. My dog hopped on the seat across from me, tongue lolling at the server as she extracted a pad of paper and a pencil nub from her pocket.

"Welcome to the One Way Café. Name's Laverne. What can I get

28

you?" She directed her question to Toby. That was strange, but maybe not as strange as allowing a dog in the café in the first place. Most places would have kicked us out by now.

Toby barked.

"Sorry, fresh out. Bacon okay?"

Another bark.

Was she *communicating* with him? Okay, yeah, this was definitely stranger than allowing a dog inside a café.

"Good choice." Laverne looked at me. "And you?"

I blinked. Stared up at her with my mouth open. "Did… Did you just have a conversation with my dog?"

"Yes." Laverne cocked an eyebrow. "Why? You the jealous type?"

What the heck? "No, it's not that, I just—"

"Good. Now what can I bring you, Miss…"

"Maria. Just … Maria." I gave up trying to understand things and fell against my seat. "We can't order anything. Toby and I don't have any money."

"You have a café card?"

The white card. I patted my pockets. Then I remembered I gave it back to Dad. "I don't think so."

"Couldn't have gotten here without it. Check your luggage."

I found the card in the front pocket of Toby's backpack. Dad must have stuck it in there.

I extended it to her. She peered at it but didn't take it from me. "You've got plenty of money on this card."

Money? Was it an ATM card? And how could she tell from looking at it? "I do?"

"Yep. What are you hungry for?"

"Um, orange juice? Toast?"

She narrowed her eyes. "I'll bring you eggs, bacon, pancakes. Some of my special blend tea, too. It'll help you make the adjustment to Sanctum. You can get real discombobulated blasting through dimensional doorways if you aren't used to it."

"Sanctum? Dimensional doorways?"

"It's all right. Sit quietly and let the truth of your altered existence wash over you. It'll all be set right in no time. You were meant to be here."

"I was?"

"Well, if you weren't, you wouldn't be, would you?" She tore off the ticket and tucked the pencil and pad back into her pocket. I was left with the feeling that there was more to Laverne than met the eye.

While she went to put in our order, I surveyed our surroundings. It freaked me out how the place looked exactly the way the abandoned café had, only clean, new, and inhabited. And minus the front door.

There weren't many customers in the place. Only Bert and another older man at the counter, two twenty-something women chatting in a corner booth, and a guy in a black sweatshirt hoodie in the booth next to mine. He was lying face down on his hands, the hood of his sweatshirt pulled up to cover his face, a cup of untouched coffee on the table in front of him.

Bert stood, adjusted his overall straps and his cap. "Nice to meet you both, Toby and Maria. I'm sure I'll see you around. Dead End isn't a big town—not this part of it, anyway. The basement at City Hall is another matter." He smiled and I just nodded, because the things he and Laverne said made zero sense to me, and I didn't think I was emotionally ready to hear him explain further.

As Bert passed the booth of the man with his head down, he reached out and patted him on the shoulder. "You come see me if you need anything."

The man nodded without lifting his head, and Bert sighed and walked out.

Laverne brought breakfast a couple minutes later. She served Toby's in a blue ceramic dog bowl with the words "The Boss" scrawled across it, and served me a blue ceramic plate with enough food on it to feed a large, hungry family.

"Wow, thank you, but I can't eat all this."

"Believe me, you'll eat it. Soon as the time shift hits you, you'll be as hungry as a chimera in spring. Then you'll want to hibernate like one." She looked at her wristwatch. It had a white leather band, and the face was shaped like a daisy. "Should hit you right about … now. I'll be back in a bit to refill your tea."

My stomach dropped into my shoes. Not because I was scared, but because I was freaking *starving*. In fact, I'd never been so hungry in my entire life and that was saying something, because I once ate a half gallon of rocky road ice cream and still had room for a hamburger and fries.

I shoveled the pancakes into my mouth, chewing, slurping down orange juice, chomping eggs and bacon, guzzling tea—and I didn't even like tea all that much—until the only things left on my plate were a drop of maple syrup and my licked-clean fork.

"Oh my gosh, I ate it all." I let out a silent burp. "I'm a pig."

"It'll go away after a couple of days. The hunger. It's just your body's way of replacing the calories you burned on the trip over. The fatigue is harder to shake." The soft male voice came from the next booth over. The head-down-hoodie-man. Except his head was up now and he wasn't a man at all. He was just a big teenager. A handsome big teenager with wide strong shoulders, dark brown skin, and a flat half-frown on his face.

"Hi," I said. "I'm Maria and this is Toby." My dog jumped up and peered over the back of the booth seat.

"Samuel. Where did you come from? On the other side, I mean."

"An abandoned café a couple of hours west of Tucson, Arizona."

"Did you see anyone else at the café? A woman?"

"There was no one there when I arrived. A bunch of bad people showed up after." One especially bad person with silver hair who had better pray I never see him in the flesh or astral form again.

"Oh." Samuel stood.

Holy crap he was tall—as tall as Laverne, at least. He had the kind of muscles you get when you spend a lot of time in the gym working with heavy weights. The guy looked like the teenage version of The Rock.

I'd have talked to him more, but I was pretty sure I was going to be busy now that I was smack in the middle of a nervous breakdown. Because, as I'd determined between bites of pancakes, if Bert was right and Toby and I weren't dead, that had to be what was happening. I'd been captured by the Kilshaw Agency and they'd drugged me, and this was all a hallucination.

Dad was right. I read too much urban fantasy, and it was starting to show.

Because there were no such things as dimensional doorways and cafés that went from condemned to pristine at the twist of a lock. Waitresses in cafés did not take orders from dogs, and they certainly did not serve them at the table, though they really should—at least the polite ones, like my Toby.

Samuel tossed a white card on the table. It looked like the one I had. The plastic rectangle lit up like a Christmas ornament, then went dark again. He shoved it into his jeans pocket. "Thanks for the coffee, Laverne. See you tomorrow."

Without a glance back, he walked out.

"No you don't, Samuel Bekker." Laverne burst out of the kitchen clutching a paper bag and hustled out the door after him. I watched through the glass as she handed him the sack and hugged him. He took the bag and the hug with a nod and a smile, then ducked his head down and jogged to the road.

I wondered why the café patrons seemed so worried about Samuel. I wondered why he'd left without even a polite goodbye to Toby and me. But most of all, I wondered how long it would be before the meds wore off and I was face-to-face with the monsters at the Kilshaw Agency.

That had me wondering. How long had my delusion been going on? Was Aedan real or was he part of my delusion?

I didn't know how I felt about that. On the one hand, I'd like to know I hadn't been hallucinating this entire time. On the other hand, if he was real, he was a giant liar, and I hated his stupid guts.

"Weird stuff going on, Toby."

My dog barked back at me, but I didn't speak dog, so I had no idea what he said. I giggled a little. *Speak dog.*

I finished my second glass of tea. It tasted real.

Laverne reentered the café, two men in their late sixties on her heels. One was tall and slim, with thick silver hair, dark olive skin, and what looked to be a permanent scowl etched into his face. The other was short, with pale white skin, graying auburn hair, and a wide happy grin that dimmed slightly when it landed on me.

The shorter one reached behind him for the taller one's hand, and they both stared at me as if I were a monkey on display at the zoo.

Finally, the short man approached my booth, cleared his throat. "You must be Maria."

In a blinding flash of clarity, I saw the truth.

I hadn't been drugged. I really was in another dimension, in a café that transcended space—and perhaps even time—in a town called Dead End.

And I was staring straight at my grandfathers.

6

AFTER BEING INTRODUCED TO MY OWN GRANDFATHERS BY LAVERNE, I paid for breakfast with the white card, gathered Toby and our stuff, and followed the men out of the café.

We all piled into their car and drove out of the gravel lot onto a dirt road with potholes like ditches, and then onto a smoother, unpaved road.

"You're Maria's child?" Abuelo Emilio, the more serious of the two, asked. He was seated in front on the passenger side with a neatly folded newspaper in his hand. The name of the paper, *Track's End Tribune*, was showing, as was a headline about a flash rainstorm that washed out Mare Road.

"Yes."

"Where is your mother?" He shuddered the words out like he didn't really want to hear the answer, but had forced himself to ask.

"She died." I swallowed. It still hurt to think about it, even after ten years. "Car accident. When I was seven years old."

Both grandfathers slumped in their seats. It was a full minute before anyone spoke again.

"We were afraid that might be the case," Grandpa Holli said, his voice soft and sad as he reached for Abuelo Emilio's hand. He'd told me what to call him when we were introduced, said "grandfather" was too formal and that everyone in town called him Holli instead of Hollister, so I might as well do so, too.

He was also the one who had told me what I should call my other grandfather. I was learning that Abuelo Emilio was a man of few words.

"I miss her very much," I said.

Abuelo Emilio nodded in response. He crushed the newspaper in his free hand.

"How old are you, Maria?" Grandpa Holli asked after an awkward pause.

"Seventeen. I'll be eighteen in a couple months."

"Are you still in school?"

"Yes. I should be, anyway. I haven't gone since middle school."

"You don't go to school?" Grandpa Holli peered at me through the rearview mirror. "Isn't it the law there?"

"Well, yes," I said, thinking that was an odd way to put it. The law *there*. He made it sound like I was from another planet. "I was on something called independent studies. I did my schoolwork alone on a computer."

"Oh. I hope you don't need a computer here. We have one, but it only works during an electrical storm, though we might get Mr. Planke to take a look at it, perhaps see if he can engineer it to function on moon phases instead of storms. Still, we'll have to send you to the high school. I don't believe there's an independent study program in Dead End. Or anywhere in Sanctum, really."

"I don't know how long I'll be here." I was reeling from the idea of life without a computer. Without the Internet. Without *social media*? "My dad's coming back for me."

My grandfathers looked at each other. "I'm sure he is," Grandpa Holli said, "but perhaps we should consider getting you in school anyway. That way, when he gets here, he won't have to rush back if he doesn't want to."

Abuelo Emilio frowned hard at Grandpa Holli. The look was the same one that had been on my mother's face the time I freed a family of lizards inside our house. Grandpa Holli nodded at Abuelo Emilio as if reassuring him.

35

"Umm, okay." That was probably a good plan. Dad and I might have to hide out in Dead End, or Sanctum, or whatever this place was called, to get away from the Kilshaw Agency. Might as well make the best of it.

Plus, I kind of did want to go to school, to at least experience it before my senior year was over. Maybe I could just try it out for a while.

I patted Toby, who was sitting like a tiny gentleman on the seat beside me. "Is Toby going to be a problem?"

"Why? Does he need to go to school, too?" Grandpa Holli asked.

Toby glanced at me and tilted his head as if to ask, "Do I?"

I scratched his furry chin. "No. I meant a problem for you. Some people don't like dogs."

"Is that so? I can't say I'd care to meet any of those people." Grandpa Holli shook his head. "To answer your question, Toby seems like a very nice canine. I'm sure we'll get along fine."

"Our Maria always had a dog." Abuelo Emilio dropped his newspaper on the floorboard and stared out the passenger side window. He and Grandpa Holli still held tightly to each other's hands.

We pulled off the smooth dirt road and onto a smoother paved one. Here, the landscape was no longer desert brush and pale flat sand. There were buildings and people and other cars. Old cars. Old-fashioned buildings. Like something out of this classic TV show Dad liked to watch where people whistled a lot because they were happy and went fishing to catch dinner and everyone greeted you with a smile.

The cars were familiar, but different, in strange and unusual ways. An old-fashioned buggy with gleaming white tires rolled past us with an enormous television antenna on the roof. A vehicle that was a cross between Dad's truck and a Mini Cooper puttered past, its small bed filled with a strange liquid that sloshed over the sides and hit the street in splashes of orange. A car the size of a little kid's ride-on toy zipped past us with what were either very young children or very small adults inside.

The people were different, too. Some were human, but others were … not. What I estimated to be a man coasted down the sidewalk in front of a grocery store on an enormous curled fin, like a mermaid. His skin was blue, and he had green hair that hung down to his waist. Another person floated over the sidewalk—a delicate woman with pale pink skin, blonde pigtails, and the pastel-shaded wings of a butterfly sticking out of the back of her dress.

I pressed my nose to the window, tried to see it all. "What is this place?"

Grandpa Holli glanced up at me in the rearview mirror again. "This is Dead End, of course."

"Is that guy from another planet?"

"Who?" Grandpa Holli peered out the side window at the merman. "Dr. Pacifico?"

"His name is Dr. Pacifico?"

"Dr. Phineas Pacifico. As far as I know, he was born in Sanctum City. That's the largest city in Sanctum. He transferred here after graduating from dental school."

"He's a *dentist*? I thought he might be an alien."

"Periodontist, actually. The only one in Dead End. We aren't a very big town, dear." The look he gave me through the mirror was tinged with pity. "I wouldn't worry about the alien thing. Dead End is quite cosmopolitan. I'm sure no one will care where you come from."

It took me a moment to realize he considered *me* an alien.

We turned onto a street lined with neat little houses. Grandpa Holli parked the car—an older model that looked new and almost, but not quite, like a Chevy—on a cement driveway in front of one of them.

My grandfathers' house was small, single story, and painted a minty shade of green. A white picket fence surrounded the yard, and a white porch railing wrapped around the house. It was the sort of place where you imagined a mom in an apron would bring you a plate of warm chocolate chip cookies and a glass of fresh-squeezed lemonade while you were doing your homework.

Looking at it made me miss my mom, but in a good way. For once I wasn't thinking about her death, but how lucky I'd been to get to eat her chocolate chip cookies. Mom's cookies were the best. None of the ones I'd eaten since compared.

We filed into the house, through the living room, and down a short hall. There were two bedrooms here, one on either end. Grandpa Holli led me to the one at the front of the house.

"It's not suited to a young lady," he said. "We use it as a guest room for when company comes over, which isn't often, so you're welcome to it. We can get some more, well, feminine things in here for you. Perhaps a dog bed."

I shook my head. I didn't want him to feel like he had to do anything special. I wasn't staying long, after all. Dad was coming back for me.

"It's very nice the way it is. Toby can sleep on a folded blanket at the foot of the bed." I searched for something else to say. "Um, thank you—for letting us stay here."

"You're our granddaughter and granddog. Where else would you stay?" His forehead wrinkled. He seemed truly perplexed.

"You didn't have to take Toby and me in at all. You don't even know us."

Grandpa Holli wandered out of the room, only to appear a minute later with a small dish of water that he set on the hardwood floor by the door.

"Please sit down." He perched on the bed and patted the bedspread.

Toby and I sat on either side of him.

"You must understand, Maria, that any reticence on our parts today has nothing to do with our happiness in meeting you. This has all been something of a shock to your abuelo and me. To know that you exist and that our daughter Maria ... no longer does."

He smiled kindly. "You see, your mother has been gone for ten years, but our child has only been dead for a few minutes." His green eyes clouded with tears. "It's difficult for us to face."

I plucked at the bedspread. "When you heard a Maria was here, you assumed it was her." God, they must have been so disappointed.

"Yes." He cleared his throat. "Try to be patient with Abuelo Emilio. He loved Maria very much. He needs to mourn her." Something told me that also went for Grandpa Holli, though he hadn't included himself.

"I understand." I really did. I mourned her every day.

"Now then. I'll bet you'd love to take a nap. Interdimensional travel is a real pain in the backside. Wears you out like nobody's business." He gave me an around-the-shoulder hug and patted Toby on the head.

"We passed the bathroom on the way in if you care to freshen up. If you're bored, there's a television in the living room and the moon is waxing with 79% illumination tonight, so we should be able to watch. I'll fix lunch in a couple of hours, but if you're hungry before that, there's fruit on the counter and drinks in the refrigerator."

He hugged me again and stood. "You're welcome here, Maria. This is your home just as it would have been your mother's, had she been the one to twist the lock at the One Way Café. I'm glad you're here."

With another pat for Toby, who had curled into a ball in the center of the bed in preparation for his usual after-breakfast nap, Grandpa Holli walked out of the room, closing the door behind him.

I reached for my backpack, unzipped the front pocket and pulled out a pile of urban fantasy paperbacks. Tucked into an Anne Bishop book was a photo of Toby, Dad, and me. I stacked the books by the lamp on my nightstand and propped the picture against them.

"Don't worry, Dad. I'll find a way to get back to you. I promise."

7

————

I'D NEVER SLEPT SO MUCH IN MY ENTIRE LIFE.

The second my head hit the pillow, I fell into a coma-like slumber. My dreams were scary and vivid, and that jerk Aedan Sterling factored heavily in several. I wasn't much for memorizing faces, but I had his engraved in my brain, along with the last words he'd said to me: *Be safe, Maria.*

It was still light out when I awoke. Groggy, I patted around until I found the bedpost, using it to hoist myself into a seated position. Someone, I was guessing Grandpa Holli, had left my slippers on the rug beside the bed. I shoved my feet into them, stood—and promptly dropped to the floor like a cartoon anvil.

"Ouch." With my cheek smushed against the floor, I had a clear view under the bed. Not a single speck of dust. There was something seriously wrong with my grandpas. What sort of people didn't have a dust bunny or two under the bed?

I blinked a few times, wiped the drool from my mouth. Looked around for my dog. "Toby?"

"Did you sleep well?" Grandpa Holli asked from the doorway. I wondered how much of my graceful fall he'd seen.

I ran my hand through my hair, which was a nest of frizz and knots, the way it sometimes got when I didn't braid it before bed. But I was sure I'd braided it before going to sleep.

"Yes, thank you. How long was I asleep?"

He glanced at his wristwatch. "Oh, I believe it's been at least fifty-two hours. Not too long. It's probably because you're still young and can adapt faster."

"Fifty-two hours? That's not *long*?"

"Well, no." Grandpa Holli smiled. "Most first-timers sleep for a full week after interdimensional travel. It puts a lot of stress on the body."

"Oh. That makes sense, I guess. I mean, I've never traveled interdimensionally before. I didn't know there even was another dimension besides my own. I thought you and Abuelo Emilio lived in Europe."

"What's Europe?"

"Um, it's a continent on my, uh, planet."

"Only kidding, Maria." He chuckled. "I know what Europe is. Sanctum is not on another planet. It's on Earth … just in another dimension of it."

"Both you and Laverne from the café mentioned Sanctum. I thought we were in Dead End."

"We are. Dead End is in Sanctum in the same way that France is in Europe."

"Sanctum is the name of this continent?"

He tipped his head to the side, squinted. "Eh, close enough. Would you like me to help you up?"

"I've got it." I tried to push myself to my feet, but my legs still weren't having it. Grandpa Holli caught me before I fell again and sat with me on the bed. "Thanks."

"Anytime, dear. Are you hungry? I was just about to fix dinner." He gave me a smile that crinkled the corners of his eyes and made me want to return it. In that moment, he reminded me of Dad so much it made my chest hurt.

Was he safe? Was he hiding in some trashy motel or was he on the road, trying to outrun the Kilshaw Agency? I needed to get him here before they got to him. The sooner the better.

"Maria? Are you okay, dear?"

Blinking away my tears, I faked a smile. "I should probably get ready." I stood, holding the bedpost for support. "Have you seen Toby?"

"He's gone on a walk with your abuelo. Third one today. Earlier he and Abuelo Emilio stopped by the café. That pup of yours has really taken to Laverne."

"She gives him bacon." Abuelo Emilio was keeping an eye on Toby? Well, at least he seemed to like one of us. "Wait, why wasn't Toby sleeping? He wasn't tired from the trip, too?"

"Animals recover more quickly than humanoid life forms." Grandpa Holli stood as I tried not to think too hard about his casual usage of the term *humanoid*. "I should get started on dinner. Do you have any requests? I was thinking either lasagna or fried chicken."

"Lasagna sounds good." Actually, anything sounded good. I was starving.

"I was hoping you'd say that. It'll give me a chance to open a jar of your abuelo's homemade spaghetti sauce. Feel free to use the bathroom to freshen up." A hint if ever I heard one. I surreptitiously sniffed myself and gagged.

"There are some toiletries in the medicine cabinet. We can get more if you need them. I understand young ladies need certain items."

Oh. My. God. No. I so wasn't ready to think in that direction with him.

"Thanks, Grandpa Holli."

"You're welcome, sweetheart. Things aren't the same here as they are in your part of the world, but we usually have an alternative. We get supplies in from the urban and farming areas fortnightly, so let me know if you have requests."

Unconsciously, I reached for my phone to search for "fortnightly" then realized it was dead and would likely continue to be so for the foreseeable future. Even if I could power it up, it wasn't as if I could access the Internet here.

Racking my brain for the meaning of the term, I thought back to social studies class—or was it history? A Harry Potter story? Anyway, I remembered that a fortnight meant two weeks. People in England used the term. So Dead End must get shipments every two weeks.

"Your bathroom things are over there." He pointed to the top of a polished oak dresser. "Hope you don't mind, but I unpacked your clothes, too."

I wasn't sure how I felt about being unpacked in this strange new world. It felt a little like I was admitting that I'd never get back home to Dad.

Grandpa left to start dinner and I tottered over to the dresser. Pulled open the top drawer and stared at the folded and organized contents. It had been a long time since I'd been able to put my clothes in an actual dresser. They were usually crammed in my suitcase because Dad and I never stayed in one place for long. We could never let our guards down. The Kilshaw Agency was always close. Hunting us.

We were never free.

The rumbling began beneath my feet and reverberated up into the walls. Shocked at my loss of control, I chanted the words Dad always used to focus me at times like these.

"Don't lose control, Maria Guadalupe."

I focused on slowing my breathing in an effort to regain control. The trembling wasn't strong, but it would be noticed if it continued, and the breathing didn't seem to be helping.

"Relax, Loops. Breathe. Just breathe."

A short yip sounded in the doorway as Toby trotted into the room and over to me, his ears and tail at attention.

"You're back." Relief flooded me as I knelt beside him.

Toby's fuzzy tail wagged and he jumped up—his way of asking to be held. He rested his head on my shoulder and let out a dog sigh. The warmth of his little body relaxed me, and the trembling faded just as quickly as it had begun.

"You'll have to be careful with that." Abuelo Emilio's voice was low and gravelly. "Magic is stronger here."

"Magic?" I tightened my hold on Toby. "What do you mean?"

Abuelo Emilio knew what I was, what I could do. I wondered if Grandpa Holli knew, too. If so, neither one seemed bothered by it.

"I mean magic. Or science, God, whatever your people call it. The force that powers your ability. However strong you were in the Other —" He said the word as if it were the name of the place where I was

43

from. "—you can double or triple that here. Maybe more. Hard to say without experimentation. That's *not* permission to experiment."

When I frowned in confusion, he said, "Think of the moon's gravity. Up there you might bounce around like a rubber ball in a room full of right angles, but on Earth, you weigh more, so ... no bounce. Sanctum is the moon and the Other is Earth in this analogy."

"Oh, I get that part. What I'm hung up on is you thinking magic, God, and science are the same thing."

For a long time he said nothing, simply stared at me the way I'd stare at someone who'd just told me she believed the earth was flat.

"*Dios*, I will never understand my daughter's fascination with that world." He whistled for Toby. "Go wash up, Maria. Dinner is almost ready, and we have a city council meeting at seven."

"Meeting? I don't have to go, do I?"

8

"THE DEAD END CITY COUNCIL MEETING IS CALLED TO ORDER." THE man banging the gavel was very tall. Not in the way that basketball players are tall, but in the way telephone poles are tall.

"How does the mayor fit in the building?" I whispered to Grandpa Holli after I'd gotten past the eye-bugging, jaw-dropping shock. We were seated in the townspeople section of the largest meeting room in City Hall, according to my grandpa. Abuelo Emilio was in a high-backed swivel chair behind a raised curved podium with the other council members.

"Look under the desk, at his chair."

"Where is his chair? I only see more torso."

"Exactly. You must have noticed that the exterior of the building is smaller than the interior would suggest," he whispered as the city reports were approved and seconded by the council. "Smaller than even this single room would suggest. And with three fewer floors."

I nodded.

"That's because the three lower floors are in another dimension. We conduct all official business in this room, but the other floors are used for non-official events, storage, and transdimensional apartments." He leaned back in his chair and folded his hands in his lap.

"Grandpa Holli?"

"Yes, dear?"

"It seems as if you think you answered my question, but I'm still confused."

"Oh, sorry dear, I forget you're not from here. Mayor Docket is able to fit in the building because, one, half of his person exists in another dimension, and two, because the part of him that serves as Dead End mayor is comprised of more than fifty percent of his total person. Anything less and he wouldn't be considered a resident." He sat back in his chair again and grinned at Abuelo, receiving a small smile in return.

Nope, still confused. However, I decided to drop it, because I didn't think more information was going to make things clearer.

"There are eight seats, but only six people are here," I said.

"Yes. One member only votes by proxy and the other member is absent."

Of the members present, I recognized Bert, the man I'd met at the One Way Café and Laverne, though she wasn't entirely present.

"Laverne?" I whispered to Grandpa Holli.

"Astral hologram, of course. Laverne is unable to leave the café property."

"Astral hologram. Of course." I patted my lap and Toby leapt from the floor onto it. His tiny head bobbed back and forth as he watched the council members speak. My dog seemed a lot more interested in this meeting than I was. Probably because I'd been to a few when Dad was a cop and had been bored out of my skull.

I hadn't had Toby then, but even if I had, Dad wouldn't have let me take him. You rarely saw terriers in city council meetings back home. One area where Dead End had it over the other world, for sure.

My hand was halfway into my backpack, fingers brushing the spine of a horror novel I'd been reading for the past week, when I heard someone from the townspeople section yell, "*It's on the agenda, Frank, and this time you'd by God better not skip it.*"

"Jeez, Dan, I'm not going to skip it. You've been harping on it for a month," the mayor replied. His voice echoed, as if he'd spoken into a canyon. No other voice in the room echoed.

"Because they're worse. So much worse."

Abuelo Emilio adjusted his black-framed glasses. "What's worse, Dan?"

"First agenda item: Danford Martindale's garden gnome," the mayor announced.

"*Gnomes*. And lawn flamingos, Frank. I told you on the phone. The jackasses are working together."

"Please approach the microphone, Mr. Martindale. Not that anyone is having trouble hearing ya," Bert said.

"And refrain from coarse language." My *abuelo* took off his glasses, rubbed his eyes.

"Sorry for that." Danford Martindale shuffled up the aisle, knitted cap clutched in his hands, his white hair infused with static electricity and standing on end. He was a small man, much shorter than the microphone, so he had to adjust the stand. The second he touched it, a burst of light the size of a summertime sparkler flew off his fingertips.

Toby let out a yip and a low growl. I patted him reassuringly.

"Good gravy," Laverne's hologram said, "he'll burn down city hall."

"Sorry. My ability is all over the place right now. I'm stressed out."

"He's a conductor," Grandpa Holli whispered to Toby and me. "He doesn't generate electricity, but he can absorb it from the environment—usually at a low-grade level."

"That's kind of amazing."

"Amazing? Perhaps. Annoying at town meetings? Always."

"Hollister, would you please?" The look on Abuelo's face when he said this made me want to laugh. I'm pretty sure that's what my books meant when they described a person's expression as "long-suffering." I pulled my hand out of my backpack and sat up taller in my seat.

Grandpa Holli adjusted Dan's mike and sat back down.

"As I was saying, I apologize about the cursing and the interruption. I'm just going straight out of my head. Carol keeps saying that's what I get for buying a house across from the sacred gardens. She's gone to her mother's until I solve the problem."

"Exactly how many garden gnomes do you have, Dan?" Bert asked.

"Started with one. Now there are thirteen." He held up a color photograph—a *real* photograph, not a sheet of photo paper printed from someone's ink jet printer—of what looked to me like a group of typical ceramic garden gnomes. Red hats, white beards, green or blue tunics, black boots… "They seem to reproduce in odd numbers, unlike the flamingos."

"How many lawn flamingos do you have?" Abuelo asked.

"Started with two." He held up another photo, this one showed average lawn flamingos, plastic, pink, long necks, metal rods for legs. Back home, Mr. Plunkett, the elderly man across the street, had fourteen of them strewn across his yard.

"And now?" One of the other city council members asked. The name plate in front of him said he was John Gale. Mr. Gale was a lanky, white-skinned, sandy-haired human who reminded me of my seventh-grade science teacher.

"Twenty-six."

"In a month?" Laverne's hologram flickered as if reacting to the shock in her voice.

"No. They've done most of the multiplying in the last week. There were only three gnomes as of midnight, but when I woke up this morning, there were nine more of the suckers on my windowsill, watching me sleep. It was unsettling, let me tell you.

"Also, the lock on my front door was tampered with, and all my boysenberry syrup is gone. Everyone knows gnomes love boysenberries. That's why we keep them in the garden altar."

"Why don't you just trap the little critters and stick 'em in a kennel until we figure out what to do?" someone called out from the back of the room.

Dan glared at the man who spoke up. "Have you ever tried to catch a greased spider monkey, Herbert?"

The man in the back whistled. "That fast, huh?"

"Ten times that fast. Those gnomes are like vapor, and that's if they're playing with you. If they're running from an enemy, the little buggers are even speedier."

Mayor Docket cleared his throat. "You mentioned the garden altar. Has anyone checked on it lately?"

Another townsperson cleared her throat and stood. "Well, no. That is, Mr. Bernard was the only Dead Ender who was allowed to enter the inner sanctum of the sacred gardens, and he passed away three months ago. We haven't gotten anyone to fill his position."

Bert slapped his hand against his forehead. "No one is replenishing the altar? I'm surprised half the trees in this town haven't attacked. If we don't get this dealt with, we'll have a lot more than thieving garden gnomes to worry about."

"They're bullies," Dan said. "The gnomes, though the flamingos are just as bad. Those blasted birds have claimed the mailbox as their territory and will only allow me to collect one piece of mail a day. If I try to take any more than that, they peck my legs until I bleed."

Abuelo glanced at John Gale. "Any ideas?"

"One. Edina?" John directed the name toward the woman who had volunteered the information about Mr. Bernard. "Would you consider taking the vacant position?"

"I don't think I'm qualified," she replied.

"There is a spiritual learning curve, but you can handle it. We supply the boysenberries, lavender, and small gray rocks for the altar. That arrangement always worked well when Bernard was running things."

"I understand that, John. The thing is, it's a lot of responsibility…"

"It's a *paid* position, Edie." Laverne rolled her eyes.

Edina nodded. "I'll do it."

"That should take care of your gnome and flamingo problem, Dan. Second item on the agenda—"

"Just wait a dang minute. What am I supposed to do in the mean-time? It takes at least a month to achieve the internal peace and horti-cultural sanctification necessary to enter the sacred gardens. By that time, the little buggers will have amassed an army."

"Why is Dan the only resident near the gardens being affected by the gnomes and flamingos?" Again Laverne's image wavered, then snapped back into focus. Her eyes were narrow and suspicious. "They don't usually bother folks that don't bother them."

My *abuelo* echoed Laverne's expression. As did the other council members.

"Oh fine." Dan threw his hands up. "When I was a kid, I entered the sacred gardens' inner sanctum without permission and stole some rocks off the altar on a dare."

Bert shook his head. "When you say kid, are you talking seven, eight years old?"

"Eighteen," Dan grumbled.

"Mystery solved. Eighteen is the age of consent." Bert shook his head. "Lawn fauna is big on retribution. They'll remember your actions for generations."

"You sound like Carol," Dan said.

"Your wife sounds like the only person with any sense in her head," someone called out from the townspeople section.

"Not helpful, Lurleen." Dan turned his pleading gaze on the mayor. "What am I supposed to do to keep the critters from destroying my house?"

"My advice? Stock up on boysenberry syrup." The mayor held up two enormous fingers. "The *second* item of the evening is the annual Dead End deworming. Is there a representative from the deworming committee here?"

"I'm here, Mayor Docket. Misha Luna." A creature unfurled itself from within a pair of dragonfly wings and levitated forward. It tapped the microphone once, sending a high-pitched whine through the room.

The dragonfly creature cleared its throat. "The committee has trapped seventy-one worm larvae this last week." There was a buzzing sound in the back of the room. "Apologies, I meant to say seventy-two. Thank you, Alvin."

I shifted Toby to the side and reached into my backpack for my book again. This sounded like boring administrative type stuff to me, even if a giant dragonfly was saying it.

Misha, the dragonfly, continued. "We're down to sixteen larvae. Half were cremated, and Chuck Stockles took the rest to his restaurant. He puts them in a slow cooker with barbecue sauce and two tablespoons of garlic. Serves the whole thing over rice."

"Isn't that dangerous, Misha?" Bert asked. "They're venomous."

"If you cook them long enough it takes the poison right out of them, though there's always a chance of paralysis—or spontaneous fur growth. I think we all remember Thelma Cole's tiger-striped beard."

"How long did it take to get rid of that thing?" the Mayor asked.

"I don't recall, but it was down to her knees by then."

I dropped the book back into my backpack.

9

TUESDAY, GRANDPA HOLLI TOOK ME TO SCHOOL. HE'D APPROACHED ME the previous night before bed and told me I didn't have to go yet if I didn't feel up to it.

When I said I was fine, he'd asked me again, just to be sure. Then again, twice before breakfast, once while I was in the bathroom braiding my hair, and three more times on the way to the car.

Although I was nervous, there was this part of me that wanted to see what a normal high school experience was like. I'd had to be home-schooled after the unfortunate pool crater incident, and I'd never really had friends before that. I wasn't smart enough to hang out with the overachievers—thanks, geometry—and I liked listening to my teachers, so I wasn't a delinquent. I was okay at sports, so not a jock, I read way too many books, and didn't wear nearly enough makeup to exist even at the fringes of the popular crowd.

"Are you certain you're ready, dear?"

"I'm sure." I glanced at his profile from the passenger seat. His mouth was set in a firm line and his kind eyes were hooded, like he hadn't gotten enough sleep. "Grandpa?"

"Yes?"

"Are you worried about me?"

He appeared to think that over before replying. "Not worried, per se. It's only that you've already been through so much. I hate to see you put yourself under more pressure. Dead End High School isn't like the schools where you're from."

"I wouldn't know the difference. I told you, I never went to high school." When he sighed, I smiled and said, "You *are* worried about me."

"I suppose I am."

"Thank you."

"Thank you?" He frowned.

"Yeah. You know, for caring about me."

"Maria, you're my granddaughter. Of course, I care."

"You just met me."

"That doesn't matter. You're Maria's child, which means you're ours, too. Your abuelo and I both care about you."

Now that I wasn't so sure about. But I said nothing, only smiled because it was nice to have someone besides Dad say they cared about me.

Dead End High was across town from my grandfathers' house. The trip took exactly five minutes, including parking the car. I'd grown up in a small town—population under five thousand—but this place was *tiny*.

"How many people live in Dead End?"

"*People*-people? I couldn't say. But the town population is 1,523—counting you." He smiled, kind eyes crinkling at the corners like Santa Claus's, though that was my slim grandpa's only resemblance to the portly present giver. "Some of us live on the outskirts, and a couple live beyond city limits."

I probably should have thought it was strange that he knew the exact number of residents, but I'd been faced with a lot of bizarre stuff since turning the lock on the café door, so on my weird-to-normal scale, it barely registered.

Dead End High School looked like a cross between a prison and a motel on a vintage postcard. Heavy black gates in front opened to reveal a two-story classroom building painted dark red with white trim and built in a boxy U-shape. The classroom doors on both floors faced each other, and a grass and cement courtyard, around which picnic tables were scattered.

Sullen-faced teenagers perched on the tables here and there. Some sat on the ground, some leaned against the walls. Three hung from the second-floor railing by what appeared to be aqua tentacles. Dr. Pacifico's kids?

Very few of the students were human, none of them smiled, and I felt intensely self-conscious the second I walked in. Yep, this was definitely a high school.

"The office is over here." Grandpa Holli led me through a door and up to a long counter separating a busy office from a waiting area where metal-legged chairs with hard plastic seats lined the wall.

"Well, hello, Holli. How are you?"

The being behind the counter sounded female, but that was the only indicator of gender. She was around five foot ten, three inches taller than Grandpa Holli, long limbed, skinnier than a runway model, and completely hairless. At least, as far as I could see.

She blinked at me. Her eyes were half the size of her large oval head, and as blue as the Pacific Ocean. She reminded me of those drawings I'd seen of outer space aliens, except her flesh wasn't gray. It was a pinkish shade of white, and mostly hidden behind a beige turtleneck sweater and tan pants.

"Hello, Judy. I'm doing well, thanks. We missed you at the council meeting last night. Everything all right?"

Judy's orb of a head jiggled like gelatin for a fraction of a second. I guessed that the movement was a nod, but it was just an impression. There was nothing on her face to support nor disprove my theory.

"Oh yes, everything is just fine. It was my turn to help with the food and supply run, remember?"

Grandpa Holli tapped his head in recognition as she spoke. "That's right. I knew that. I guess it slipped my mind after everything that happened this last weekend." He smiled down at me. "Judy, allow me to introduce the very nice reason for my distraction. This is Emilio's and my granddaughter, Maria. Maria, this is Mrs. Beeson, the school secretary."

"Maria's child? She's come here from the Other?" Mrs. Beeson sounded excited. "And Maria?"

"Gone," Grandpa Holli replied.

"I'm so sorry, Holli."

We all took a moment to wait out the awkwardness of the moment.

"Well, it's lovely to meet you, Maria." Two dots appeared in Mrs. Beeson's cheeks, though her mouth didn't change shape. Dimples? I went ahead and took it as a smile.

"Hello, Mrs. Beeson."

She clapped her slender hands together. She had no fingernails or knuckle lines, though her fingers did bend. "I have some paperwork for your grandfather—" She handed him a clipboard and a pen. "—and some for you."

I took my clipboard. "Umm, I don't have a transcript, ma'am. I was home-schooled and I didn't get that information before I, uh, came here."

"That's no problem, dear. Just list the classes you've completed, and we'll work out a schedule for you. No transcripts needed."

I plopped into a hard-plastic chair next to Grandpa Holli. "That's strange," I said for the hundredth time since arriving in town. "Usually schools demand all that stuff."

Grandpa Holli picked up his pen, jotted something on the clipboard. "Dead End isn't like other places."

Yeah, I'd kind of figured that out.

MRS. BEESON WALKED me to my first class. Well, ran me. I had to scramble to keep up with her long stride.

As I ran-walked behind her, she gave me the tour. "It's all quite logical. Mathematics there, Science back there, English classes up there." She jabbed the air with a long finger. "Electives are over here…"

I tried to retain it all, but I felt hopelessly lost. All I could think about was how I hadn't been to school in a long time. What if I made a fool of myself on the first day and became the dork of the school? It could happen. I'd read on a blog about a girl who barfed on her desk the first day of sixth grade and she was the "yak queen" until graduation.

Oh God. I really didn't want to vomit.

Or fart. That would be worse. So much worse. I'd rather vomit than fart. Burping. I'd rather burp than vomit and I'd rather vomit than fart. My stomach churned and I crossed my fingers. And my legs.

"Apologies for the interruption, Mr. Henning, but we have a new student. Her name is Maria Guadalupe Flores Thompson, but she goes by Maria." Mrs. Beeson did the dimple thing again, so I smiled back.

"Hello."

I managed the greeting without burping, vomiting, or farting. So far, so good.

"Greetings, Maria." Mr. Henning was humanoid, but not entirely human. More like an android trying to appear human. He had board-straight bronze hair down to his waist, and his skin was the shade of an old penny.

"Please take a seat next to Cindy."

He indicated a human girl—the only other one in the class—in pink shorts with fair, freckled skin, blonde hair swept into two low ponytails, and pale brown eyes. She waved at me enthusiastically while the rest of the class let out a low snicker.

I locked eyes with Cindy, tugging the straps of my backpack down to tighten it against my back and mask the deep breath I took for courage. Making a beeline to the empty desk, I tried not to focus on the sea of judgmental eyes burning holes into me. That was one of things I hadn't minded living without when I had to stop going to school.

Cindy smiled at me aggressively. To get her to stop, I smiled back.

"I'm Cindy Gale. So happy to meet you, Maria."

I wasn't sure that was a compliment. She seemed to be the sort of person who was happy about everything. "Uh, nice to meet you, too." A thought occurred to me. "Wait. Gale? Is your dad on the city council?"

"How did you know that?"

"I went to last night's meeting with my grandfathers."

"Aw, I wish I'd have been there. I don't go much because they're super boring," she said, then squealed as if she'd just met a movie star. "Oh, my Arcadia, I'm so excited. I *love* the Other. I'm a total xenophile, if you want to know the truth. I love foreign people and things, and I—"

"*Cindy.*" The teacher glared at her.

"Sorry, Mr. Henning." She smiled at me again. "We'll talk more after class."

CINDY and I ate lunch together at a picnic table near a crooked not-quite-palm tree. Most of the students sat at or around the five tables closest to the front gate. A few studied as they ate at the tables flanking the classrooms. No one sat alone, though some were clustered in groups of three or less.

They were all different. From me, from each other. Different skin color, different hair color, different number and types of appendages. Different, but also the same. Judgmental, insecure, disapproving. And several of them were staring daggers at Cindy.

I wondered who she ate lunch with when I wasn't around.

"My mom was from the Other. She came here, like you, as a teenager. I have some of her music. She was really into this group called Queen. Have you heard of it?"

"Well, yeah. They're pretty popular."

"Still? All these years later?"

"The lead singer died in the nineties, but the rest of the band tours and stuff. There was a movie about them." I peered into my zippered lunch box. Grandpa Holli had prepared a bento box with crackers, veggies, meats, and cheeses. He'd included some sugar cookies, an orange, and a bottle of water.

"Oh no, don't tell my mom Freddie Mercury is dead. She'll cry." Cindy frowned into her paper lunch sack. "Basil, tomato, and mozzarella again. Would it kill her to make me a peanut butter and jelly once in a while?" Her eyes widened. "Is that salami?"

I picked up a neatly sliced square. "Yep."

"Wow, you're so lucky to live with your grandparents." Cindy watched, wide-eyed, as I unloaded the bag. "I'd love a lunch like that. It looks like the sort of stuff my parents eat when they drink wine."

"Have some." I nudged the bento box toward her.

She shook her head. "I shouldn't. It's your lunch."

"I don't mind sharing."

"No. I don't want to be pushy. People are always telling me how insensitive and rude I am, and I know they're right. I don't want to do that with you."

Weird. Cindy was energetic and kind of loud, but she wasn't bossy or rude. "It's not pushy if I offer."

"No, I don't want to mess up." She pulled her hands into her lap.

"It's fine." I whipped my lunch around and circled the table to sit beside her. "So, you're human?"

"Yeah, I'm human." Her hands weren't in her lap. They were tucked under her thighs as if she had to restrain herself to keep from reaching out.

"Like me."

"Am I like you?" Her gaze flickered to the boisterous students at the tables by the front gate. "You should know, humans aren't all that respected at this school. Especially humans with no abilities. The others can be pretty mean about it. I just think you should know it's a risk eating lunch with me, and I'll understand if you want to move."

"It almost sounds like you're warning me of the dangers of being your friend."

"They might pick on you the way they do me."

"They sound like a bunch of a-holes."

She snorted out a laugh. "Is that short for assholes? Do people where you come from say it like that? I love it."

"We say it the other way, too. Why do they pick on you?"

"My mom comes from a long line of healers, and my dad is a seventh-generation tracker. The Gale family is responsible for all the cartography we have of the Beyond. He's always either out scouting locations, at meetings, or locked in his office working on his maps. Mom's usually in her garden tending her herbs, or in her greenhouse bottling her tinctures. And then there's me."

"You?" I frowned.

"Who isn't a tracker or a healer." She nodded too much, too quickly. "I'm a nothing."

Someone had said those words to her. I knew it as surely as I knew my own name. Probably someone seated at that table she kept sneaking glances at. I wanted to lash out at those stupid kids, but my anger was a dangerous thing and I couldn't indulge it, even for a new friend. Abuelo Emilio said abilities were stronger here, and my ability had been strong before arriving in Sanctum.

"I don't know. You seem nice to me."

A shy smile curved her lips. "Thanks."

"Besides, abilities aren't all that great," I said. "Sometimes they get you in a lot of trouble." And sometimes they hurt people you never intended to hurt.

"Maybe, but on this side of the universe, it's better to be a trouble-maker than a nothing."

There was that word again. Nothing. I didn't know what to say to make her feel better, so I said the first thing that popped into my head. "You know, I haven't gone to a real school in a long time. I was worried I might throw up in class on my first day."

Cindy shot me a side glance, then ducked her head and giggled. "I always worry about things like that. I tend to make scenes."

I piled some salami on a cracker and topped it with brie. Grandpa Holli really had no idea what teenagers ate.

"Also, I was worried I might fart." I handed her the cracker. A laugh burst from her—quick and short like a hiccup—as she took it from me.

"That would be awful." She happily bit into the cracker. "Even if you had farted, I'd have still been your friend—if you wanted me to."

"I'd want you to." I made a cracker for myself, took a bite.

"Good." Cindy dusted crumbs off her hands as she chewed. "But I have to tell you, if you'd pooped your pants in class, I'd have had to walk away. There's no coming back from that one."

This time a laugh burst out of me. "Good thing I didn't poop my pants then."

"Yeah." Cindy grinned. "Good thing."

10

"So, you think your dad will be able to come here?" Cindy asked, after I told her how I'd ended up in Dead End.

We were at the same picnic table we'd sat at during lunch, but it was three o'clock now—was I ever glad they used normal days and time here, one less adjustment to make—and we were waiting for my grandfathers to pick me up.

"Sure. Why wouldn't he?"

For the first time in our short acquaintance, Cindy didn't smile, and she didn't answer my question.

"Cindy?"

She bent her legs to her chest and wrapped her arms around them, then rested her chin on her knees. "Because it's kind of impossible."

"What do you mean?" I tried to ignore the rising panic.

"Well, unless you have a café card, you can't find or enter the One Way Café, which is one of only a couple of ways you can get to Sanctum from the Other. Café cards are for residents."

"I wasn't a resident."

"You said you used your mom's card. The cards themselves aren't hard to get—we all have them—but they are hard to get across the Divide."

"Divide?"

"The barrier that separates Sanctum from the Other."

It was apparent I had a lot to learn. "So, I guess you couldn't just go buy one of those cards and mail it to someone back home."

"Well, no. But that's not so strange. We can't send mail to anywhere west of Dead End because of scavengers, and we can't travel north at all." She pointed toward a range of snow-peaked, purple mountains on the horizon. "Not since the trains stopped running."

"Why did the trains stop running?" I hopped along the conversation, feeling a lot like Alice must have felt when she dropped into Wonderland.

"Marauders. Rippers. Monsters. When my dad was a kid, there used to be a bunch of towns in the Beyond. There was a railroad that led straight through it to the ocean. He swam in it as a little boy."

"Where are the people now?"

"The ones who survived live in the towns and cities east of Dead End. My dad says we're the last bastion of the civilized world to the west. He sometimes talks like that—my mom says he's cute when he's pompous. Gross." Cindy stood, dusted off the back of her shorts. "Looks like your ride is here. My mom should be here soon, then."

I turned to see Grandpa Holli standing at the gate. He was pink-cheeked, like he'd exerted himself coming to get me.

"Come on. I'll introduce you," I said.

"Oh, I already know your grandpas. They're friends with my parents. Also, we only live a block down from you all." She walked to the gate with me, waved. "Hi, Mr. McCain-Flores."

"Hello, Cindy. I see you met my granddaughter." His chest puffed out a little when he said that. It had puffed out when he'd introduced me to Mrs. Beeson, too.

It suddenly dawned on me that Grandpa Holli was *proud* that I was his granddaughter. Proud of *me*. I wouldn't have thought it would mean so much, but it did, especially after Abuelo Emilio's cold indifference.

"Yes, sir. I'm glad you got her signed up for school. Maria and I are in all the same classes—*oh my Arcadia*, what a handsome dog." That Cindy referred to Toby as handsome rather than cute made me like her even more.

Toby raced up the sidewalk and launched himself into my arms, tail wagging furiously. "Hey, guy, I missed you, too."

Grandpa Holli glanced over his shoulder. "Your abuelo must have let him out."

Abuelo Emilio was in the passenger seat of their car with the door open and his nose in a newspaper. It looked like the same one he'd been reading this morning—the *Sanctum City Times*. He read the newspaper the way most people watched TV or read books. I had no idea what could possibly be that interesting; it wasn't as if Dead End had a lot going on—if you didn't count the lawn gnome attacks and the giant worm hunting.

On second thought…

I introduced Cindy to Toby, and promised I'd meet her tomorrow morning at the picnic table by the meridian tree. It just looked like a twisty palm to me, but I nodded as if I understood what she was referring to and waved goodbye.

Grandpa Holli, Toby, and I strolled to the car. "Did you and Cindy really eat your lunch under a meridian tree?"

"Yes."

He pursed his lips. "What time?"

"We're dismissed for lunch at 12:15. Why?"

"Nothing. Nothing at all to worry about. As long as you're never near a meridian tree at noon or midnight. That's when it blooms."

"Blooms? Isn't that a good thing?"

"Not if you want to eat your lunch. The meridian tree has a six-foot-long tongue and a sense of smell even more developed than this gentleman." He helped Toby into the back seat and I followed. "It loves meat."

I grimaced. "We need to find a different table."

"Only if it's noon or midnight. Their feeding window is five minutes long, so plan accordingly and you'll be fine."

"What's that, amor?" Abuelo Emilio turned down the car radio. I heard the brassy strains of a mariachi song in the background. The music reminded me of Mom. I pictured her flicking her long black hair over her shoulders and swishing an imaginary skirt around as she danced with Dad and me.

"Maria says they've got a meridian tree in the courtyard at the school."

"That right?" He frowned at me.

I nodded.

"Stay away from it at noon and midnight or it'll eat your lunch and chew on your hair."

"Good point, Emilio." Grandpa Holli started the car and pulled out of the lot. He drove about twenty miles an hour, yet no one honked at him or even sped past like they were angry. People either waved and went around, or matched his speed. "I forgot about the hair chewing."

I touched my braid. It hung to the middle of my back—the perfect length for grabbing. "It eats hair, too? Why doesn't the school chop it down?"

"That would be cruel. It's a living thing, after all," Grandpa Holli looked horrified.

"Okay then, why not move it to somewhere away from the high school?"

"Because we'd have to listen to it whine for months as it re-acclimated." Abuelo turned the page of his newspaper. "Nothing whines worse than a meridian tree that's been uprooted."

"Remember when Bert Mackey had to pull out that one by City Hall because it was infested with root-eating vermin? We could hear it wailing in the pest control office for two weeks straight. Bert nearly lost his mind during the healing process."

I leaned over the front seat. "What happened?"

Grandpa Holli shrugged. "Bert was finally able to get rid of all the root bugs and replant the tree. Once it was back in its spot, the tree shut right up."

11

_____

"WHERE CAN I GET A CAFÉ CARD FOR MY DAD?"

I'd asked this question a good five minutes ago, and had yet to get a response from either of my grandfathers. We'd gathered around the kitchen table with milk and a pile of snickerdoodle cookies Grandpa Holli had baked while I was at school—which was why his face had been red earlier. His skin had flushed from the oven heat.

"Talk to Laverne at the One Way Café. She's the lead guardian of our side of the Divide." Grandpa Holli studied the cookie on the napkin in front of him like it was a magic 8 ball. "But getting it to your father is another thing altogether."

Abuelo bit into his cookie, chewed, swallowed. "There's no way to do it."

"Then how did I get this one?"

"Your mother took it with her. Not only that, but she gave you her name so you could use it."

"Her last name here was McCain-Flores. My last name is Thompson."

"I would imagine yours isn't listed as Thompson on your birth certificate. Maria would have made sure of that."

I pressed my finger into the cinnamon in the center of my cookie. "Okay, but she left this place, so it must be possible."

"That was years ago. Back then, the rippers were ... less volatile. They've been getting worse in recent years. No one from Dead End would dare to cross through one. The last person who tried was torn to shreds." Grandpa Holli shivered.

Cindy had mentioned those things. "What exactly are rippers?"

"Tears in the fabric between worlds that allows us to travel from one world or universe to another."

My mind was working overtime, trying to rewire itself as I took in all this new information, so I chewed my cookie quietly and gave it some time. When it was finished, I looked at Abuelo Emilio, who had picked up his newspaper again.

"How did my mom manage to get through the rippers before they became ... unstable?"

"Maria wanted to leave Sanctum. She was determined to find a way to see the Other. I don't know why." Abuelo lowered his newspaper just enough so I could see his eyes. They didn't look happy.

Grandpa Holli glanced over at him, then cleared his throat and stood. "Emilio, weren't you supposed to meet with Bert about the next supply run?

My abuelo folded his newspaper and glanced down at his wristwatch. "Yes, amor, I do. At five o'clock."

"Well, you'd better get going if you want to make it on time."

I looked back and forth between the two. It was obvious that my question had been a sensitive one, though I hadn't meant it to be. Even though I knew finding out the answer would be helpful, it didn't seem like the best time to dig in my heels.

"I've got homework." I stood and slung my backpack over my shoulder.

"You go ahead then, Maria. I'll start on dinner and call you when it's ready. Emilio, do you want me to save you a plate or do you think you'll be back in time?"

Abuelo Emilio stood as well and tucked the folded paper under his arm. I felt like he was watching me even though he was facing Grandpa Holli. "Save it, please. I'll be home tonight."

He walked out, Grandpa Holli following behind him. I glanced over to where Toby was curled up under the table, on the lookout for dropped food.

"Did you sense the weirdness too, or was it just me?"

Toby blinked.

"Thought so. Nothing gets past you."

The pup's tail slid back and forth across the floor in a lazy wag. I knelt to scratch his ears as Grandpa Holli strolled back into the room.

He smiled at me and began clearing off the table, picking up our crumpled napkins and cupping his hand to scoop up the crumbs left behind.

I tried to help, but he waved a dismissive hand. "I appreciate the offer, but I can handle a few crumbs on my own. You go ahead and work on your homework."

"Are you sure? You're always cleaning up."

"Oh, not always. When I retired, I didn't cook or clean for nearly two years. Emilio did it all. I'd spent forty years in a kitchen and figured that was enough." He carried the crumbs to the trash can. Dumped them and the napkins inside, and dusted off his hands.

"Forty *years*?"

He nodded. "I owned a restaurant on the east end of downtown Dead End called *East End Eats*. We served soups, salads, artisan pizza, that sort of thing. I sold the business to Chuck Stockles, who turned it into an exotic barbecue." He gave me a stern look. "Do *not* order the slow-cooked limpid worm there."

"I remember. Thelma Cole's beard."

"Exactly. Took her six months to get rid of it. And when the sun hits her just right you can still see a tiger-striped five o'clock shadow."

I had to cover my mouth so I wouldn't laugh.

"It's not entirely unattractive on her. She did say she would have preferred one not quite so vividly colored." Grandpa Holli didn't try to hide his laugh. He did it right out loud and wiped his eyes when he was through. "Anyway, I realized that it wasn't the cooking or cleaning I hated, it was doing it for customers. I don't mind when it's Emilio and me. And you. So, go on and do your homework."

"If you're sure."

"I'm sure, Maria."

I snagged my backpack and headed toward my room.

Out of the corner of my eye, I spotted the Ghost of Asshat Past twiddling his fingers at me. He melted through my closed bedroom door. My smile slid off my face.

How in the world had Aedan found me here?

I MADE a beeline into my room, shut the door, and threw my backpack onto my bed.

"What are you doing here?" I wanted to yell, but my grandfather was in the house, so I settled for a furious whisper.

Aedan Sterling, in astral form, leaned against the wall by the door. The smile on his stupid, handsome face annoyed me so much my heart beat faster. Yeah. I'm sure that was the reason. What else could it be?

"I'm not going into the bathroom with you. I don't want to talk to you. Go away."

"Come on, Maria." His eyes went wide. "Whoa, *I can talk*."

"How convenient. Anything else you want to tell me, *mentiroso*?" Liar was a pretty benign insult considering what I really wanted to call him, but it would have to do for now.

"I didn't know I could do that here—wait. What does *mentiroso* mean? Because it doesn't sound flattering."

"Google it, jerkface."

"Hey." He took a gliding step forward. "Look, I didn't lie. I'm as surprised by all this as you are."

"Right. You know what? I liked it better when you were mute. Can you do it again for old time's sake?"

I sat on my bed, retrieved my calculus textbook and a notebook from my backpack. "Now, if you don't mind, I have homework to do."

Aedan sighed. "I understand why you're upset."

"Do you? Then by all means let's hear it." I sat up and folded my arms over my chest.

"You feel betrayed." He spoke slowly, as if he were thinking carefully about his next words. "You think I only got close to you because I work for the Kilshaw Agency."

"I *trusted* you, Aedan. I was vulnerable in front of you. I told you things I never told anyone else. We kiss—" I stopped short and gritted my teeth, looked away. "Yeah. I'm feeling betrayed."

Aedan was quiet for so long I had to check to see if he was still in the room. He was, but he looked pained, as if what I'd said had truly hurt him.

Oh no, uh-uh, I'm not falling for this. I got up and walked across the room, turned my back to him. "If that was all you had to say, then go."

A familiar breeze blew against the back of my neck. He was behind me. I knew it without even having to turn around.

"That kiss was real. It had nothing to do with Kilshaw."

There was no way I could feel his breath on my ear, his hand on my shoulder, the warmth of his body behind me, but I shivered as if I could. Then I shook the feeling away because it was all an illusion, a trick he was playing to get me to trust him. Again.

"Is that right, *mentiroso*?"

"Okay, that's it. I'm looking up that word when I get home."

"Here's an easy one for you. Assface."

"I deserve that."

"Satan."

"All right, take it easy."

"Son of a—"

"Totally got the picture now."

I swung around to face him. "How am I supposed to believe that your apology is real?"

Aedan's expression was grave. "I never lied to you while in this form. The agency can't hear me, so why would I?"

I rolled my eyes.

"Hey, if I was really a bad guy, would I have helped you with the door? You wouldn't have gotten here if I hadn't helped, remember?"

Okay, that part was true. If he hadn't helped me turn the lock, the agency would have captured me with ease.

I still didn't trust him, though.

Aedan leaned down, rested his forehead against mine. As angry as I was with him, I wished I could feel it.

"You don't trust me, but you liked that kiss."

"Shut up." I really hoped he couldn't hear how hard my heart was beating. I was supposed to be mad at the jerk. I *was* mad at the jerk.

"Maria, how do you feel about Brussels sprouts?"

My eyes widened and I stepped back, bumping into the dresser behind me. "Okay, you need to go. Now. That's my grandpa."

"Do you forgive me?"

"Forgive you?" I threw my hands up. "Are you kidding me? Get out of here before he sees you. If he can see you, that is, I'm actually not sure how that works here. I'm not sure how anything works here, to be—"

"Maria?" Grandpa Holli sounded closer.

Aedan cocked his head, grinned. "Tell me you forgive me, and I'll go."

"Seriously? Is this important right now?" I whisper-yelled.

"Yes."

"Okay, fine, I forgive you. Happy? Now please go."

"You don't mean it."

"*Of course* I don't mean it," I snapped. "If you want my true forgiveness, you have to earn it."

Grandpa Holli knocked on my door. "Maria? Are you asleep?"

"Earn it?"

"Yes, leaving now would be a good start."

"All right. But I'll be back." He disappeared.

I dove onto my bed, tried to look like I'd just woken up from a nap. "Come in."

"Maria? Are you asleep? I thought you were doing your homework."

I fake-yawned. "Um, I got sleepy."

Toby yawned for real. He'd slept through my entire conversation with Aedan. What happened to barking when the Kilshaw Agency was near? Come to think of it, he'd never barked when Aedan visited me in our motel rooms either.

"How do you feel about Brussels sprouts?"

69

"I like them." I added another fake yawn for good measure.

"Good. The garden had an abundance of the things this year and we need to get rid of them. See you in a few minutes for dinner."

"Okay, Grandpa."

Toby followed him out. I took one last look around my room for any ghosts or other transparent lurkers. My gaze snagged on the picture of Dad, Toby, and me I'd propped against my books on my nightstand.

Every time I looked at it, I got a pain in my heart. I missed him so much. I had to find a way to get him to Dead End—or get myself back home.

I'd ask about it at dinner. Surely my grandpas would help me find a way.

12

THEY FROZE ME OUT.

I went after Grandpa Holli first, who told me not to worry because everything would work out, that everything was fine, and *did I like the chicken?*

Later that evening, I approached Abuelo Emilio. He didn't even lower his stupid newspaper—a different one called *Beyond's Edge Courier*. He responded to my questions about how to get home with grunts and shakes of the *Courier*.

Frustrated, angry, and bored without my cell phone—it had been days since I'd charged it and it was dead, plus no service—I decided to take Toby for a walk.

"Sorry about your blog going offline," I said.

Toby shook and trotted down the sidewalk after me. He didn't seem as upset as I was about not having a cell phone or Internet access. Then again, I was the one who had to type out all his blog entries. He was the idea dog.

We walked a half mile until we were near the outskirts of town. I realized I was heading for the One Way Café. Maybe I didn't yet have a way to send Dad a café card, but I was going to make sure I had it when the opportunity to get it to him came up.

I mean, how could there be no way to return to my own world? It didn't make sense. If there was a way in, there had to be a way out. I just needed to find it.

My grandfathers were not going to help me, that much was obvious. Maybe Cindy knew something. Or Laverne. Or that guy I met in the café—Samuel.

Toby and I walked until the road ended and the café loomed ahead, the waning sun reflecting off its shiny aluminum siding. I wondered if Laverne got much business. It was nearly seven o'clock, dinner time for some people, but the small gravel lot near the entrance was empty.

I stomped on the bottom step leading up to the café, shaking the desert dust off my shoes so I didn't track it inside. Toby did a polite all-over-body-shake and I pushed open the door.

The café was empty. The jukebox in the back was silent. No one sat at the counter or in any of the booths, and Laverne was nowhere to be seen. Toby and I took a seat at the booth where I'd eaten enough pancakes to make a lumberjack ashamed and waited.

Laverne emerged from the back, which I assumed was the kitchen, and hustled to our table. "Hello again, Mr. Toby and Miss Maria."

"Hi, Laverne. Do you work here all the time?" I asked.

"Oh, no. I was just going home—I live behind the café in one of the apartments."

I'd seen the outside of the café, and there didn't appear to be anything like an apartment building out there. I hadn't even seen a toolshed. Maybe she lived in a room behind the café. A studio apartment. Yeah, that made sense.

"My niece is usually here at this time, but she was feeling under the weather, so I'm filling in while she takes a nap in her apartment."

"Behind the café?"

"Yes."

Mayor Docket and his existence in two worlds at once came to mind. Parallel universes seemed to be a common thing here. That was a good thing. A very good thing.

"Can I get you something to eat?"

"Just a Dr. Pepper for me, thank you."

Laverne looked at Toby. He didn't seem to have any problem communicating on his own, so I left him to it.

He barked twice and Laverne scrawled down whatever it was he was saying on her order pad. She glanced up at me. "We don't have anything called Dr. Pepper here, but we have soda pop. That okay with you?"

"Sure."

She brought my soda, and a bowl of water with ice cubes for Toby. Spoiled dog. While he slurped, I tossed my card on the table and watched it light up.

Laverne perched on a bar stool facing our booth. "I imagine you didn't come here for the pop. Not many townsfolk here this time of day."

I pocketed my card and took a sip of my drink. It wasn't Dr. Pepper, but it wasn't bad. "I noticed that. Why? It's not that late."

"Not good to be outside the city limits after the sun goes down. Danger lurks in the dunes. In the mountains. In the Beyond." Laverne said this with a faraway, spacey look in her eyes.

"What sort of danger?"

"Marauders. Wizards. Other things." She stood and peered out the window, arms akimbo. "Better drink up and get going. Sun's going down fast tonight."

"Okay. Laverne?"

"*Drink.*"

I slurped half my soda in one gulp. "Look, I need a café card. Can I get it here?"

She reached into her pocket, pulled out her pad and pencil stub. "Name?"

"Robert Thompson."

"Relationship to you?"

"He's my dad." My sadness must have leaked into my voice, because Laverne's gruff expression softened.

"Maria, you do understand that the problem isn't getting a café card."

"I've heard that."

"There's a reason this place is called the One Way Café. It's nearly impossible to breach the Divide between this world and yours."

"But what about parallel universes? Like Mayor Docket … and your apartments?"

She sighed. "The apartments exist in a pocket dimension, not a parallel universe. Mayor Docket's universe is easily accessible from Sanctum—as are thousands of others. Just… not yours. I'm sorry."

"But I have to do something." I played with my straw. "I can't leave him there alone."

She gave me a long look, then put the pad and pencil in the pocket on her left hip and withdrew a white card from her right pocket. "You'll have to load it with funds from the bank if you want to use it to pay for meals and such, but if you can get it through the Divide, it'll work to bring your dad over."

Her forehead creased as she picked up my soda glass and Toby's half-empty dog bowl. "Now, you two get going. I don't like the looks of that dust cloud rolling this way. It's got some evil in it."

ALTHOUGH I THOUGHT it was strange that Laverne was so freaked by a dust storm—I was raised in a desert town, they happened all the time —her worry was contagious. I hurried out of the café and toward town, anxious to get to the paved road and sidewalks.

The sky grew darker by the second and, with it, my fear. Grains of sand stung my skin, my hair blew into my mouth, and dirt assaulted my eyes. Evil dust cloud was right. Blackened clouds loomed over the landscape like an omen of bad will.

Scooping Toby up, I shouldered through the worst of the wind and ran to the main road. I'd just set my pup back on his feet when there was a loud belching sound.

"Gross, Toby."

He darted to a small mound of sand to my right, showed his teeth, and growled. The fur on his back stood on end. The mound began to tremble. Toby gave it one last snarl and ran behind me. He was shaking so hard his growls sounded like underwater gurgles. With an explosive thrust, a man-sized, barrel-chested, translucent-skinned worm burst out of the sand and slammed onto the blacktop in front of us.

I stared at the hideous thing. "No."

The worm hissed. Its breath was spoiled milk laced with cat urine. I had to fight not to throw up.

The worm wriggled closer, the sound like someone stirring a bowl of thick cottage cheese. Though it had no eyes, I could tell it was focused on Toby by the way it slithered in his direction.

"What do you want?"

The thing let out a squeak that sounded like a scream, strident and piercing, and undulated toward us.

"Stay away." I swung my hand toward my dog, who was quivering against my calf. "Don't touch him." If the worm heard me, it didn't act like it. "*Don't touch him,*" I yelled as I backed away, shooing Toby behind me.

My anger activated my ability, and the ground beneath my sneakers rumbled like the hungry stomach of a god. I gritted my teeth and tried to slow my breathing. I was tired, frustrated, and scared to death.

The worm let out a steaming hiss—the sound of a boiling kettle if it doesn't have one of those whistles on the spout—and opened a mouth that half circled its head. A ten-foot skinny purple tongue rolled out and wrapped around Toby's body like a lasso. Jerked him toward the worm's mouth.

"*Toby!*" I jumped on the tongue between Toby and the worm. Yanked at the thing where it was wrapped around my dog's furry body. The tongue was strong—a slimy, leathery muscle. It wouldn't budge.

The rumbling under my feet turned into a cracking sound, like thunder rolling closer.

"Let him go, *please.*" I don't know why I said please. If the beast didn't pay attention to my yelling, it wasn't going to pay attention to my begging.

Toby yelped in wheezy puffs of air. I pulled my knee to my chest, then stomped my heel into the worm's tongue. Did it again. Again. It didn't even slow the beast down.

Tears rolled down my face as I threw myself on the tongue, wrapped my hands around the belt of muscle, and held on. I would not lose Toby. I'd lost Mom, Dad, and my world. It wasn't fair of the universe to ask me to lose something else.

"*Stop it.*" I choked out the words.

Shallow fractures appeared on the blacktop. If this thing took Toby, it was taking me, too. I would throw every drop of power I had into the ground and swallow up the three of us in a crater deep enough to reach the blazing center of the earth.

I rolled closer to the worm's gaping mouth. Close enough to see its teeth. Clear, rectangular, and jagged—sharp. Toby gasped out a weak little bark.

"*Don't take him,*" I shrieked. Hysterical with panic, I pulled my legs up to my chin and kicked at the teeth. It was like kicking a steel door. The energy reverberated back up my legs and hips.

I wasn't going to be able to save Toby. I couldn't fight this thing. It was too strong and too relentless, and I'd never been either of those things.

The fight drained out of me. I wrapped myself around my dog and, just as I had that day at the pool back home, waited for the darkness to take me.

Whomp.

The blade of a solid black ax slammed into the narrow space between the worm's mouth and Toby and me. The creature screamed, its mouth shooting out a yellowish liquid I took to be blood, seeing as how it was squirting out of one end of its severed tongue. With a frantic twitch, the worm reared back, let out another squeaking scream, then rammed itself back into the sand hole it had popped out of.

The detached tongue relaxed, releasing Toby. My pup lay panting on his side, but his eyes were bright. "You're okay." I pulled him into my arms, kissed his furry head. "You're okay."

"Yeah, he's a strong little guy."

Samuel Bekker, the cute guy from the café, knelt beside Toby and me. He wore jeans and a black T-shirt, and his biceps made the sleeves seem too tight as he wiped the ax head on his jeans, then slid the weapon into a leather loop on his back.

"Thank you," I whispered.

His upper lip curled. "What are you guys doing out here after dark? It's not safe."

"I know that *now*." I shivered, hugged Toby close.

I felt Samuel's gaze on me, probably judging my stupidity on a scale of one to ten and giving me an eleven. It annoyed me, but he was right, so it wasn't as if I could argue.

"Come on, you two." He helped me to my feet.

"Okay." I shivered and Toby did, too.

"Uh, Maria?"

"Yes?"

"I think we both agree I saved your life, right?"

"Right. Thank you."

"You're welcome." He frowned at the deepening cracks in the asphalt. "Can we agree that the danger is now over?"

Shifting Toby higher in my arms, I said, "It would seem to be, yes."

"Then could you do me a favor?"

"What is it?"

"Can you please stop shaking the earth?"

13

"W-What makes you think it's me?"

Fear sent icicles into my blood, and Dad's voice into my head. *You can never tell anyone what you are, Loops. It's too dangerous.*

"Uh, because you're an earthmover? Look, you were scared and probably pissed off at the limpid worm, so you made the ground shake. No big deal."

"I'm an earthmover?"

"Well, yeah. It makes sense, doesn't it? Your grandfather is one, and that sort of ability is usually inherited."

The ice in my blood melted. "Grandpa Holli?"

"No, your other grandfather. Emilio Flores."

"Oh. I didn't know." But I should have. He was my mother's father. Apparently, they'd shared more than eye color and an affinity for mariachi music. "I don't really tell people about it."

"That's weird. It's a cool ability." He jumped to the side when a crack in the road widened. "Usually."

I needed to make it stop. "Can you give me a minute?"

"Yeah, sure."

I closed my eyes and let out a long breath. Another. Again, I heard my dad's voice: *"Relax, Loops. Breathe. Just breathe."*

As my brain and body calmed, the rumbling slowed. Toby helped. Just knowing he was all right made me feel balanced.

When it had stopped, I opened my eyes and caught Samuel staring at me. "I don't understand why you don't talk about your ability, but hey, it's your life. Thing is, I need your help. So, we're going to have to talk about it a little."

"No." I took a step back.

Samuel's eyes narrowed. "Don't you even think about running."

"I wasn't." I was. It was a reflex, something Samuel wouldn't understand, living in a place where, apparently, people told anyone and everyone what they could do.

"Right." One eyebrow shot up. "You ever heard of the ripper fields?"

I shifted Toby in my arms. He was quietly snoring now, exhausted from the ordeal. "I've heard about rippers. My abuelo said they're tears in the fabric between worlds. He didn't say anything about a ripper field, though."

"It's over there." Samuel pointed to the west side of Dead End. The sky over that area was different from the rest of town. It was gloomy, dark as night, with stormy purple clouds overhead. "Did you know rippers can be used as doorways to other worlds?"

"Yes. I also heard that the last person who tried to cross one was torn to shreds."

"Not true. I saw the last person who crossed to your world from here. I watched her walk through the ripper, and I saw her standing on the other side. She was fine."

Could it be true? Could the answer I'd been looking for have fallen right into my lap? It sounded perfect.

"What's the catch?"

Samuel frowned. "What makes you think there's a catch?"

"There's always a catch when something seems perfect. So, could you please get on with it? I'm cold, covered in worm gunk, and I want to take my dog home."

He sighed. "The catch, as you say, is that the rippers have been getting more and more unstable. The odds of us finding the one that leads to your home—at least, right away—are pretty slim."

"How slim?"

"Struck by lightning, hit by a meteorite, surviving-an-encounter-with-a-chimera slim. But not impossible."

That's the second time someone had mentioned a chimera. I hoped it was just a figure of speech, but this was Dead End, so anything was possible. "My grandfather told me that the rippers have killed people. Are you saying he lied about that?"

"It wasn't a lie. But those people died because they tried to cross *unstable* rippers. Stable rippers are few and far between, but they do form naturally. The thing is, you and I don't have to wait for one to naturally form because you can stabilize them."

"Me?"

"Yes, you. You're an earthmover." He folded his arms over his chest. "How do I know more about this than you do? According to my sister, Mr. Flores is the strongest earthmover in Sanctum. I heard your mom was strong, too. Didn't she teach you anything?"

"She taught me how to hide," I said.

"If she left here through a ripper, she either found a stable one or she figured out a way to stabilize one with her ability. Too bad she didn't teach you how."

"I didn't even know she was from here."

The half-truths and lies by omission were starting to add up. My mom had never told me about her part of the world, and now my grandfathers were keeping me in the dark about how I could stabilize a ripper. The fact that they were keeping something like that from me made me angry, and a little sad.

"You need to back-burner whatever is causing that look, Maria. Get all moody and pissed off later. I need an answer. Will you help me?"

"When you ask all sweet like that, how can I refuse?" I smirked. "Why do you want to get to my world so badly?"

"There's someone there I need to find."

"The person you said you saw go through? The one you asked me about when we first met?"

Sadness seeped into his eyes. I knew that look all too well, because

I'd seen it in the mirror every morning since Dad left me behind. Samuel had lost someone important to him.

"Will you do it?" he asked.

"I have a condition."

"What is it?"

"If I help you stabilize the ripper enough for us to pass through, you have to promise to help me find my dad."

"All right."

"He might be with some very bad people."

"Not a problem."

I wasn't sure about that, but I decided to take his word for it. "I have no idea how to do this ripper-stabilizing thing."

"Yeah, I know. Your ability works similarly to mine, so I've got some ideas."

"You're an earthmover, too?" I perked up. It would be nice to know someone like me, someone who wasn't ashamed of what we were.

"No, I'm not. But my ability relies on vibrations, same as yours. Like I said, I've got some ideas. Is it a deal?" He thrust out his hand.

I hesitated, though I didn't understand why. If helping Samuel was going to get me to Dad, there was nothing to hesitate about.

"It's a deal."

"Can I come, too?"

"Sure, if you want to." After school the next day, Cindy and I were sprawled on her bedroom floor painting our nails prismatic black. It was the only bottle of black polish I brought with me, and she was fascinated with the color. "It's not like I have any idea what I'm doing."

"Why don't you know more about your ability? Kids here usually learn from their parents or, if they have an ability their parents don't have, another adult with that ability teaches them."

Toby popped out from under the bed with a lime green sock in his mouth.

"Like some sixth sense big brother/big sister program?"

"I don't know what that means." Cindy patted Toby on the head, and he dropped the sock and licked her. "It's a mentor-mentee relationship, if that helps clear it up."

"My mom taught me some things. Mostly how to suppress my ability. But she died when I was seven, and my dad's ability was different. He did the best that he could."

"I'm sorry you had to hide." She patted my shoulder with the heel of her hand so as not to smudge her nails. "So how did you learn to control it? From what I hear, earthmoving is one of the more difficult abilities to wield." Cindy wiggled her black sparkly toes in front of a small metal fan that looked like it belonged in a museum.

"I didn't learn, really. I sort of squeeze it down deep, try to calm myself. It doesn't always work." I put my toes next to hers and let the air flow dry the polish. "What else have you heard about earthmovers?"

"Only the stories, same as Samuel. That you're supposed to be able to stabilize rippers, that your kind is responsible for rippers in the first place, you know, the stories."

"*What*?" Toby trotted over to sniff at the polish, so I screwed the lid on tighter. "My kind is responsible for the rippers?"

"You haven't heard the story?"

"No, I haven't. I think I'd remember something like that. Tell me."

She peered at her painted nails, frowned at a smudge on her thumb. "There's a legend about a group of Sanctum revolutionaries who overthrew the Elite Council."

"Council? Like the one your dad and my grandpa are on?"

She shook her head. "*Elite* Council, not city council. Sanctum used to be a dictatorship rather than a democracy—or maybe you'd call it a meritocracy? This was years ago, when my grandma was a kid. We learned about this in civics, but you missed that lesson."

First time I ever regretted missing a lesson.

"Who was the dictator?" The big ones I could think of from my world's history were Saddam Hussein, Chairman Mao, Hitler.

"It wasn't a person, it was people. The Sanctum Elites. Families with powerful abilities. The more powerful you were, the higher in the council you rose—usually by killing the people above you. Lots of people died before The Seven started the revolution."

"The Seven?"

"Seven of the most powerful Sanctumites to ever inhabit these lands joined together and put an end to that regime. But in doing so, they created enemies. One of those enemies killed the original Seven in retaliation, but seven more rose to take their place."

"This sounds like a fantasy book."

"It does, huh? But it's no story." She switched off the fan and we went to sit on her bed. "When the next Seven cornered this enemy, they worked together to get rid of him. It was said the earthmover caused the rip in the Divide, and the other six shoved the enemy through it. So, in a way, they saved the day, but it came at a cost. The Divide weakened and more rips appeared. Now there's a lot of them."

"In the field outside of town?"

"Yeah. That field is the only place in Sanctum where the Divide is entirely unstable. My dad said that Dead End was founded to monitor the weaknesses in the Divide."

"Are you saying they created this whole town because of that field?"

"Well, yeah. The town is like a watchdog." Cindy smiled down at Toby. "Dead Enders keep an eye on the rippers and the things they attract."

"What, exactly, do they attract?"

"Dangerous creatures from the Beyond. Used to be that things like the limpid worm that attacked poor Toby stayed away from populated areas. But the rippers have drawn them here. We get a few in town every year. More lately, for some reason."

Did Abuelo Emilio know anything about the earthmover who created the first ripper? Very likely. Would he tell me about it if he did? Not likely. Unless I published my question in one of those newspapers he always had his nose stuck in, he probably wouldn't even hear me.

"Maybe your abuelo knows something about it. He's an earth-mover. Plus, he's on the city council."

"So's your dad."

"Yeah, but my dad won't talk about anything that isn't public knowledge. I mean, how many times can you hear about the dream sprite invasion of '15? Boring."

"See..." I rolled off the bed and to my feet, gathered up my polish, remover, and cotton ball. "That sounds like the opposite of boring to me."

"Dream sprites are these little pests that feed on the energy we release during sleep. If you don't ward your house against them, they can put you in a coma or even kill you if they take too much, which they almost never do because killing your food supply is pretty freaking stupid." She rolled her eyes. "See? Boring."

"You and I have very different definitions of that word."

"Well, we are from different realms."

"True." Speaking of realms, I had another question for her. "This is going to sound weird, but in my world, I had this other ability."

"Another ability?" Cindy's eyes widened. "That's unusual, even for Elites. What is it?"

"I can see, uh, ghosts." I thought of Aedan drawing messages for me in the bathroom. He hadn't been a spirit, but I still thought of him that way. Not that I wished him dead or anything, but things between us had been easier when I thought he was. "The spirits of dead people."

She gestured that I should continue. "And?"

"That's it. I kind of thought that was enough."

"Not really. We get spirits popping in now and then." She shrugged. "Especially during a spectral storm."

"*Spectral storm?* What's that?"

"So you know when the veil between the spirit world and ours thins, pressure builds up between the dead and the living, and it culminates in cyclones of spirits attacking the town?" Cindy admired her fingernails.

"No, I do not know. Great. Another thing to freak out about."

"It's no big deal. It's why every house in Dead End has shaman-blessed storm shutters. One or two is no problem, but if you start seeing a bunch of spirits, tell your grandpas so they can activate the shutters."

"And I'll do that," I said dully. "Because that's a thing that people actually do here."

"Exactly. Nothing to worry about." She stood, gave me a quick hug. "I really do hope you get to the Other soon, Maria. To find your dad, and also because we're going to need more nail polish. This stuff looks amazing on us."

14

"WHAT KIND OF WARDS DO WE NEED TO BLOCK OUT DREAM SPRITES?"

I set a bowl of white rice on the table and took a seat beside Abuelo Emilio and across from Grandpa Holli. We were having stir fry. I only recognized two of the vegetables in the dish, and I still wasn't too sure those orange things were carrots.

"The standard ones." Grandpa Holli passed me the rice. "Don't worry, we had the city shaman by a couple months ago to renew them. Why? Have you been feeling fatigued?"

I shook my head. "I'm fine. What about shaman-blessed storm shutters?"

"Those are up-to-date, too. We had them re-blessed after the spectral storm last year. Is something wrong?"

"I just realized there's a lot that I don't know about Dead End." *Smooth segue, Loops.* I heard the words in Dad's voice, and had to hide a smile.

"What would you like to know?"

The opening I was hoping for, though I had hoped Abuelo Emilio would answer instead of Grandpa Holli. "Cindy told me that Dead End hasn't been around all that long."

"It was established fifty-one years ago." He smiled at Abuelo. "I've lived here for forty-three years. Emilio and I met around that time."

He leaned in, as if about to tell me a secret. "He applied for a dish-washer job at the restaurant. This was before he went to work doing maintenance for the city, of course." He smiled. "Married him two years later, and we've lived here ever since."

"Best years of my life, amor." Abuelo winked at Grandpa Holli, who smiled shyly.

Yet another way Dead End had it over my world. Forty-one years ago, on my side of the Divide, they would have had to hide their love or be persecuted for it. And that would have been impossible. Their love was too big to hide, too awesome. It was in the way they seemed to know what the other was thinking, in the glimmer in Abuelo's eyes and the spark in Grandpa Holli's smile.

When my mom told me stories about her parents, she told me her one dream was to find a love like theirs. She and Dad had loved that way, but they didn't get forty-one years together. I wish they had.

I took a bite of something that looked like broccoli, but tasted like potato. "What do you know about the earthmover who opened the first ripper?"

Abuelo Emilio took a sip of water before responding. I half-suspected he was the one who had opened that ripper so long ago, but he didn't react in any way suspiciously. Just sipped his water and set his glass down. "What do you want to know?"

"Was he related to us?"

"You assume it was a he?"

"I think everyone does. Cindy said that's how she heard the legend."

"Legend? That's an odd way to put it."

"Oh, you know how people love to talk, Emilio," Grandpa Holli said. "Why make up a story when you can create a legend?" He jabbed his fork into the thing I'd thought was celery but now believed to be in the legume family. "The whole thing was blown out of proportion."

Now that was odd. Abuelo Emilio was as calm as a sleeping kitten, but Grandpa Holli appeared rattled.

"Do my questions bother you?" I asked.

"No." Abuelo took another bite, chewed. "You can ask anything you like. We may not always be able to answer, but we'll try."

"Thank you."

He nodded. "May I ask you a question?"

"Of course."

"What sort of mother was our daughter?"

I hadn't expected that. A jolt of pain went through me as I tried to explain. It hurt to remember her, but it also hurt to forget, and I'd rather have the sting of remembrance than the empty sadness of forgetting.

"She was always smiling. There was this positivity around her, like a forcefield. Like you." I indicated Grandpa Holli with a tilt of my head.

Tears filled his eyes, but he looked away before I saw them fall.

"Dad said she was brilliant. So smart he had to work to keep up with her beautiful mind." I smiled at Abuelo, because I was pretty sure he was like that, too.

"Your father loved her."

"They were very happy together. I think he would have chosen to die with her if it hadn't been for me. Taking care of me became the focus of his life. He never dated anyone else as far as I knew."

My grandpas seemed happy with my response. "It was our fondest wish that she would know love. Although she didn't have it for long, at least she had it." This time, Abuelo Emilio gave me a broad smile, the first one since I'd arrived. I was embarrassed by how much it meant to me.

"Yeah. I hope I find a love like theirs someday. Like yours."

Grandpa Holli reached across the table to pat my hand. "We wish that for you, too."

"Digging the black polish. It looks good against your pretty brown skin."

I dropped the urban fantasy book I was reading and let out a gasp, my heart thundering in my chest. "Aedan."

"The one and only."

My ghost ex-boyfriend—pseudo-ghost boyfriend? —was glowing in the dark like a real ghost.

"Are you dead?"

"Wow, could you at least look sad while you ask that?"

"Uh, sorry. I'm sort of used to thinking of you that way." I leaned out of my bed and scooped up my book. "And then, after you sold me out, wishing you that way."

"Brutal. No, I'm not dead. I'm just getting really good at this astral projection thing. I think it has something to do with this place."

"Dead End? Or Sanctum?" I asked.

"Your bedroom." He grinned.

"I liked you better dead." I turned away from him. "Go away."

"Can't. When I'm astral projecting myself over here, I can only be where you are. You're some kind of anchor for me." His smile widened. "Hey, how about you take me on a tour of the town?"

"At—" I glanced at the analog clock on my nightstand. "—2 a.m.?" *Uh oh.* I'd lost track of time while reading again.

"Yeah. Don't be afraid. I'll protect you."

"Seriously? You're incorporeal. And you just told me that if something were to attack me, you couldn't even leave me to get help."

"I can scream really loud."

"Go away. I hate you. Goodnight." I pulled the covers over my head and flopped onto my pillow.

The bed didn't depress beside me, but I felt him there anyway.

"Get off my bed."

"Let me lie here with you for a while. It's not as if I can get you pregnant in this form."

I threw the covers back and came face to face with him. "That was rude, and you are disgusting."

"I know. I meant it to be. It's the only way I know to get you to listen to me."

His voice sounded different tonight. Sadder, softer. I didn't trust it.

"What's the matter? Long day at the office trying to kill people like me?"

"I would never have let them kill you, Maria."

"And I'm supposed to believe you."

"I wish you would." He sighed. "Let me lie here, please? I promise I won't be rude anymore. I just want to be here with you."

"Why?"

"Because I'm tired." He grinned. "Why? Were you hoping for something else? What were you thinking?"

"Stop wiggling your eyebrows like that. It's not sexy, it's pervy. I'm asking why you want to lie here, with me. You could just stop projecting and go to sleep in your own world."

"I rarely sleep in my world."

It wasn't a lie or exaggeration. I felt it in his tone.

I moved over, gave him room. "Why not?"

He curled up on my pillow, crossed his arms. "It's hard to relax when you're a prisoner."

"You didn't look like a prisoner to me. You looked like a jailer."

"There are different kinds of prisons, Maria. You of all people should know that." He rolled over, gave me his back. It was weird having a guy in my bed. He was a projection, so it's not as if there was anything happening, but it still felt like something Dad would freak out about.

But then, he wasn't here.

"Aedan?"

"Hmm?" He sounded sleepy.

"Who are you, really?"

He rolled over, bringing himself nose to nose with me on the pillow.

"Just a boy lying beside the girl he likes."

"Stop it. I'm tired of games, Aedan. Tell me who you are."

"Really?" He propped his head on his crooked arm, reached out as if to touch my hair.

"Yes."

"I'm the son of a devil and a saint. I'm a nomad in the world, too different to be fully understood by anyone here, and unwilling to hide myself away, so I keep moving. I pray for the day I find a place where I can rest. Running is exhausting."

"You sound like you're in the middle of a mid-life crisis," I drawled.

"Yeah. I'm nineteen, but I'm aging in dog years. I wish I could touch your hair. It looks so silky." He leaned closer, rested his forehead against mine. I pretended I could feel it. "Will you run your fingers through it, Maria? Tell me what it feels like?"

I should have refused. Told him to stop being a perv.

I didn't.

Because the embarrassing truth was, although I didn't trust Aedan, I really, really liked him.

Slowly, I stroked my hand over my hair. Sifted the loose strands through my fingers. "It's soft right now. It's always soft after I condition it."

Aedan reached his hand out, put it through mine. "What does it smell like?"

"The shampoo Grandpa Holli bought me."

"Be more specific."

"Fine." I sniffed the ends of my hair. "It smells kind of like these flowers my mom used to love. Sweet peas. They died fast and the petals were like tissue paper, but while they lasted, the scent filled the entire house."

"Nice."

Tears filled my eyes. "It's been a long time since I remembered the sweet peas." Guilt filled me up. I'd forgotten about my mom's favorite flower.

"Gardenias," Aedan said, a minute or so later.

"Huh?"

"They're these fragrant flowering bushes. My mom used to plant them every place we lived. She smelled like sunshine and gardenias." He smiled. "I'd almost forgotten that."

I laid back on the pillow. "I don't trust you."

"I know."

"I don't forgive you, either."

"I know. But you feel it, don't you?"

For a few seconds I didn't say anything. The only sound in the room was my heart beating in my ears. "Feel what?"

"Whatever this is between us."

I didn't bother lying. "Yes."

"I've had girlfriends, Maria. Probably too many. But I have never felt like this about anyone. And I've only been near you in the flesh one time."

"When you led the Kilshaw Agency to me, you mean? Nearly got me killed?"

"I apologized for that. Explained…"

"Aedan, if you hadn't told your bosses where I was, I'd be with my dad right now instead of crying myself to sleep every night because I miss him so much." Instead of plotting to do something incredibly dangerous to try and find him again.

"You really believe that if we hadn't tracked you down that day at the café, you'd still be with your dad?"

"Of course."

"It never once occurred to you that the café where we found you was the place he'd been heading toward, though I admit by a circuitous route, all along? Could it be possible that I didn't tell anyone where you were, but that the Agency anticipated your destination?"

It had occurred to me, all right. But I wasn't admitting it to him.

"This place, Dead End, was your destiny, Maria." Aedan stood, hesitating by the bed. "I think you know that somewhere deep inside."

"What I know is that the first guy I ever liked betrayed me, and now my dad is gone. *That's* what I know."

"I'm the first guy you ever liked?" He grinned, completely missing the point—probably on purpose. Ugh. I wish I'd kept my mouth shut.

"Go home, Aedan."

For once he did as I asked, and disappeared.

15

"I'VE NEVER RIDDEN A MOTORCYCLE BEFORE," CINDY YELLED IN MY EAR.

Having grown up in the desert, I had experience with quads and motorcycles, so I was driving. Plus, Cindy was terrified of the thing.

"This isn't a motorcycle," I yelled back. "It's an ATV."

We hit a bump and she locked her hands tighter around my waist, but didn't move her chest any closer to my back—which I thought was odd given how nervous she seemed, but understandable. Some people were particular about how they were touched by others.

Either that, or she'd stuck snacks in her sweatshirt pocket and didn't want to crush them. I was hoping for the latter, because I'd forgotten to bring any and it had been four hours since lunch.

"ATV?"

"All-terrain vehicle." I came to a halt close behind Samuel's quad. His was midnight blue, while ours was highlighter yellow and looked newer.

"If you mess up that quadricycle, I will lose my mind," Samuel said.

He'd told us the same thing three times before we left. His face had been all stern and solemn, his shoulders stiff as he patted the seat. "This is Mica's ride and she never lets anyone on it—not even me."

"Why is she letting us now?" I asked.

"She doesn't know."

That didn't sound good. "Why not?"

"Because she isn't here. Let's go. Hurry up."

"It's Mica, isn't it?" I narrowed my eyes. "She's the person you're looking for. She's who is on the other side of the Divide."

"Mica is his older sister," Cindy said.

Samuel's jaw hardened as he regarded her. "Let's get going."

That had been twenty minutes ago. Now we were standing at the top of a sand dune, staring at a wavering mirror image of ourselves. I glanced at Cindy. She had both hands tucked in her sweatshirt pocket and didn't look all that impressed. Samuel wore the same expression.

I was low-key freaking out. All I could think of to say was, "Whoa. Wow. *Wow*."

This was the Divide. It wasn't what I had imagined at all. Nothing like the borders between countries or continents back home. This was a real, touchable … thing.

The sand was warm dusty powder beneath our feet. Trudging through sand dunes was a bit like what I imagined walking through fresh snow would be like—if I wasn't careful where I stepped, my foot would sink down and slide out from under me. Since I'd never seen snow except on TV, I had to guess.

"What are those?" I indicated a pile of bleached white bones.

Cindy craned her neck. "Looks like mostly *chupacabra* bones."

"Wait, back up. *Chupacabra? The Chupacabra?*"

"*A chupacabra*. They travel in swarms." Cindy continued as if we were discussing what grasshoppers eat or where swallows nest and not the bones of a fictitious blood-sucking monster. "They like to hunt out here. Lots of food."

I kept waiting for the punchline. She couldn't be serious—could she? "But *chupacabras* aren't real."

"You really need to get it through your head that things are different here than they are in the Other," Samuel said.

He had a point. I mean, I'd seen giant worms, bug people, aliens, a merman, and a mayor so tall he lived in two different dimensions at once. Compared to that, a *chupacabra* didn't really seem that far-fetched.

"Those, though," Cindy pointed to a six-by-ten-foot stack of carcasses. "I don't know what those are."

"Cattle. Cows." My breath caught. "Sliced in half."

"Those are *cows*?"

"Yeah." I recalled the news on the radio in Dad's truck. "Apparently they're finding the other halves of them on my side of the Divide. No one knows how it's happening."

Samuel side-eyed the cows, said nothing.

Cindy pulled a grotesque, worm-like creature out of her sweatshirt kangaroo pocket. It wriggled in her grip, drooling slime all over her hands.

"*That's* what you had in your pocket? *Gross*. I thought you'd brought snacks," I said.

"You need to see what you're getting into." Cindy's pretty, normally carefree face tightened with worry. "This seems like a good time for a demonstration."

"Demonstration?" I scrunched up my nose at the odor. It smelled a lot like that putrid worm that had tried to kill Toby. "With that thing?"

"That's the plan."

"Hey, she doesn't need to see that." Samuel tried to snatch the slimy creature out of her hands. Cindy sidestepped him. She was faster than she looked, something that surprised me—Samuel too, if the look on his face was any clue.

"I knew you weren't going to tell her." Cindy scowled. Under other circumstances, the dirty look would have been cute on her pink-cheeked face, but she was dead serious.

"Tell me what?"

"How *bloody* dangerous this is."

Whoa. I'd never heard Cindy curse before. Even if it was a British curse and didn't sound as bad as my own swear words, it was probably the equivalent of the F-word to Cindy.

"I intended to tell her. I just wanted to ease her into it. Hand over the limpid worm larvae, girl."

"My name is *not* 'girl.'" Cindy drew herself up to her full height. She was small, but she was formidable when furious. Prettier, too, which I don't think I found as interesting as Samuel did.

"Cindy, then. Hand it over." He did a "gimme that" gesture with his right hand.

That was a mistake. Samuel had vastly underestimated how pissed off Cindy was.

"Go jump into a *chupacabra* swarm." She pulled her arm back and chucked the larvae into the nearest shimmery spot on the Divide.

It exploded with a wet splat. Half of it slithered down the barrier to land in a pile of what looked like raw hamburger meat on the sand.

I plopped on my butt. Slid about three feet down the dune. "Oh my God."

"That's why I wanted to come with you today, Maria." Cindy stood over me, hands on hips. "I wanted you to see firsthand what a dangerous idea this is."

"It's not dangerous," Samuel said. "Not for her."

"It is dangerous. You just don't care as long as you get what you want."

Samuel's dark brows formed a vee between his eyes. He took a menacing step toward Cindy. "You don't know me."

"I know what I see," she replied.

"You only think it's dangerous because you don't know what it's like to have an ability. How can you possibly understand us?" Samuel took another step. "Someone like you—"

"Oh, just say it. Someone like me." Cindy spoke through gritted teeth. "A *lesser*."

They both stopped talking then. Samuel's face softened a little and he took a step away from her without breaking eye contact. "That's not what I meant."

Two bright red spots formed on Cindy's pale cheeks. "I know what I am."

"I'd never use that word. It's a stupid slur," Samuel said.

My head whipped back and forth. I felt like I was watching a tennis match at twice the speed. Obviously calling someone a "lesser" was a huge insult.

"It's the truth, though, right?" She shrugged like it didn't hurt her feelings, but I knew Cindy well enough by now. It hurt. A lot. "*Your* family was one of the Elites. The powerful, the chosen. While *my* family—"

"My family was also one of the first in the revolution." He thumbed toward himself while he spoke. "Some of the first to join in the fight against the abusive Elites. So don't give me that. Besides, all that stuff happened forty-something years before we were born. Why are you so mad?"

"It's funny." Cindy wasn't laughing. "How you all think the revolution solved the problem. Elitism is alive and well, Samuel Bekker. I'm proof of that."

I could tell Samuel wanted to argue, but he was staring into Cindy's eyes as if she were some new and interesting lifeform he was attempting to communicate with for the first time, and he couldn't seem to put together words.

Finally, he said, "I shouldn't have said that about you not understanding."

Cindy swiped her cheeks with the back of her hand. I thought I saw tears in her eyes, but they were gone before I could be sure. "Maria is my friend. I won't let you use her."

Samuel stood statue-still for a full minute. He let out the long, deep-lung breath he'd apparently been holding. "Fair enough." His gaze shifted to me. "If you still want me to teach you, I will. But what Cindy said is true. It's dangerous. I would have told you, but I wanted you to help me. I was wrong."

"Thank you." I reached for Cindy's hand, gave it a quick squeeze, released it. "You're a good friend."

She smiled and the red blotches on her cheeks lightened. "So are you."

I picked up a handful of sand, let it filter out through my fingers. "Despite what you've done, Samuel, I still want to learn. But you have to promise to be straight with me. If something is dangerous, I deserve a warning."

"What level of danger merits a warning?" he asked.

"How about you err to the side of caution and tell me everything."

"Fine. Can we get started?"

"We probably should. I told my grandpas I was studying at the library with Cindy. It closes at eight and I have to stop by for at least a few minutes so it's not a total lie." I didn't like lying to my grandfathers, even if it was for what I thought was a good reason.

"I have a book on ancient herbal remedies to pick up, too." Cindy slid down the hill, landing on her feet. She kicked the worm bits away from the Divide, dug a hole in the sand with her shoe, and nudged the bits inside.

"Why is she burying that thing?" I asked.

Samuel glanced back over his shoulder. I had no idea what he was looking for, as there wasn't anything behind us save for the distant mountain range.

"It's food," he said.

"For who?"

"Not who. What," he said. "Now let's get started."

He scooted down the dune, leaving me standing alone with visions of worm-gobbling *chupacabras* dancing in my head.

16

MOST PEOPLE MY AGE GOT TO SPEND FRIDAYS AFTER SCHOOL MAKING questionable decisions about alcohol and drugs and birth control. I was way luckier than that. I got to get yelled at by Samuel.

"Call your ability. Bring it to just below the surface. Keep it at a gentle simmer."

I tightened my muscles, tried to force it to the surface.

"Relax. Let it flow into you."

This time I inhaled through my nose, exhaled through my mouth, then tried to force it to the surface.

"You're forcing it."

"How else am I supposed to make it work?"

Samuel paced ten steps away from me, then ten steps back. "This is unreal. How do you not know anything about your own ability?"

Offended, I said, "I know how destructive it is and I know how to suppress it. Don't tell me I don't know anything about my ability."

His expression grim, Samuel nodded. "Fine. Do it again. This time, slide beneath it, case it up the way you'd help a baby bird to fly."

Cindy grinned. She'd plopped in the sand beside the ATVs and was quietly watching us.

I shook my body the way I'd seen boxers do before a match. Rolled my neck, bounced on my toes, took another deep breath and reached.

The earth trembled.

"Slow down. Easy."

"I'm trying. My ability is either off or on. There is no simmer setting."

"You can control it. Cradle the energy in your palms, ease it upward."

The ground shook beneath me and I dropped into sand up to my kneecaps.

I tried again. Dropped to my thighs.

Samuel waited for the trembling to stop, then edged close, toeing the line between solid ground and quicksand. I waded as close as I could to him and accepted his outstretched hand, letting him slowly pull me out and slide me over to hard-packed earth.

"Again. Slowly."

"Tell me why you want to get to my world so badly you're willing to risk going through a ripper," I said, "because I'd like to know exactly how far you plan to push me."

"That's my business."

"*You were right before. It's his sister,*" Cindy yelled.

"*How do you know so much about me?*" Samuel yelled back.

The red blotches sprang to her cheeks again. "It's a small town."

It was the truth. Dead End was a small town. But I had the feeling there was more to Cindy's knowledge of Samuel than town gossip. I wasn't telling him that, though. Girlfriends stick together.

"What happened to your sister?"

"She went through a ripper. I want to get her back. Now concentrate."

"Had a feeling it was something like that." I did the body-shake thing again. "You could have just told me. I understand what it's like to be separated from the person you love most in the world."

He scowled at me. "*Concentrate.*"

"So we're not bonding?" I gave him an over-the-top sad face. "Aww, I was so hoping for a hug."

Cindy snickered.

"Maria…"

I reached for my ability again. This time I didn't close my eyes. This time I stared right at a ripper and let loose.

Not my greatest idea, seeing as how the ripper immediately doubled in size and let out a sonic boom sort of crack that I felt in my chest.

"Be careful," Cindy said. But she might as well have been in another universe with Samuel and the animal bones and the cattle carcasses. My entire focus was on that glimmering rip in the fabric of the world.

I pushed a little harder, and the ripper quadrupled in size. In the upper right corner, the mirror image surface swirled. It reminded me of a whirlpool on a calm lake.

A whip-whooshing noise, like the sound of the silty wind during a dust storm, made it hard to hear anything but the beating of my own heart.

"Maria, reel it in. You aren't ready for this." Samuel's voice was a mouse whisper from a mile away. I could barely make out the words.

Another push, and the whirlpool cleared. Through it I spied a sliver of the night sky, which was odd, since it was the middle of the day. I wanted to see more, so I gave another push.

And another.

The next thing I knew, I was flat on my back. The ground was shaking so hard I'd sunk several inches into the sand.

"Look." Samuel pointed to the corner where the sky was still visible. A large bird with a red featherless head and two-toned black-brown wings flew toward the opening.

I cringed, recalling what had happened to the thing Cindy had thrown at the ripper, but the bird didn't disintegrate or slice in half. It soared through the ripper with no resistance, and landed on the pile of dead bones.

Cindy jogged up to us. "What the goddess is that?"

The bird glared at me through shiny brown eyes. Hissed.

"Looks like a buzzard," I said.

"That's not a Sanctum buzzard." Samuel couldn't seem to take his eyes off the thing.

"Vulture, then." I made a note to find out what a Sanctum buzzard was.

The bird flapped its wings, hopped off the bones, and stomped toward us.

"He looks angry," Cindy said.

I shrugged. "He just looks like a vulture to me."

"No, Cindy is right. He looks mad." Samuel glanced up at Cindy. "You wouldn't happen to have brought two limpid worm larvae, would you?"

With a proud smile, she produced another fat, wriggling larva from her sweatshirt pocket. A string of mucus extended from the worm to her shirt. "I was worried the first one wouldn't work."

I frowned at her. "We are bleaching that sweatshirt, Cindy."

Samuel took the thing from her and chucked it at the buzzard. The bird snatched it up, then flew toward the mountains outside Dead End with its prize dangling out of its mouth.

"Nice throw," I said, "now help me up."

Cindy peered at the shallow hole I was lying in. "Maria, the ground is still shaking."

I'd noticed, seeing as how I was now lying in a two-foot-deep hole with a blanket of sand over me.

Samuel said, "Relax your hold on the power inside you. Let it spin out until there's nothing left."

I did as he said. By the time I regained control—*Had I ever actually had it?*—the hole was four feet deep.

Samuel did an army crawl to the edge of the hole. "Where did all the sand go?"

"Below the surface," I said, dusting myself off. "Help me up."

He went flat on his belly and reached over the edge. I grabbed his extended hand. With him pulling and me using my legs and free hand to climb, I made it out. I didn't know what his ability was, but I wouldn't have been surprised if it was some supernatural weightlifting power. The guy was athletic and very strong.

We climbed to the top of the dune where Cindy was waiting, and squinted at the ripper.

Samuel grinned. "It's closed now. You did it."

"It's still there," I said.

"Yes, but it's closed. That's the important thing."

"It's also bigger." About four times as big as it had been when I started messing with it. "Should we be worried?"

There was a rumbling and a trembling beneath us, and then the short dune we were standing on collapsed in on itself, dumping all three of us on our butts in the sand.

"Yes." Cindy stood and dusted off her shorts. "I think we should."

EVERY DAY for the next week, I went to Samuel's house after school and practiced in his backyard. Cindy came, too. She said she wanted to be sure he didn't try to deceive me again, and I believed her. But I also thought she might like being near Samuel. It was pretty obvious he liked being near her.

"Concentrate."

"Sam, if you say that one more time, I'm going to open up a hole in the ground and drop you in it."

"I'll stop saying it if you start doing it. And my name is Samuel. My dad's name was Sam."

"I'm trying. Shut your face and let me focus, Sammy."

This exercise was about control. Samuel's idea was to have me "dig" holes with my ability and cover them back up. So far, I was able to make a hole long enough to lie down in, six feet deep, and cover it back up. A grave. I was pretty proud of that.

Samuel was less proud. He was impatient and pushy, and getting on my last nerve. "Get moving."

Cindy's, too. "We've been at this for three hours. Give her a break."

"Take a break at home. We only have another half-hour before the first of my neighbors gets home from work, and she needs to double the size of that hole without losing control and pulling someone's tool shed underground."

"Double it, why?" Cindy asked.

"I told you I was sorry about that," I said.

He glared at me. "It's about control, Cindy."

Wincing, I continued, "I pushed the shed back up. Sure, it's a little caved in, but—"

"*Concentrate*," he snapped.

I did, and this time the hole was bigger, though not double the size. My head hurt and my nose was running. I was so done.

I sniffed. "I think I'm allergic to something in your backyard, Samuel."

Cindy handed me a tissue she pulled from her front pocket. "You have a bloody nose." She rounded on Samuel. "We're done for the day."

"Cindy…" I began.

"Abilities don't come without a price," Samuel said.

"Push her too hard and you'll lose your *tool* to get through the Divide." Cindy was like a wolverine when she felt I was threatened. I don't think I'd ever had a friend who defended me so passionately.

I slung my arm around her shoulders. "I'm okay. We'll do another ten minutes and then head home. Grandpa Holli's making paella. Want to stay for dinner?"

"Oh, my goddess, yes. We're having kale again. Kale. I will walk through the first ripper you stabilize if you tell me there's no kale on the other side."

"Sorry."

"Ugh. I should have known a stubborn vegetable like that wouldn't be content to be only on one plane of existence."

I had just closed another not-big-enough hole, when Samuel's head shot up. He cocked it to one side, looking a lot like Toby when he hears the mail carrier on the street outside.

"What is it?" I asked.

He held his finger to his lips to shush me. Closed his eyes. Tipped his head from side to side.

Cindy and I looked at each other. Shrugged.

Samuel's eyelids popped open and he ran for the gate. "Need to alert emergency services. We've got a horde coming our way."

"Horde?" I looked at Cindy. "Horde of what?"

"Worms."

17

"CAN'T YOU JUST CALL AN EXTERMINATOR?"

"No, because the phones have been non-functional since the last full moon." Cindy was clearly a better runner than I was, because I was huffing out every word between desperate gasps of oxygen.

"So what ... do you do, write ... letters?" Strangely, that idea horrified me almost as much as the worm horde. Dad used to make me write thank you notes for birthday gifts, and by the time I got them all written it was practically my birthday again.

"Or telegrams. The telegraph in the basement at City Hall works most of the time."

Telegraph? Guess I could kiss my cell phone goodbye. I pumped my arms and sprinted to keep up with her.

"How did he—" I pointed to Samuel, who was way ahead of us. Or, I should say, pointed to the dust cloud he'd left in his wake, because I sure couldn't see him. "—know the worm horde was coming?"

"Samuel is a Seismo."

"Which means?"

"Long story short, he hears really well. He can track vibrations above and beneath the earth, and pinpoint the location of a disturbance with near-perfect accuracy."

I slowed down a little. "Guess I know … how he figured out I was … an earthmover."

"That or he just assumed. Everyone knows your grandpa is one."

"So, how do you know all this … about Samuel?"

"Everyone knows. Samuel is a legacy talent. He comes from a long line of Seismos. When an ability is passed through families in its purest form, it gets stronger for every successive generation. I've heard rumors that Samuel is a seventh generation Seismo. That makes him very strong."

"Wonder how many of us have had earthmover abilities. I'm sure of three, at least."

"It's probably more. You're also strong."

We jogged a little slower. I suspected it was because Cindy felt sorry for my lack of athleticism. It had been three years since the swim-team tryouts, and it showed.

"Hey, Cindy?"

"Yeah?"

"Do you think Samuel's hot?"

"Hot?"

"You know, good-looking. Cute."

"Wow, what a great way to put it. He's definitely *hot*." She clamped her teeth together on the last T. Every time I used a word in a way she wasn't familiar with, she latched onto it with the tenacity Toby reserved for his favorite chewy.

"You like him?" I waggled my brows at her. "You know, *like* him, like him?"

"Even if I did, it wouldn't matter. He's an Elite and I'm a lesser."

"That shouldn't matter if you like some—"

"*Holy Beyond*." Cindy's eyes were wide and unblinking, her voice hushed. "I've never seen so many at once."

We skidded to a halt in the middle of the street in front of Chuck's Exotic BBQ, across from McCarty & Martin's Grocery, and catty-corner from Planke's Metallurgy & Energetics. Dr. Pacifico's dental office was on the corner of Dead End Avenue and Main Street, and City Hall was a block away toward the middle of town. There were a couple of other storefronts on the short street, but they either had no sign or the business name was written in symbols I didn't understand.

"This isn't normal?"

"No."

There was a part of me that was glad of that there might not be any emergency measures in place to deal with it. That it wasn't a normal Dead End occurrence.

I grabbed Cindy's arm, pulling her into the narrow alley between the grocery and a shop that sold what appeared to be some sort of incense. When I was sure the creature couldn't see us, I let go of her and shook my head it to clear it.

"Dang, that thing has a loud hiss."

Cindy did the same. "Yeah, well, look at the size of it."

The hissing limpid worm was coiled like a fat bedspring in the middle of the street. It was twice the size of the one that had tried to eat Toby, and there were four of them.

Five. No, *seven*.

Seven ten-foot-tall, five-foot-wide, clear-skinned worms.

The hisser dragged its large body into a half circle and lurched down the street behind the others. Now all seven were undulating in the direction of the high school. Unfortunately, Sunshine Elementary was a block closer.

As if on cue, three of the worms banked right and slithered toward the elementary school.

"Isn't school out?" I asked.

"Yes, but there are afterschool programs. Mr. Skip teaches chess."

We followed the worms that had diverted toward the school, keeping our distance. A group of five elementary students huddled beneath a tree that looked like a palm—but one could never be certain in Dead End. Mr. Skip, a mostly human-looking male with a bird-like face, was doing his best to shield the kids, his winged arms spread wide.

"Why don't they run?" I asked Cindy.

"They can't. Look."

The three worms halted in front of the group. One of the worms let out a pulsating sound I'd only heard in documentaries about killer whales.

"What the heck? It's using echolocation to find them."

"How do you know about echolocation?" Cindy asked.

"Some animals from my side of the Divide use it instead of sight. Bats, dolphins…"

"You're right. The worms are blind, so they respond to the reflection of the sound to identify objects. People. The tree is helping to confuse the sound reflection. It's hiding the children, but it won't last long." Cindy let out a whoosh of breath as the noisy worm thumped the ground in front of the tree with its head. "Oh no. It found them."

My feet started moving almost before I made the decision to run. A wailing alarm rang out over the city. Samuel had finally reached Emergency Services. Problem was, even if he showed up now, he'd be too far from the children to do anything.

People filtered out of the stores and offices down the street and gathered on the sidewalk across from the school. One raised her hand, and a fireball flew from her fingertips and hit the noisy worm in the face—or whatever was on the front end of his body.

It left a char mark on his diaphanous flesh, but didn't faze him much.

Dr. Pacifico threw open the door to his dental office and propelled down the sidewalk on his fin. The way he moved reminded me of an ice skate blade gliding across an ice rink. He made a clicking sound with his tongue, then flung his long green hair over one blue shoulder, puffed out his cheeks, and blew in the direction of the worm on the left, the one now nearest the children. A crystal blue ocean wave formed beneath the creature and lifted it fifty feet in the air.

"Whoa." I sounded dumb, but what else could I say when faced with a merman periodontist who could summon tidal waves out of thin air?

After another click of his tongue, Dr. Pacifico inhaled, and the wave disappeared. The enormous thin-skinned worm dropped out of the sky and splatted on the street, worm guts splashing everyone unfortunate enough to be standing nearby.

"Ugh." Cindy swiped the smelly fluid out of her eyes.

Attracted by their fallen comrade's guts, the other four worms changed direction and fell upon the corpse like a mob. They consumed every scrap, crushing its cartilage with their teeth and making rude slurping sounds with their long tongues. Then, as one, all six worms turned back to face the children and the chess teacher.

"Okay, we're way worse off now."

Cindy gripped my shoulders. Shook me. "Make a hole. A deep one. Bury them."

"*What?* I can't bury one of those things. You saw me today. I can't even make a hole big enough to bury Samuel in, or I'd have done it the twentieth time he told me he couldn't believe I was this inept at using my ability."

"You can do it. I believe in you."

"Cindy, I can't..."

"You have to. There's no time. Dr. Pacifico can't do it again. He needs to recover." We both glanced at the dentist, who was sprawled on his back, gulping air.

"But..." The rest of my sentence died as the first worm cleared the sidewalk six feet from where the children were huddled. "Okay. I'll try."

WE MOVED CLOSER, well within tongue-grabbing range of the worms.

I pinched my eyes closed. Tried to concentrate, but all I could think about was how scared I'd been when that worm wrapped its sticky tongue around Toby.

Nothing.

But then, my ability had never been affected by fear.

Fisting my hands at my sides, I tried again. There was a slight rumble beneath my feet. Problem was, that's not where I needed it to be.

"Something is happening, I can feel it," Cindy whispered. "Uh, FYI, so can the limpid worms."

My eyes flew open.

As one, six worms pointed their empty faces at me. Six tongues flicked out. One of them slapped Cindy's shoes and tried to wrap around her ankle. She managed to sidestep out of its reach and we both backed away down the street, drawing the worms with us. Another tongue whipped out like a lash, leaving a bright red mark on her calf.

"*Don't touch my friend,*" I yelled.

This time when I thought about how these things had tried to eat my dog—and now Cindy—I didn't get scared.

I got angry.

Without thinking, I reached for my ability. Forced myself to relax into it—the way Samuel had taught me. Once I stopped trying to force it, the power flowed into me. When I had it simmering nice and easy, I let my gaze drop to the ground beneath the worms.

And then I turned up the heat and waited for it to boil.

This time, when I felt the rumbling, it wasn't under my feet. I pushed harder, and a sound like the cracking of a thousand whips at once rent the air. The children clapped their hands to their ears. The Dead Enders on the sidewalks did the same.

Hairline cracks appeared on the blacktop, spidering the surface of the street. I pushed a little more, and the cracks widened. The whip-crack sound, which was coming from under the street, grew louder. The worms' full attention was on me now. From the corner of my eye, I saw Mr. Skip lead the children away.

"Maria, they're getting closer," Cindy whispered, "*Hurry.*"

More anger. I needed more.

My mind flipped through traumatic memories... Mom's death and Dad's abandonment of me at the cafe—but that only made me sad—Kilshaw and his goons—that made me fearful—and finally landed on the one person capable of making me want to choke the life out of him with every stupid word out of his lying mouth.

My not-a-ghost ex-boyfriend, Aedan.

I hit the street below those worms with all the anger of a woman scorned.

The road fractured and ragged chunks of blacktop stuck up in the air like broken glass, stabbing into the worms' skin, making them hiss and shriek.

It wasn't enough.

I pictured Aedan's smart-ass smile and sent another jolt of energy into the ground beneath the smashed-up street.

The worms let out a scream like so many foghorns as a yawning chasm opened beneath them and swallowed them—and the street—in one giant bite.

18

THE NEXT THING I KNEW, I WAS FLAT ON MY BACK ON THE GRASS IN A puddle of worm gunk, with my grandfathers and Cindy kneeling over me.

"She's fine, Hollister," Abuelo Emilio was saying, "considering what she did. I would have expected more blood than this."

Grandpa Holli dabbed at my mouth with a handkerchief. It came away stained red and brownish green. Worm insides. Blech.

Abuelo stood, crossed his arms over his chest. "Tell your grandpa you're all right. He's worried."

"I'm okay." I was impressed the lie came out as steady as it did, because I felt anything but okay.

"No, you are not." Grandpa Holli dabbed my mouth again. His hand was shaking. "You're covered in blood. It's coming from your nose, your mouth, even your ears. What were you thinking? You could have been killed."

"She was thinking that if she did nothing, those children would die." Abuelo lifted a silver eyebrow. "That's not true, by the way. Emergency services would have taken care of it with liquid nitrogen. It's the cleanest way to kill them."

"Cleaner than burying them under ten tons of soil?" Cindy asked.

I smiled at her. She was always sticking up for me. I'd never had a friend like that before.

"I did what I thought I had to." With Cindy and Grandpa Holli's help, I sat up. A speed metal band was playing a rage song inside my skull, but I didn't throw up and I thought that was pretty amazing. "Are those things dead?"

Grandpa Holli nodded. "They could not have survived you dropping them that deep."

My eyes settled on the enormous sinkhole in the middle of the street. "I don't want anyone to fall in."

"Oh, the city will put up a safety barrier," Grandpa Holli said.

"I'll come back later tonight and see what I can do to fill the hole." Abuelo Emilio pulled a folded newspaper out of his back pocket and tucked it under his arm. "Let's go home. Dinner is almost ready."

AFTER DINNER—WHICH Cindy didn't stay for since the tension between my abuelo and me was "thick enough to spread on a cracker," as Dad liked to say—things got quiet. The sort of quiet where you're waiting for something loud to happen and when it does, you aren't ready for it even though you knew it was on its way.

Grandpa Holli excused himself from the table, saying he had a headache, and left the room. He hadn't cleared the doorway when Abuelo asked, "Where did you learn to do that?"

"Use my ability? I've had it all my life."

He shook his head. "That level of control only comes with practice."

"I've been practicing."

"With whom? Cindy? Or Samuel Bekker?"

The way Abuelo said Samuel's name made me second-guess telling him the truth. It was obvious he either knew or strongly suspected what was going on. In the end, though, I didn't lie. I'd never liked lying, partly because I'd had to do so much of it back home. There, no one could know what I was or what I could do.

"Samuel. Cindy goes along for moral support."

"That young man wants you to get him through a ripper so he can find his sister, right?"

"Yes." *If you already know the answer, why ask?*

"So, he's using you."

"And I'm using him. I told you I was going to find my dad."

The creases between his eyebrows deepened. "You have no idea how dangerous that is."

"I've seen the animal bones out there." I folded my unused napkin, tucked it under my plate. I hadn't eaten much. My stomach wasn't all that happy with me. It had a lot in common with my abuelo.

"You think the danger lies in a pile of animal bones?"

I swallowed. "Tell me, then. How dangerous is it? Because no matter what you tell me, it won't matter. I'd walk through fire to find Dad."

"Will you risk getting yourself, Cindy, or the Bekker kid killed? Because that's what's going to happen. You aren't strong enough to hold a ripper long enough for someone to walk through."

"Can you?"

The answer was in his eyes. He could do it.

"Teach me how, Abuelo. Or help me do it," I begged.

"No."

The word was a slap in the face. "Why not?"

"Because it's dangerous in more ways than you can fathom." He stood, gathered up his newspaper. "You need to accept that you cannot return to your side of the Divide. If your father is meant to be here, he'll find a way."

Wishful thinking. That's a great life philosophy. Except for the part where it never works.

"You know, I'll say one thing for Samuel, Abuelo. At least he doesn't make me feel like garbage for using my ability."

His brows dropped over his eyes. "I won't tell you again, Maria. Leave the rippers alone."

And with that, he left the room. Guess we were finished talking about it.

I gathered up the dinner dishes and washed them. Wiped down the stove, the counters, the table. When neither grandfather appeared, I decided to go to my room.

"Come on, Toby. Let's get you a fresh tie."

As I passed the doorway leading to the grandpas' bedroom, I paused. They were arguing.

"...then why don't you show her, Emilio?"

"I made that mistake once..."

"...you're making another one now..."

"Amor, you don't understand."

"Then explain it to me."

I hung my head. My grandpas loved each other so much the emotion radiated from them like the heat from the sun, warming everything it touched. Mom had told me about it when I was a child. How much she'd loved being loved by them.

And now they were fighting because of what I had done. Mom would be so disappointed in me.

"We should have never come here, Toby."

───────

I PUSHED OPEN the door to my bedroom and nearly jumped out of my skin.

"How long does it take you to eat dinner, Maria? I've been waiting for *hours*."

As my pulse wound its way back to normal, I covered my shock with annoyance. It wasn't difficult with the astral-projecting dream boy smirking at me. "Go away, Aedan."

"Why?" He tilted his head to the side. "What's going on?"

"Nothing."

"You used to tell me everything."

"I used to tell you some things, and that was before I knew you were a lying jerkface."

"Come on. Talk to me."

It was wrong.

It was probably stupid.

But my emotions were all bottled up inside me and I had to talk to someone before I exploded. Cindy wasn't around, and if I tried hard, I could ignore the stupid things Aedan had done and remember who he was before, when I liked him so much. Besides, with him on the other side of the Divide, it wasn't as if the information would mean much to him.

I told him everything.

"You were able to open a ripper long enough to let something pass through?" He looked impressed. "I disagree with your grandpa. You're definitely strong enough to hold a ripper open, you just need practice. It had to take a lot of strength to open that hole in the street today, too."

I shrugged. "My abuelo doesn't think so."

"He's worried about you. Isn't that what grandpas are supposed to do? I don't have grandparents, but I've heard this is how it usually works."

"He's not worried about me. Grandpa Holli, maybe. But Abuelo? He can't stand me. I think it's because he was expecting my mom that day in the café. Not only was I not Mom, but I also had to tell him his daughter was dead." I sniffed. "I mean, I get it. Compared to her, I must be a huge disappointment."

"I doubt that's true," Aedan said gently.

"God, I just want to go home. Thanks for making that impossible, you ass."

"My employer did that, not me." He paced in front of my dresser. "You said your other grandpa was okay with you being there, didn't you?"

"Yeah, but they're arguing about me right now. I'm causing problems between them."

"Maybe they already had problems and your being there is just making them worse."

"You said that like you think that would be better. How is that better, you giant dork?"

He winced. "In my defense, it sounded nicer in my head."

"You should have kept it in there." Toby sniffed around the place where Aedan's shoes would be if he were corporeal. "Why doesn't my dog freak out when you show up? He doesn't care for ghosts."

"I'm alive. Maybe he can tell the difference."

"I wish he couldn't so I could give him a treat every time he growled at you."

"Mean," Aedan said, but he smiled.

"Go away."

"Why? So you can wallow in self-pity?"

"Yes. Now go, beat it, skedaddle. I've got a lot of wallowing to do."

"*Skedaddle*? You sound like a grandma."

"Yeah, well I live with two grandpas. You pick up things. Go away."

"Are you sure you want me to go? I could listen in on your grandpas. Find out what they're arguing about."

I sat cross-legged on my bed, patted the comforter. Toby hopped up beside me. His bow ties were neatly laid out in my nightstand drawer where Grandpa Holli had left them after washing and starching them. And *ironing* them.

I think retirement was boring Grandpa Holli right out of his mind.

"Why does your dog wear ties?" Aedan watched as I slipped the new bow tie onto Toby's collar and refastened it around his neck.

"Why do you wear clothes?"

"Because I don't want to start a riot."

I burst out laughing. "A riot of police fighting over who gets to arrest you for indecent exposure?"

"A riot of people attracted to my hot body." He swung his hips in an exaggerated dance move.

I laughed again. "That dance was *not* hot."

"Maybe not, but it made you laugh."

"Was that your intention?"

He lifted a shoulder, plopped on the bed. "I wouldn't have minded if you had been overcome with passion."

That got another laugh out of me. "Aedan, why do you keep coming to see me?"

"Because I like you."

"So much that you had no trouble betraying me. If I was still over there, you'd do it again in a heartbeat."

"Would I?" He scooted closer to me on the bed. "If you recall, I'm the one who helped you turn the lock."

"Yeah, I've been meaning to ask how you knew to do that."

"I've known about Sanctum my entire life. My ancestors were from there."

"Really?" I sat up straighter on the bed. "Who were your ancestors?"

He gave me a *duh* look. "Uh, they're all dead. I don't think you know them."

"Wow, I was just asking. You've become a real smart-ass since you gained the ability to speak."

"I was always a smart-ass. It's just there's no way to express sarcasm when writing on steamed mirrors."

There was no winning with the guy. My best course of action was to ignore 90% of what came out of his mouth and shoulder forward.

"Was your mom from Sanctum?"

He shook his head. "She was from over here. Had no idea what she was getting into when she married…" He let the sentence trail off. "I don't want to talk about her."

"Why not? We've talked about my mom."

"Because it's too sad and I don't like sad things."

"What's sad about it?"

He fell back on my comforter, stared up at the ceiling. "Tell me the saddest thing you can think of."

"Someone being hurt. Animal, human."

"And why would someone hurt someone else?"

"Because they're an a-hole."

"People aren't generally born a-holes. How do they become one?"

"I don't know. They're crazy? Abused themselves? Lonely? Unloved?"

"I mean, that's kind of it, right? If all good things come from love, then don't the bad things come from the absence of it?"

I relaxed against my pillow, pulled Toby onto my lap. "Your dad didn't love your mother?"

"She was a means to an end." He smiled grimly.

"So, what does that make you?" I asked.

"An end."

19

SCHOOL WAS DIFFERENT THE DAY AFTER THE WORM INCIDENT. THE students who had pretty much shunned Cindy and me before were now saying hi to us in the halls, smiling at us—I even got a high five.

"*You*, not us." She hugged her books tighter to her chest as we walked toward our final class of the day. One of her blonde braids was flipped over her shoulder, while the other bounced against her back. "You're the one with the ability."

"Nah, I think it's both of us."

"I could save a school bus full of newborn kittens and I'd still be a lesser to them."

"Samuel said that's a slur. Why do you keep saying it?"

"I've been called it all my life by people like that. If I say it first, it takes some of the sting out of their insult."

"Hey." I nudged her. "Are you sure you aren't overreacting?"

The hurt in her eyes made me wish I could take the words back. Her shoulders hiked up to her ears as she brought her books up against her chest like a shield.

"Cindy, I'm—"

"It's fine. We should get to class."

Cindy left right after school for a dental appointment, and Samuel had decided we should take a break for the day and meet early Saturday morning at the ripper field instead. He'd said he had things to do in preparation. I hated to think what he was preparing for. Samuel thought I was ready to create a stable doorway to my world, but he was desperate, and desperate people don't always think straight.

Abuelo's words echoed in my head. *Will you risk getting yourself, Cindy, or the Bekker kid killed? Because that's what's going to happen. You aren't strong enough to hold a ripper...*

I walked home alone. I couldn't help but stop to look at what used to be a smooth asphalt road in front of the elementary school. Although I didn't regret helping the kids, I wondered if I could have avoided causing a miles-deep crater to erupt in the middle of town if I'd had more control. And that made me angry at Abuelo Emilio all over again, since he could teach me control if he wanted to.

You aren't strong enough to hold a ripper...

I hung back behind a tree, watching as a street crew jackhammered blacktop into manageable chunks. One of the workers appeared to have some form of telekinesis, because large chunks were rising into the air and being dumped into a truck, and there wasn't a bulldozer or any other construction machine in sight.

"We saw you do that yesterday," a voice behind me said.

Startled, I spun around. When I saw who it was, all my muscles tightened up.

Gilda Bond. Cheerleader, Solstice Maiden—which I took to be something like homecoming queen, except with less football and more celestial stuff—and all-around Dead End High School mean girl. Most of the cheerleaders I'd met were okay, but Gilda and the two snobs she was with today did not fall into that category.

"Hey," I said. Killing it with the communication.

"You're really powerful," she said.

"Uh, thanks." What was I supposed to say to that?

One of the other girls spoke up. I thought of her as Thing One, like in the Dr. Seuss book. I really should learn her name. "My dad says you're even more powerful than your grandfather."

"Yeah," Thing Two said, "Mine, too."

Gilda gave the girls a withering look and they shut up. "There's a party Saturday night, if you're interested. At the Beyond border northeast of town."

"Party?"

"Yeah, the moon is waning, so we've got a good chance of seeing the mountain chimera."

All of it, every last word, meant nothing to me. "Umm, thanks. I'll talk to Cindy about it."

"You do that," Gilda said, her voice like a gong inside my brain. Holy crap, I didn't know what her ability was, but my head felt like I'd drunk a slushy way too fast. "And one more thing."

"Yeah?"

"Some of us like to showcase our abilities out there. Not everyone has the greatest control, so, you know, watch out." She turned on her heel and flounced away, her waist-length orange hair bouncing against her back. Six palm-sized butterflies alighted on the ends.

Where had they come from? I hadn't seen any butterflies earlier. *What the heck was her ability?*

Maybe I'd find out if I went to the party.

I scrunched my head between my shoulders and fast-walked past the city workers cleaning up my mess as I headed home.

───────

"WHAT'S A MOUNTAIN CHIMERA?" I parked the ATV at the base of a different dune to the last one, this one a little farther away from the Divide.

"Why?" Cindy let go of my waist and climbed off.

I told her about Gilda's party.

"Bunch of stupid-rears," Cindy said.

"You mean dumbasses."

"Yeah. Dumbasses. The mountain chimera isn't something to be fooled with. If they aren't careful, they'll antagonize her and she'll attack."

Samuel, who'd beaten us to the dune by five minutes, chuckled. "I'd pay money to see those conceited elitists running for their lives from the mountain chimera."

"That wasn't nice, Samuel," Cindy said.

"It wasn't? Good. I properly expressed myself. My English teacher is always telling me I need to work on that."

"So, you guys don't like Gilda?" I asked.

Cindy sighed. "It's not that I don't like her. It's more that we don't move in the same social circles."

"And Gilda has no problem letting her know that," Samuel said. "Wait a minute. Tell me you aren't thinking of going to this stupid party."

"I don't know. I'm kind of curious about it. I've never been invited to a party before—well, since I was a child, anyway. It might be fun." I nudged Cindy. "Want to go?"

"I can't. I promised my mom I'd help her with the canning. Our sparrowberries are going crazy this year." She smiled, but it seemed dimmer than its usual thousand-watt glare.

Samuel eyed Cindy, a muscle in his jaw pulsing. When he noticed me looking at him, he cleared his throat. "To answer your original question, the mountain chimera is a creature that lives in the mountains separating Dead End from the Beyond."

"They're called the Chimera Mountains," Cindy said, "in honor-fear of the mountain chimera."

"Honor-fear?"

"Yeah, it's when you honor someone not because you admire them, but because—"

"You fear them?"

Both Samuel and Cindy nodded. I thought about it a moment, realized the term actually made a lot of sense, and brushed past it to get to the heart of what I really wanted to discuss.

"Please, you guys, tell me there isn't a real chimera up there."

A few months ago, I'd read a horror novel in which a mythical chimera terrorized a small American town. I'd loved the book, mostly because it terrified me. I liked being scared in fiction. I liked it in real life a lot less.

Cindy laughed. "Oh, no. Only a fire-breathing monster with a lion's head and a goat's body and a serpent's tail."

"That sounds like a real chimera," I said flatly.

"No, the real chimera lives far into the Beyond. Now *she's* scary. Part Tyrannosaurus Rex, part sand demon. Has about ten heads, all of them awful. She hardly ever comes close to populated areas, though. Last time was, what," she looked at Samuel, "six months ago?"

"Yeah. At Track's End. Ate someone's pet tarantula and went home. She was only in the area for a couple of hours."

"That's all she did in two hours? Just ate someone's pet?" I mean, it was sad, but it wasn't as horrifying as I'd imagined.

"Well, it takes a while to eat a two-hundred-pound spider," Cindy said.

"The exoskeleton on one of those things is like a bulletproof vest," Samuel said. "Don't you have tarantulas in the Other?"

"Yes and no, and please stop saying things that scare me."

"Don't worry. The mountain chimera isn't nearly as bad as the Beyond chimera." Cindy smiled in that way that told me she was a little bit lying, but also telling the truth.

"Yeah." Samuel pulled a water bottle out of a pack tied to his ATV. "But then everything is worse in the Beyond. The deeper you go, the more dangerous it gets."

"Remind me never to go there." Useless words. I wasn't going to need a reminder.

Samuel downed half the water, then capped the bottle and set it in the palm of his right hand. Closed his eyes.

"Let's get started."

The sloshing water in the bottle stilled. Samuel kept one foot planted and took small steps with the other—like a human drawing compass—keeping the water in the bottle surprisingly level as he turned in a semicircle.

I started to ask him what he was doing, but I recalled Cindy's words from a few days ago and held my tongue. *Seismo ... hears really well. He can track vibrations above and beneath the earth and can pinpoint the location of a disturbance with near-perfect accuracy.*

So, I figured this all had something to do with his ability, and waited to see what would happen.

Although Samuel hadn't made any abrupt moves, the water in the bottle began to slosh around. His eyelids popped open and he pointed at a section of the Divide just beyond where the water had reacted.

"There. That ripper is partially below ground. Perfect for walking through. Come on."

20

I wasn't sure about this. A hundred negative possibilities sprang up in my mind at once, and I froze.

"Try again. Here." He held out his hand. "I'll help you tune into the vibration."

With a wide-eyed look at Cindy that she returned with a brow waggle and a grin, I took Samuel's hand.

"Ease up. I'd like to be able to play the piano after this is all over." I yanked my hand back.

"Sorry. Guess I don't know my own strength." He took my hand again, this time more gently. "You play the piano?"

"No. Always nice to have the option, though."

One side of his mouth tilted. *Document the date and the time, Samuel Bekker almost smiled.*

"Let your consciousness slide into the vibrations of the ripper. It's like music. The symbols don't make sense to everyone, but to the people who can read it, it's a wordless poem straight to the heart."

I made a face at Cindy and mouthed, "He's a romantic."

"I'm not a romantic," Samuel said. "I can read vibrations and hear well. You can't whisper to keep me from hearing you, and when I'm connected with the vibrations of the atmosphere, you can't even move your lips without me hearing."

"Fine. I still think you're a romantic." I squeezed his hand and closed my eyes.

"*Concentrate*," Samuel said through clenched teeth.

"You know, you repeating that actually makes it a billion times easier to focus."

"She's being sarcastic," Cindy said.

"Yeah, I got that," Samuel grumbled.

It took a few minutes, but I was finally able to tune in to the ripper. Once I latched onto the vibrations, I didn't need Samuel to lead me to them anymore.

"Now bring your ability to a simmer." He released my hand. "When you get it there, blend the vibrations."

I was getting better. In only one week, I'd learned to simmer. I hadn't, however, learned to blend. "How?"

"The way I told you. Slide in and hold until it feels right."

"That sounded dirty," I said, and Cindy giggled.

"Do you want me to start saying 'concentrate' again?"

"I'm sliding, I'm sliding." I eased the vibrations I created close to the vibrations of the ripper. Sped mine up until they matched. Slid them together.

My mouth fell open. "It worked."

"Great. Now hold it steady," Samuel said.

"Uh, guys…" Cindy said.

"Steady, Maria. You're throwing too much into it."

"I'm doing the best I can, get off me."

"Guys?"

"Hang on, Cindy." I scowled at Samuel. "You made me mess up. Be quiet and let me do it again."

"You're too emotional. Just—"

"I'm *what*? I swear, Samuel Bekker, if you don't shut your cake-hole, I'm going to show you emotional."

"*Guys!*"

"What?" Samuel and I snarled.

"Look. Right side of the ripper."

We did, though I kind of wished we hadn't. "Not another worm."

"Don't be a wimp," Samuel said. "This one is half the size of the one that came after you and your dog."

I pictured that stupid worm with its stupid tongue around Toby. "Kill it with fire."

"Fire doesn't work on these things." Samuel stomped through the sand to his bag, held up an ax. "How about I kill it with this?"

"Works for me."

Cindy cringed. "I wouldn't do that."

"Why not? They aren't pets, Cindy. Those things are dangerous to people and dogs, and must be stopped," I said.

"They're dangerous to all kinds of creatures, not just people and dogs. I'm not trying to make it a pet, I'm trying to tell you I saw it swallow a lizard," she replied, as if that were a good reason not to kill the thing.

"So, it's a lizard murderer. Now we have an even better reason to kill it. Samuel, whack it."

"Nope." Samuel lowered the ax.

"What the heck? What's wrong with you? Chop-choppity-chop its head off."

He sighed. "Do you have skunks on your side of the Divide?"

"Sure. Black and white, small and cute, spray stuff out of their butts that smells like rotten eggs? Why? Do you have them here?"

"Sure," Cindy replied. "We have skunks, moles, gophers, dograts, dragon-squirrels…"

"What are dograts and dragon-squirrels? Please don't say rats as big as dogs and squirrels as big as dragons." I crossed my fingers.

"Well…"

"Use your imagination," Samuel snapped. "So, you've been sprayed by a skunk before?"

"Me? No. I've never been sprayed, but I've smelled when a car has hit one. Nasty stuff. What's that got to do with this?"

Cindy said, "You don't want to kill a limpid worm while it's digesting food, if at all possible."

"Why not?"

"If you don't time it just right, the worm explodes on impact, coating you in its digestive juices."

I made a gagging sound. "That does not sound nice."

"It's not. A limpid worm's digestive fluid is skunk ... times ten," Cindy said.

"Let's not ax it."

"Great idea, Maria," Samuel said wryly, as he pointed to the ripper. "Hey, you're still holding it."

"I am *not* holding that thing."

"Not the worm, the ripper."

"Oh. I am, huh? I kind of forgot I was doing it."

"Look, the limpid worm is going through the ripper." Cindy grabbed my elbow. "Should we let it? Do you guys have limpid worms there? I don't think you do. We probably shouldn't let it—"

"It's coming back." Samuel came up on the other side of me. "Nice work, earthmover. The worm is nearly through. I knew you could hold it." He slapped me on the back.

I'm sure he meant well.

It was a congratulatory sort of slap—a "good job" slap.

But it was enough of a distraction that I lost my grasp on the ripper. It destabilized and slammed shut, catching the worm between both sides of the Divide. Sliced the thing in half.

Then it exploded.

I WAS on my fifth shower.

Well, it was the same shower, just my fifth time soaping up my entire body, turning off the water while the soap sat on my skin for ten minutes, then washing it all down the drain.

Grandpa Holli gagged when I walked in the door. He told me to get in the bathroom and stay there while he went out to buy some kind of special soap from the local herb and mineral apothecary.

"Doug down at Dent's Apothecary said this should take the edge off." He handed me a burlap bag the size of a woman's purse through a crack in the door. "Lather up, including hair, and leave it on for 10 minutes. Repeat until your eyes stop watering. What were you thinking, taking an ax to a recently fed limpid worm?"

"Well, Grandpa, I don't know what I was thinking. However, I can guarantee that I will never do it again."

He backed away from the door, swiped at his watery eyes. "There's also a cleanser for the bathroom itself in there. Scrub it down when you're finished showering. And dump your dirty clothes out the window. I'm going to burn them."

"There's no way to save my jeans?"

"No. I'll have to burn them, sprinkle sage over the ashes, and bury them ten feet below ground."

Kill it with fire, I'd said. Guess the worm had the last laugh. Stupid worm.

I washed off lather number five, sniffed myself, gagged, and lathered up again. Turned off the water and perched naked on the side of the tub inside the dark blue shower curtain as the soap tingled my skin.

"Jeez, how long does one shower take?"

I slipped off the edge and back into the tub, nearly ripping the shower curtain off its rings in the process. When I had my balance again, I shoved the thin plastic aside and scowled at the astral projection slouched against the sink.

"Aedan, get out of here."

"I've been waiting in your room forever."

"Get out, you ass."

"Relax, I can't see you behind that thing." He did an exaggerated sniff. "I think I can smell you, though."

"Shut up. You can't smell anything. You're an astral projection."

He laughed. "Only teasing."

I put my hand around the edge of the shower curtain and gave him a one-finger salute.

He laughed again. "How did it go at the ripper fields today?"

I whisked the shower curtain shut. "How do you know I went there?"

"It's the only place you go besides school, the blonde girl's place, and that boy's house. You should stop doing that, by the way."

"Doing what?"

"Going to that guy's house."

"His name is Samuel and I go to other places, too."

"No, you don't. You have no social life. Almost as bad as when you lived here. You've got the blonde girl and the big dude, but that's about it."

I turned on the shower water. Rinsed off. Sniffed.

Better. Not great, but better.

I lathered up again.

"I'll have you know I was invited to a party tonight." To which I had no intention of going.

"You won't go."

"Why do you say that?" I poked my head out from behind the shower curtain. Aedan leaned on the edge of the sink, checked himself out in the mirror. He was a little less substantial today, more like an actual ghost.

"You're not the type to party."

He was right, but I was pissed. "I am exactly the type to party, which I will prove to you tonight when I do, in fact, party."

"So, you're going to hang out with a bunch of prissy girls from school. Big deal."

I let the shower curtain drop. "Guys will be there, too."

"No."

"Yes, there will be. Gilda said lots of people go."

"Oh, I figured you were telling the truth. I'm saying 'no' as in 'I forbid it.'"

"*F-Forbid* it?" I laughed so hard I nearly slipped again. "Tell me, on what planet does that kind of crap fly?"

He didn't speak for so long, I thought he might have disappeared.

"I admit, that was a little ... chauvinistic of me."

"A *little*? That was the textbook definition of a male chauvinist. It's like you were practicing for a test." I shoved the curtain aside again, peered out at him. "A-plus, by the way."

"I've always been an overachiever." He turned away from the mirror and looked at me. "Don't go."

"Why not?"

"It's dangerous."

"What makes you say that?"

"The things you can do," he said, "there are people on your side of the Divide who will try to use you for their own purposes. You have to be careful who you trust."

"Was it heavy for you? That last statement?"

"Heavy?"

"Yeah, because it felt a little like *irony* to me." I snickered.

Aedan shoved away from the sink. "You know what? Go if you want to, but don't subject me to your Dad joke puns. That's cruel."

"My puns are great. But, if it bothers you, don't worry; I won't pun-ish you anymore."

It was dumb, but I laughed myself silly to spite him as I rinsed off the last of the lather, tucked a towel around me, and shoved the curtain all the way aside. My fingertips looked like raisins and my skin was raw from the scrubbing, but I smelled better.

"Good thing we're in the bathroom, because I might barf after that last joke."

"You can't barf. You aren't even real."

He zoomed over to me. Not walked, not ran, not floated. He *zoomed*. "I am real, Maria. You can bet on that."

My heart started flipping around in my chest the way it always did when he was too close. Why couldn't I hate this guy? It really wasn't fair the way his eyes glimmered, and that dimple in his cheek deep-ened whenever he looked directly into my eyes.

I cleared my throat. "I meant you aren't corporeal."

He stepped into my space, put his face in mine. "Not here, but I am very corporeal. And you and I have unfinished business, so no kissing other people."

"We are not together, and I will kiss whomever I damn well please."

"Oh yes we are together. More than you know." He leaned in to kiss me, and I let him because I'd been thinking about that kiss back in the motel bathroom and I wanted to see if what I'd felt then was real or imagined.

Aedan's mouth was soft and cool, and even though I knew it was a trick of the mind, that there was no way I could be feeling anything from him, my pulse reacted as if he were standing in front of me. I was suddenly very much aware that I was only wearing a towel and less than half of my normal skin surface after all those showers.

"Be careful at that party tonight," he said. "Watch out for the chimera. I hear those things are nasty."

"Wait. How did you know about the chimera? Are you *spying* on me again? Aedan? *Aedan?*"

He winked at me and disappeared.

21

I couldn't decide if it was when the telepathic girl in the cropped top told everyone what color panties I was wearing or if it was when the shirtless drunk boy with pyrokinetic abilities burned the sleeves off my top, but somewhere between 8:15 and 8:20 p.m., I realized this party sucked.

"Maria, you made it."

"Gilda?" I squinted through a haze of blue smoke flowing from the nostrils of a guy with what appeared to be steel spikes for hair. As far as I could tell, his special ability was being a human fog machine.

I waved my hand to clear the air, and came face to face with Gilda and her two-cheerleader entourage.

"Enjoying the party?" She said it with a smile so plastic I thought I heard it crack.

"Yeah, sure." A pair of ripped-up boxer shorts floated past my head and I recoiled. "There's definitely a lot going on."

"You're not used to hanging around other Elites."

These guys were Elites? Huh. I'd expected them to be more impressive, I guess. Like Samuel. The abilities I'd seen tonight were more like tired party tricks.

"You look nice," I said.

Gilda wore a tight gold minidress with matching heels so high they didn't make sense. Her makeup had been applied by either a makeup artist or a fairy godmother, and her orange hair was in perfect ringlets down her back. Not a strand out of place.

It really was too easy to hate her.

"Thanks, Maria." She looked me over. "You look nice too."

I stopped myself from smoothing the non-existent wrinkles of my off-the-shoulder sundress. I did look nice. The olive green made my skin look brown and healthy. I'd put my hair up in a tight bun and even worn my favorite gold hoop earrings. The ones so big I could wear them as bracelets.

The sound of an air horn drew my attention to the DJ table.

The DJ, a humanoid guy covered in gray reptilian scales, made the air horn sound again. Only thing was, he didn't have an air horn. The sound was coming from his nostrils. What the heck was with these people and weird nose tricks?

One more piercing honk and everyone, excluding myself and Gilda, let out a sort of battle cry in response.

I blinked. "What was that about?"

"Chimera must be close by," Thing One said from behind Gilda. She sounded as excited about seeing a chimera as I felt about it, which was ... not at all.

"Don't worry, Tamara. If she gets too close, Zack will take care of it." Gilda seemed very sure of this. "He told me he's been running drills in his backyard."

"He passed out ten minutes ago," Thing Two said. "Ethan and Harper are practicing their telekinesis on him."

"Zack is helping the Bradford twins?" Gilda sounded doubtful.

"It's more that he's not putting up any sort of resistance to them building a rock wall around him."

"Why are they doing that?" I asked.

"They need the training. Right now they can't lift more than five pounds, and the only way they can get stronger is with practice." Thing Two rolled her eyes. "And duh, also, because it's fun."

It didn't sound fun to me, but maybe I was missing something.

"Look." Thing One pointed to a pile of dirt that had erupted into a volcano a couple hundred feet from us.

"Chimera?" I really hoped I was wrong. The opening at the top of that dirt pile wasn't small.

Gilda stomped over to where a guy with a crew cut, and a letterman's jacket with more patches than the number one cookie seller in a Girl Scout troop, was sprawled inside a half-formed stone crypt of sorts.

"Wake up, Zack." She grabbed him by the lapels of his jacket.

"Ten more minutes, Mom," he mumbled.

"*Now*." Gilda used that deep voice again—the one that had made my head hurt yesterday.

"Siren." Thing Two, whose real name I'd found out was Ava, gestured toward Gilda with her chin. "In case you were wondering what her ability is."

The only siren I knew about was a mythical creature that lured sailors to their death with her voice. I wondered what bizarre Dead-Ender twist Gilda's siren ability had.

"Lemme sleep," Zack murmured. "Just a little nap."

"*The chimera is here*," Gilda said.

Her voice made my teeth hurt as if all the nerves had been exposed to cold air at once.

"I thought sirens had *beautiful* voices," I said.

"Some do," Thing One—Tamara—said. "Not this one, but some do."

"I got it, Gilda. Get off my back." Zack pushed to his feet, toppling one side of the rock wall. A confused look crossed his face as he patted his jeans. "Where the hell are my boxers?"

Ethan and Harper snickered.

"*Nice*." He swung around too quickly, tripped over the other side of the rock wall, and landed in the dirt. He flopped onto his back and squinted up at the rock-levitating brother-and-sister team who were now cackling with laughter. "Thanks a lot, assholes."

He somehow managed to push himself to his feet.

"Are you sure this is a good idea?" I sidestepped Zack as he weaved through our small group. "He seems too drunk to handle a chimera." Not that I knew what it took to handle a chimera, but if I was guessing, I'd have said Zack was not the guy for the job.

"I told you," Gilda said, "he's been training. Now, come on. We don't want to miss this."

GILDA, her entourage, and I made our way to the front of the crowd. There had to be thirty teenagers gathered there, drinking beer and waiting for the chimera to show up. For most of them, though, I was pretty sure the main draw was the beer and not the chimera.

"*Move.*" Gilda used her siren voice, so people listened to her and stepped aside.

I rubbed my temples. I was going to have a headache tomorrow.

Excited murmurs moved through the crowd.

"She's *here.*" Gilda's eyes lit up. "This is going to be amazing, Maria."

I followed her line of sight and swallowed a yelp.

The creature that burst out of the dirt volcano had to be twenty feet tall. It was crimson, had a lion's head and a goat's body, and long, scaly arms and legs. It looked like a sunburned gecko on steroids.

That was pretty unusual, but the weirdest part of all was her "tail." A black-and-red-banded serpent-like creature protruding from— cohabitating in? —the place where her tail should be. Its diamond-shaped head hissed and spat at the spectators.

Holy crap. Cindy hadn't been kidding. "That is definitely a chimera."

"Duh," Tamara said.

Zack planted himself around thirty feet from the chimera's toes and stared the creature down like it was high noon in the wild west. If a tumbleweed had rolled past, I wouldn't have been surprised.

"*Ladies and gentlemen, are you ready to watch me tame this chimera?*"

A few people from the crowd clapped, and a group of guys dressed in letterman jackets gave some spirited backslaps and hoots from the far side.

Zack put his hand to his ear. "I. Can't. Hear. Youuuuu."

The crowd erupted in applause and cheers.

As if he were a pro wrestler hyping the crowd, Zack ran along the front row, giving high fives to everyone he passed. When he reached

Gilda, the girls, and me, he stopped and moved closer, one brow raised as he looked me over.

"Hey, aren't you that chick from the Other who took out those worms the other day?"

"Yeah." I had no idea where he was going with this.

"That's pretty *hot*." His breath smelled worse than exploded limpid worm goo. With every exhale, it was as if he were releasing demonic entities from the pits of Hell.

"Uh, thanks?" I backed up a step.

"God, this is pathetic. Even for you, Zack." Gilda put her head in her hands.

Ignoring her, Zack stepped into my space. "Hey, girl, are you really an earthmover?"

"Well, yes, I guess I—"

"I know you are. Because you are officially rocking my world." Zack winked and smacked me on the butt. "Cool earrings."

Oh *hell* no. He did not just do that. I narrowed my eyes, hands balling into fists at my sides. The earth beneath my feet rumbled softly. I couldn't hear it with everyone yelling, but I felt it.

I took a deep breath and tried to think calming thoughts.

"If you've finished making an ass of yourself, Zack, could you do your job and handle the chimera?" Gilda inserted her siren ability into her tone. "*Now.*"

"Get off me, woman." Zack clapped his hands over his ears and scowled at Gilda before giving me another wink.

Surprisingly, the creature had not moved any closer during all this. She seemed fascinated by Zack's antics; her fire-red eyes tracked his every move.

"Let me show you posers how it's done." Zack did a full body shake as he faced the beast. I assumed this was to loosen up his muscles, though I wasn't sure for what.

"Oh good, he's not dead yet. I was worried I'd missed it," a deep voice to my right said.

I knew that voice.

"Samuel? What are you doing here?"

"I could ask you the same thing." He looked entirely at ease, so casual it was as if he'd been standing beside me all night long. "Did you not hear anything Cindy and I said about the mountain chimera?"

"I did."

"Yet you came anyway." He motioned to the crowd around him. "Was it everything you hoped for and more?"

No. Not even close. "It's been ... interesting."

Damn Aedan. I wouldn't be here if it wasn't for his stupid mouth. And my pride. But mostly his mouth.

Zack began bouncing on his toes.

Samuel grinned. "*Yes.* He's shadow boxing. Things are about to go south."

"Nothing is going south," Gilda snapped.

"If you think Zack can pull this off, you're as delusional as he is," Samuel said.

"He's an Elite," she replied, as if that explained it.

"What exactly is his ability?" I assumed it was something other than being an insufferable ass, though he was pretty good at that, too.

"He communicates telepathically with animals," Gilda replied.

I waited for the rest. Surely that wasn't the extent of what he could do. The guy was about to take on a twenty-foot-tall lizard monster with a freaking *snake* for a tail.

"You're waiting for her to tell you what ability he has that would enable him to handle a chimera, aren't you?" Samuel murmured, keeping his eyes on Zack as he spoke.

"Uh-huh."

"Yeah, there isn't one. Unless drunken bravado is an ability."

"So, that's *it*? He just going to *talk*? The way he acts, I thought he could at least throw fire at it or something."

"It'll be fine." Gilda glared at me. "Everything is *fine*."

Zack strutted over to the chimera, speaking to it as he stomped around. Although I couldn't hear what was said from this distance, given his posture, attitude, and state of drunkenness, I'd bet every word overflowed with arrogance.

"On a scale of one to ten, ten being royally, how screwed are we?" I asked Samuel.

"Us? Maybe a three. Zack? Royally plus ten."

The chimera's tail wagged slowly back and forth as Zack drew closer to it. The serpent head flicked out its tongue.

"See, I told you it would work." Gilda said, looking pleased.

Zack pointed to the ground. "Down, beast."

The crowd oohed and aahed as the chimera slowly lowered herself to the ground and released a loud yawn.

"You've got to be kidding me," I whispered.

"It's not over yet." There was a thread of glee sewn into Samuel's words. "Wait for it."

Zack turned his back on the creature, shot the crowd a movie star smile, and assumed a superhero pose. "See, I told you I had it all under *contr—*"

The chimera lifted a red-scaled hand the size of a twin mattress and backhanded drunken Dr. Doolittle across the lot, sending him headfirst into the DJ table with a loud crash.

"Wow. He did better than I expected." Samuel reached for his ax.

The chimera threw her head back and let out a deafening screech. Samuel gritted his teeth, dropped the ax, and slapped his hands over his ears. The chimera's cry had my ears ringing, so I could only imagine what it had done to someone as sensitive to sound as he was.

I scooped up the ax, gripped his muscled forearm, and pulled him along with me as fireballs began raining down on our heads.

22

EVERY TIME THE CHIMERA SCREAMED, SAMUEL BENT OVER AND DRY-heaved, which slowed us down. This was a problem because the chimera's screams were not the most dangerous thing about her, and, I was beginning to think, neither were the fireballs.

The beast raised herself to her full twenty feet and stretched out her hands. Fire erupted from her left palm, shot ten feet into the air, arced, and splashed into her right hand.

"What is she doing?" I yelled to Gilda. She was on Samuel's other side. Her sidekicks were puffs of wind on the horizon.

"Getting ready to attack," she yelled back.

"She hasn't attacked *yet*?"

"With those wimpy fireballs? No way. She's just warming up."

Wimpy? The last one hit three ATVs and left nothing behind but a smoking hunk of tire.

"Samuel, you have to run." Gilda was careful not to use her siren voice on him, which I thought was uncharacteristically nice of her. I'd expected her to have ditched us by now, but she'd stayed when everyone else passed by.

"Please, Samuel," I said. "We have to move faster."

He grunted and hurled himself forward, shambling over the dusty scrub like Frankenstein's monster, Gilda and I running alongside.

Even in those ridiculous heels, she outran me. Samuel moved like an athlete, and it was becoming an effort to keep up with him, too.

"Did anyone get Zack?" I puffed out the words.

"Couple of his football buddies dragged him away," Gilda replied. "I checked. Everyone is out of there."

The siren surprised me at every turn. Just when I thought I had her pegged as shallow and insincere, she did something that made me rethink my opinion of her. It was confusing.

"Why is the chimera attacking now? Did Zack really make her that angry?"

"No." Gilda leaped over a large rock. "Zack is annoying, but he's not enough to provoke this sort of response. There's something else, something she wants enough to come into town to look for it."

"We can't let her reach Dead End." It would be catastrophic. The limpid worms were bad enough, and they weren't a sliver as intelligent as the chimera had proven to be.

"Can you do something?" she asked. "With your ability, I mean?"

I glanced over my shoulder. The chimera was following close behind, though at a leisurely pace. Probably thought she had all the time in the world to deal with us puny beings. "She'd have to stop long enough for me to dig a hole. Or we could lure her into a hole I dug, but at the rate she's moving, I don't think there's much I can do."

"So, we just need her to stop?"

"Well, yeah, but even then I'm not sure I could pull it off."

Gilda and I quit talking, instead putting all our energy into running for a couple of minutes. If I were her, I'd have twisted my ankle by now, but she didn't seem to have any trouble at all. Was that part of her siren ability, running in high heels?

"It's not as if digging holes is the only thing you can do," she said.

"Yeah, I can also half-ass stabilize rippers," I muttered.

The chimera had paused to dig under a tree, so the three of us took the opportunity to catch our breath.

"Looks like she found a snack." Samuel indicated the chimera with a head flick as he jogged back to us. "You guys are slow."

"Maybe we're tired from hauling your heavy butt around," I said.

Gilda frowned at Samuel. "Why does Maria think the only thing she can do with her ability is dig holes and stabilize rippers?"

"Before I started working with her, she didn't know that much," he said. "She's from the Other. You know the stories. People there don't acknowledge abilities, much less understand them."

"But her mother was an Elite," Gilda said, "her grandfather, too."

"She died when I was seven."

"Elites start training as soon as they are able to respond to discipline. I was sixteen months old. Samuel was..."

"A year."

"I was taught to hide mine," I said.

"That's awful." Gilda's pitying look annoyed me, but she wasn't wrong. Why hadn't my mother taught me more about my ability? For that matter, why wouldn't my grandfather teach me now? It's almost as if they were ashamed of what we could do.

"Diversion." She clapped her hands together. "We need one. To give you time to dig."

Bad idea. "The limpid worm hole was a challenge for me."

The three of us started running again as the chimera uprooted the tree she was digging under and chucked it over her shoulder.

"And that hole wouldn't be big enough to keep a chimera contained. The only reason it worked with the worms was because they have fragile skin. The fall, coupled with the dirt she piled on top of them, burst the things open like a ripe melon dropped from a rooftop." Samuel glanced over his shoulder, grabbed my elbow and Gilda's, and ran faster. "Mountain chimeras have skin like a military tank. Unless Maria digs a hole to the earth's mantle and drops her in, burying her won't work."

"*Chimeras?*" I huffed out the word. "Plural? There's more than one?"

"Uh, yeah. Everybody has parents." Samuel hoisted me up by my arm until my toes barely touched the ground. "The others are deeper in the Beyond. This one hunts in the mountain range closest to Dead End."

It was a weird time to get desperately homesick, running for my life as I was, but I did it anyway. In that moment, I missed Dad and our side of the Divide more than I had since entering Sanctum.

"The bunker is over there." Gilda pointed to a cluster of meridian trees. These trees were twice as big as the one by the lunch tables at school and they looked menacing—if trees could look that way—which they obviously could, since these were totally pulling it off.

I got a cramp in my left calf and let out a yelp.

"*Move.*" Samuel scowled. "It's almost midnight."

FIVE MERIDIAN TREES came alive at the stroke of midnight. Thankfully —or sadly, depending on how you looked at it—we were not near them at the time.

"Bunker is a no-go," Samuel said.

"I've got an idea." Gilda slammed on her brakes out of the reach of the first tree. "Cover your ears."

We did as she said, but I could still hear her, could feel the gut-clenching intonations of her powerful voice as she sang to the trees. One by one, branches drooped and trunks bent as if collapsing under their own weight as she lulled them to sleep.

Samuel ran, so I ran, too. When we reached a steel door set into the ground, he pointed at me with his elbow. "Spin the wheel."

The thing reminded me of something out of a war movie, like a hatch door in a submarine. I was a desert kid. I'd never seen a sailboat in person, much less a submarine. But I yanked on the wheel anyway.

"Two hands." Even with his hands covering his ears Samuel cringed as Gilda hit a particularly low note. I almost threw up. If we survived this, I was investing in a strong pair of noise-canceling headphones.

I gripped the wheel with one hand on top and the other on the bottom, and turned. The wheel made a grinding, rusty noise as if it hadn't been used in a long time, but it moved. I pulled the door open and went inside, climbing down a short ladder to a dirt landing. Samuel followed.

Gilda kept singing until she reached the door. When she stopped, the trees immediately snapped awake, faced her —which made no sense seeing as how they didn't have faces, only mouths—and let out a series of shrieks.

"Uh-oh." She scrambled inside and yanked the door shut. Something hit the door with a loud *thrump* and she turned the wheel, which spun more easily now that I had loosened it up.

Samuel leaned against the dirt wall across from me, his breathing ragged. Gilda half-slid down the ladder to land on her knees in the dirt, chest heaving, blood oozing out of her nose.

"Here." I handed her one of the pressed linen handkerchiefs Grandpa Holli always made me carry for some weird reason. A handkerchief and a granola bar. His idea of a survival kit.

She pressed it to her nose. "Thanks."

"That way." Samuel pointed to another door. This one also had a large wheel mechanism in the middle of it though it was an actual door, not a hatch.

The front room of the bunker was surprisingly comfortable. It was stocked with fresh water, snacks, and a bed, table, and chairs. It looked the way I imagined a bomb shelter from my side of the divide would look, only with more rooms.

"You could fit the whole town in here," I whispered.

"That's the idea," Gilda whispered in reply. "Four quadrants branch off from the main room. Beds, supplies, weapons. Enough for the entire town to live on for six months, if necessary. Reinforced steel and seven shaman blessings. Even a Beyond chimera couldn't bring this thing down."

Samuel, pale and covered with sweat, slid all the way down to the floor. Blood dripped down the sides of his neck.

"Oh no, Samuel. Your ears." I hurried to his side.

He gritted his teeth. "I'm aware," he whispered. "Could you give me a minute? I know you mean well, but every word you two say sounds like artillery fire."

Nodding, I moved closer to Gilda. She sat on the edge of the bed with her head back, my handkerchief pressed to her nose.

"Are you all right?" I whispered.

"I'll manage." She glanced in Samuel's direction. "How is he?"

"His ears are bleeding and extremely sensitive right now."

Samuel covered his face with his hands. "Please shut up."

Gilda quieted her voice. "You wouldn't happen to have another one of these handkerchiefs, would you?"

I shook my head.

"I'll see if I can find something in the supply boxes." She kicked off her heels and padded barefoot across the room to a set of floor-to-ceiling shelves.

Worried, I returned to Samuel. His eyes were closed, and his breathing had steadied. I looked him over but didn't dare speak.

"I feel you staring," he whispered. "Mouth the words if you have something to say. I'll be able to hear you."

We can't stay here, I mouthed. *The chimera is going to hurt someone.* I thought of Zack. *Someone who doesn't deserve it.*

Samuel breathed in through his nose, then out through his mouth. At first I thought he hadn't heard me, so I repeated myself. He held up his hand, cutting me off mid-sentence.

"I heard you. Just trying to get my bearings back."

Given the lack of color in his cheeks, I didn't doubt that. The distant sound of the chimera wreaking havoc outside drew my attention.

What do we do?

Samuel opened his eyes. "We need a plan."

We need help.

"That too," he replied.

The outer hatch creaked open and slammed shut. Samuel grunted in pain. The wheel on the inner door spun slowly.

Gilda looked over her shoulder at me. "Cover his ears."

I knelt beside Samuel and did as she said.

"Who is it?" Gilda asked with her ability. I knew Samuel needed my hands more than I did, but it was hard to resist the urge to cover my own ears when she did that.

"Maria? Samuel? Are you guys in there?"

I shot to my feet and hurried to the hatch door. "Cindy?" I grabbed one of her hands away from her ears and yanked her all the way inside. "What are you doing here? You could have been killed. The meridian trees... and there's a chimera running around out there... How did you get in?"

She glanced at Samuel and whispered, "It's after midnight, so the meridian trees were no problem. And the chimera isn't out there anymore."

"Where is she?"

"Headed south."

"Toward town?" Samuel grimaced. It seemed even the sound of his own voice hurt his ears.

"Yeah." Cindy's natural smile slipped off her face. "Toward the north end of town. *Your* neighborhood, Samuel and Gilda."

23

"I HAVE AN IDEA," CINDY WHISPERED.

"What if Maria created a hole large enough to capture the chimera's feet?" Gilda whispered, in deference to Samuel's ears. "If we held her still, perhaps one of the fire abilities could attack."

"And burn down half the town in the process?" Samuel leaned his head against the wall. "No, thanks."

"See, the thing about chimeras—"

"What about the Johnsons?" Gilda rolled over Cindy again. "Their son Matt froze a swimming pool solid last summer."

"It was winter, and it wasn't solid," Samuel said.

This had to be one of the strangest conversations I'd ever had, as we were all doing our best to keep our voices soft.

"Chimeras have thick hides," Cindy said. "External attacks are useless. You have to—"

"What about Javier Rivas?" Gilda asked. "He turned a meridian tree to stone. Fossilized the thing."

Samuel rubbed his chin. "Rivas might work."

"Why do you keep talking over Cindy?" I asked Gilda. Frankly, I was getting pissed off about it.

"I was under the impression that we were in a hurry, so why would we choose to waste even more time?" Gilda finally looked at Cindy.

"Not to be cruel, but you have no abilities. We need an Elite to deal with this thing, and the only two people who know every Elite in town are Samuel and I."

"Not every problem requires an Elite to solve it," Cindy said.

Samuel tilted his head, regarded her with that quizzical, interested look he seemed to save just for her.

Gilda noticed. Her face screwed up, then flattened. "Well, of course *you'd* feel that way." The condescension was thick. "And no one would blame you for it, but it's simply untrue. Now, please, be quiet and let us figure this out."

Although I didn't appreciate the way Gilda spoke to my friend, I had to admit she kind of had a point. If you had people who could set things on fire or freeze them or fossilize them with their mind, you probably didn't have to call on emergency services very often.

"Understood." Cindy pasted on that unhappy smile she often wore at school. "I should get home."

"I'll go with you," I said.

"No, you should stay here and try to figure out how to handle this mess. I'll talk to you tomorrow." She opened the bunker door. "One thing, though. You're wrong, Gilda."

Gilda sighed. "Again, I understand why you'd feel—"

"I know every Elite in town. *Every single one.* I have to. It's a matter of survival for my kind." She dug in the pocket of her jeans, pulled out a tiny plastic container. "Here. I had a feeling you might need these. Chimeras are notorious screamers." She tossed them to Samuel.

He stared at the object in his palm for several seconds.

"What is it?" I whispered.

"Earplugs." He put them in his ears and smiled. "Thank you, Cin—"

She was already gone.

"Fossilize a mountain chimera? Are you freaking kidding me?"

Javier Rivas stood on his front porch in a pair of plaid pajama bottoms and nothing else. He looked to be around eighteen or nineteen, and I was pretty sure he worked out daily. Maybe even twice a day, with abs like that.

"You took out a meridian tree," Samuel said.

"That was blown out of proportion. The tree was sick and it wanted to die. I wouldn't have done it otherwise. I'm not a freaking monster."

"But the mountain chimera is," Gilda said.

"Is she?" Javier narrowed oak brown eyes. "Or is she a Beyond creature who was minding her own business when a bunch of partying teenagers disturbed her hunting grounds?"

Boom. Got it in one.

I had a feeling I was going to like Javier despite the fact that we were from very different worlds. Not only dimensional worlds, either. He was standing on the porch of a house the size of my middle school gym, on a street with three others like it, and they all reminded me of the scale model I made in fifth grade of the San Juan Capistrano Mission. All white-painted brick and tall arches and red clay roofs. Rich people houses.

My grandfathers, and Cindy's family, had modest suburban houses, a lot like the one I'd grown up in. Samuel lived in a big house on the outskirts of the nicer part of town, but Javier was in his own category. His family had to be loaded. I wondered what they did for a living, or if they needed to do anything...

"Javier, please help—"

"No, Gilda. I'm not cleaning up the mess made by a bunch of smug-ass Elites who think everything they do is acceptable because of their birthright. I'm not part of that and I never will be, revolution or not." He shook his head at Samuel. "I thought you were different."

"Hey, I came along after the fact. Don't blame me for this mess." Samuel crossed his arms over his chest. "But I'm not going to abandon my town to an enraged chimera either. Sometimes we have to clean up messes we didn't make."

Javier dropped his chin to his chest and groaned. "That's how you're going to play it, Bekker?"

"Yep," Samuel replied.

After another louder groan, Javier let loose with an explosion of

Spanish curse words that all basically meant the same thing. He was going to help us.

He disappeared into his California mission mansion, returning a few minutes later dressed in jeans, a plain white T-shirt, and white sneakers that looked almost, but not exactly like, Converse. Without a glance at us, Javier strode across the lawn and down the sidewalk. We followed close behind.

As we moved through the neighborhood, a few sleepy townsfolk emerged from their homes, took one look at the chimera, and scurried back inside, slamming their doors behind them.

"I'd drive, but no way am I letting a chimera mess up my car. I just got the thing," Javier said.

Samuel shrugged. "Just as well. Looks like she ended up closer to this side of town anyway. Turn right at the next street."

Javier hung his head, shoved his hands into his pockets. "I won't kill her."

"You may have to."

"I hate this." He let out another string of Spanish curse words, some I'd never heard before—and Mom had been a colorful curser. Then he glanced over his shoulder at me and frowned. "You killed the limpid worms, right?"

"Yeah."

"How did you feel about having to kill them?"

I had to think about that. If pressed, I guess I'd say it hardly bothered me at all. All I could think about was saving those kids. But I sensed that was not the answer he wanted, so I said, "Conflicted."

"Liar." He laughed. "You felt nothing."

"Fine. I felt nothing. One of them tried to kill my dog." I threw that in there in case he was lumping me in with Gilda's crowd. "The others tried to attack some little kids. I wasn't thinking about the worms then, and I don't think about them now that they're dead."

He slowed a little, let me catch up to him. "Okay, but you do think about your dog."

"That's different."

"How?" His dark eyes smiled at me though his mouth remained a straight line.

"Toby is a sophisticated animal. He's kind to all living things—except for spiders. He eats spiders."

"No, it's different because you've anthropomorphized him." At my confused look, he said, "You've *humanized* him. You've attributed to Toby traits that you value as a compassionate being, but the truth is, if he was out in the wild, he'd have to kill to eat, to survive. That's all the chimera is doing. It's really all the worms do, though they do have to be thinned out or they'll overrun the town."

"The city council is working on deworming the town." I jogged to keep up with him.

"Yeah, they do it every year. It's a humane way of dealing with the issue. Unlike what we're about to do now." He slid to a stop and pointed at the sky. "*That's* her? Sweet Arcadia, she's grown by five feet since I last saw her."

"Yeah. She's not hard to pick out in a crowd," Samuel said.

True. Being twenty feet tall gave the chimera one disadvantage. It made her very easy to spot from pretty much anywhere in town. If Javier had taken a moment to look up when he was standing on his front porch, he would have seen the top of her head then.

Javier opened and closed his mouth like a fish on dry land. "I should have left this to my dad. Even if I wanted to, I couldn't take her on." But he continued walking, so I took that to mean that he would at least try.

We caught up with the chimera at the park between Samuel's neighborhood and the rest of the town. Oddly, she wasn't throwing fireballs or screaming, or doing anything, really. She'd simply plopped down in the center of the park, crushing about eight trees beneath her, and was pawing at the ground with her massive claws.

"What's she doing?" Gilda asked. We were across the street from the park, on the concrete steps of a vacant house.

Samuel looked at Javier. "Do you know?"

"This is a new one for me."

"She seems sad," I said, "but calm. If Javier tries to hurt her, she'll be mad. And probably a lot less calm."

"Then what do we do?" Gilda threw up her hands. "Call in a psychiatrist? Maybe a shaman? Doug the apothecary?"

None of us had a good answer. So, we sat there and thought, and kept our voices low so as not to disturb the creature. It was shortly after Gilda threw up her hands for the sixth time, and right after Javier said he was going home because he had to work in the morning, that we heard the singing.

The song was gentle and serene, a pretty lullaby. It was beautiful. I glanced at Gilda, but her mouth was pinched shut.

The singer emerged from the trees to the right of the chimera and I caught my breath.

"*Cindy.*"

24

"CINDY," I WHISPER-YELLED.

She didn't hear me, of course. She was far too busy singing a children's song to a creature who could end her life with one bite of her snake tail.

"What's *she* doing?" Gilda snarled. "She's going to get herself killed. We told her we'd take care of it."

"And we seem to be doing a bang-up job of that," Samuel muttered, his gaze fixed on Cindy.

"Who is she?" Javier asked.

"My best friend," I replied. My best friend who was scaring the bejeezus out of me. "Her name is Cindy."

"Cynthia *Gale*?" Javier appeared fascinated. "I haven't talked to her since we were kids. She looks ... different."

"She looks like she's about to be eaten by a mountain chimera." Samuel started across the street, but halted at the curb.

Cindy continued singing as she stepped in front of the chimera. She had a burlap sack in her arms, and as she sang, she reached into the sack and extracted several small, translucent-skinned worms.

"Is that limpid worm larvae?" Javier asked.

"Yeah. She appears to have an unending supply of the things," Samuel grumbled.

"Not unending," I said, as we jogged up to where Samuel was. "She told me they're attracted to the peaberries in her mother's garden. Cindy's in charge of deworming the garden at home."

"Brilliant idea." Javier stared at Cindy, interest sparking in his gaze.

Cindy's melody reached an end. She laid the larvae in front of the chimera in lines like tally marks. She then took a step back and went to her knees, hands folded neatly in her lap.

"Revered Chimera, we humbly request you to pass through our lands without bloodshed. Our deepest apologies for disturbing your hunting." Cindy's voice was calm and clear as she addressed the creature, nothing like her usual chattering self. "We have brought an offering to demonstrate our sincerity and respect."

The chimera's snake tail slithered to the grubs, flicked its tongue out as if to examine them, then slithered in front of Cindy. I would have freaked out and run like a man in a hockey mask was chasing me with a machete, but she remained still.

Samuel took a step. I don't think he meant to, but he was staring at Cindy with fear in his eyes and he just moved.

"Easy," Javier said. "She's doing great."

"She's a fool," Gilda spat. "This is no place for her kind. She'll be killed."

"Yeah, you mentioned that, but look at her over there, not getting killed." Javier gripped Samuel by the shoulder. "She's invoking the respect and apology ritual. I heard my great-grandfather talk about it once or twice, but thought the lyrics had been lost over the years. I'd totally forgotten about the worm larvae, too. It's a delicacy for many Beyond creatures."

"Then why isn't the chimera eating the worms?" My hands were clenched by my sides. I felt sick to my stomach with worry for my friend.

"She's deciding whether or not to take the offering," Samuel said. "The next few minutes will determine whether Cindy, and Dead End, lives or dies."

"I can't stand this." My teeth were clenched so tightly my jaw was throbbing. "It's been six *hours*."

"Six *minutes*," Javier said. "But I get you."

"Be quiet," Gilda said. "Don't draw the chimera's attention to you."

Funny she should mention that, because that was exactly what I intended to do. Dig a big hole with my ability, draw the attention of the chimera, grab Cindy, and make a run for it.

Samuel's gaze was locked on Cindy's back. "She's moving."

The chimera extended an index finger. The clawed tip was as big as Cindy's head, which I got to compare easily because she was *reaching for Cindy's head.*

"No." The word punched out of my lungs.

The claw retracted and the tip of the chimera's fleshy finger grazed the front of Cindy's face. Her head tipped to one side as she regarded the human seated in front of her.

"I think she wants her to sing," I said.

Cindy got the message and began singing the lullaby again. The melody washed over us in placid waves. As her soft voice weaved with the night sounds of the town, the chimera picked up the larvae, one by one, chewing slowly, timing her meal perfectly so that the last bite coincided with the final notes.

When the creature had finished eating, she stood, nodded at Cindy, and walked calmly out of the park. As she reached the edge of town, she let out one last scream, though this one sounded joyous rather than furious, then took off at a run toward the mountains and disappeared into the night.

We *flew* across the street. Samuel beat me by a few strides, but I got the first hug. I pulled Cindy close and squeezed her hard. I needed to make sure she was still here, still real, still alive.

"You scared the crap out of me." I was crying and I couldn't recall starting. "Don't ever do something that dangerous again."

"Let the girl breathe," Javier said.

"That was irresponsible and stupid." Gilda tipped up her chin and huffed. "You put yourself and the town in danger. We asked you to leave it to the Elites, didn't we? But you had to get involved, and now—"

"—the chimera is gone. Without hurting anything but a few trees and Gilda's pride," Javier finished.

Gilda pressed her lips together until they were thin and bloodless. Threw her hair back, crossed her arms.

Javier smiled down at Cindy. "That was some fast thinking. How do you know the ritual?"

"I learned it when I was little." Her voice was sweet and brittle, like sugar glass. Her face was washed out and her hands were trembling. She appeared to be in a state of shock.

"You were brave as hell out there, Cindy." Samuel cupped her face and turned her to look at him. "Thank you."

"You're welcome," she said, and threw up.

"I LEARNED the ritual as a kid. No big deal. I'm sorry about your shoes."

"They'll wash," Samuel said.

We'd walked to his house since it was closest. Javier had offered to walk Gilda home, so it was just the three of us. It was half past two in the morning and I was probably on restriction for the rest of my natural life, but Cindy and Dead End were safe.

Totally worth it.

"You're going to make me barf again. Quit squeezing me so hard, Maria."

"I can't. You could have died out there tonight. I'm never letting you walk home alone again. Jeez, Cindy, what were you thinking? You should have waited for us, told us what you were doing."

"She tried." Samuel kept his eyes on Cindy as he spoke to me. "We were too stupid to listen."

"It's okay. I'm used to being ignored by Elites." Cindy had washed up in the bathroom and was now seated on the sofa beside me, across from where Samuel paced the length of the living room. "Is this really your house?"

"Of course, it is." Samuel had scowled at Cindy's *used to being ignored* remark. "You've seen it before."

"Not the living room. We're always in the garage or outside. I love the colors."

He shrugged. "My mom loved orange and my dad liked dark blue. After my parents died, my sister and I didn't want to change it."

"Why would you? They're happy colors." Cindy yawned, and hugged an orange and gray sofa pillow to her chest. I had a similar one in blue on my lap.

"Yeah." Samuel stopped pacing. It was almost comical, the way he watched Cindy. As if she was some sort of magic trick that, if he studied her closely enough, he'd figure out how the magician made the rabbit disappear. "Who taught you that ritual?"

"Was that Javier Rivas with you tonight?" She plucked at the corner of the pillow. I wondered why she was dodging Samuel's question.

"Yes. Why?" His frown deepened.

"Umm, because he's super hot?" I waggled my eyebrows at her. Samuel resumed his pacing, stomping a little harder than necessary in my opinion.

Cindy yawned again, then laughed. "No, it's that I haven't seen him since before I left Dead End."

That snagged my attention. "I thought you'd lived here your whole life."

"My parents have, but I went to live with my grandmother at Track's End when I was in the second grade. I didn't return to Dead End until last year, when she passed away."

"I'm sorry for your loss," I said.

"Thank you. I loved her very much. She was like me. A lesser."

I really didn't like that word.

Cindy smiled when she saw my frown. "It's okay. She knew what she was, too. She always said, 'Those self-important Elites are thinking it anyway. Best just to put it out there yourself. That way they can't hurt you.'"

"If your parents lived here, why did you live with your grandmother?"

"Bullies." Samuel looked grim. "*Elite* bullies, right?"

She nodded. "It was hard when they only called me names, but when a couple of Elite girls dragged me to the monkey bars and kicked me until they cracked a rib, my parents said it was too dangerous for me here and sent me to Grandma. She home-schooled me so I could learn in peace."

"I'm sorry for that," Samuel said.

"Why? You never picked on me."

"I didn't stand up for you, either. I could have. I *should* have."

"Thanks for being sorry." She didn't let him off the hook for failing. I liked that about her. "You know, Mica helped me that day."

Samuel's head whipped around. "My sister helped you?"

Cindy nodded. "She sent one of her friends to get a teacher, then ran over and lay across my body. Mr. Wheeler said if she hadn't stopped those girls, they might have killed me. It's happened before." She glanced in my direction. "Mr. Wheeler was my second-grade teacher."

"*Happened before? Killed* you? What the hell is up with these Elite jackasses?"

"Umm…" Cindy wrinkled her nose. "*You're* an Elite, Maria."

"No, I'm not. I don't want to be lumped in with those losers. No offense, Samuel."

"None taken. I don't want that either, but I am an Elite and so are you. You can, as Javier and I have, choose not to be around the worst of them, but that choice doesn't take away what you are. Your ability dictates what you are."

"But you're not a *jackass* Elite." Cindy nudged me.

"Thank you," I said.

"You know, that sounds like something Mica would do. Thanks for telling me that." Samuel let slip a smile.

"You're welcome."

The way they were looking at each other made me feel like a third wheel, so I decided to change the subject before they forgot I was in the room altogether.

I tucked the pillow on my lap behind my back and stifled a yawn. I was tired, but wired, and I didn't know if I'd ever get to sleep. "Tell me about these ritual things."

She shrugged. "Rituals are the old way. Years ago, Sanctumites lived in the Beyond. We were able to coexist with the creatures there because there were understandings between us and them. Respectful boundaries, offerings, songs, blessings, prayers ... things like that. But people got tired of these things and moved out of the Beyond. Within two generations, all the rituals were lost. Completely forgotten."

"If they're lost, how do you know them?"

"My grandma's side of the family passed them down through the lessers. This was before the revolution, at a time when our kind were still being rounded up and sent to work farms by the Elites. Keeping the rituals alive meant my kind would be safe in the Beyond if they saw the chance to escape the farms."

"Rounded up? They were sent there for their own good," Samuel said. "To keep them safe from harm."

"Keep us safe? It was to keep us *oppressed*. If a lesser showed the slightest bit of intellect, they were silenced. We lessers might not have abilities, but we aren't fools. We learned to play the game long ago."

"You almost make it sound as if the Elites back then were afraid of your kind," he said. "But what would they have to fear?"

"Our numbers," Cindy replied. "For every Elite like you, there are three lessers and four mid-caste—people with low grade abilities, Maria."

First I'd heard of the term, but it made sense.

"They knew that if the lessers ever teamed up with the mid-caste, they'd overthrow the Elites' fascist regime. And if they were able to pull some powerful Elites over to their side?"

"They'd start a revolution. Which is exactly what happened fifty years ago." Samuel appeared nonplussed. "We've always been taught that it was rebellious Elites who engineered the revolution."

"Yeah, well, revolution or not, our governing systems are still mostly run by the wealthy Elite class. There's no way they'd admit they were defeated by a bunch of no-and-low talents."

Something odd happened then. Samuel began to laugh. Not just laugh, but *guffaw*. I'd never had a reason to use that word before, though I'd come across it occasionally in the books I read, but there was no other way to describe it. The guy was definitely guffawing.

Cindy squeezed the pillow tight to her chest. Stared up at Samuel with hurt in her eyes. "You don't believe me."

"Oh, I believe you. It makes perfect sense," he said, between laughs. "I want to record the look on Gilda's face when we tell her. The exact moment when she runs through the probabilities and arrives at the same conclusion I did."

"What conclusion?" Cindy asked.

"Why would Elites ever surrender power? The answer is, they wouldn't unless they knew they couldn't win. And the only way to win a war is with a bigger and better army."

I wasn't sure that was entirely true, but it sounded good. Also, it was kind of fun to watch Samuel crack up like that, so I kept my rebuttal to myself.

"Hey." I grabbed the pillow behind me and chucked it at his head when he flopped onto the floor. "Quit it. You freaked her out."

He wiped his eyes. "Sorry. I really do believe you."

Cindy tossed her pillow at him, too. "You should. Your grandparents were part of the last revolution. Part of the 'rebellious Elites.'"

"I know. I always thought that was cool."

"Okay, so it's been a fantastic history lesson, but why did your grandma teach you these rituals if you don't have to escape those awful camps anymore?"

"Partly tradition, and partly because the creatures are moving closer." Cindy yawned for the third time, and this time I did too.

Samuel stopped laughing. "Closer?"

"Grandmother noticed it years ago. There were creatures in the mountains that used to live in the desert region. The *chupacabra*, for instance. You remember the bones, Maria?"

How could I forget? "Did she teach you a ritual for the *chupacabra*?"

"She taught me how to respect them and how to be respected by them. Nothing is certain with a *chupacabra*, though. They're unpredictable. Grandma always said the best way to deal with one was to avoid them in the first place."

"Exactly how many of the old rituals did your grandma teach you?" Samuel asked.

Maybe it was just me, but he sounded like he was humoring Cindy.

There was the slightest edge of condescension in his tone that grated on my nerves.

The smile she gave him was of the "go screw yourself" variety. It was my new favorite expression of hers—so long as it wasn't pointed at me.

"*All* of them."

25

Even though Cindy lived farther from Samuel than I did, I walked her home. After the events of the evening, along with her retelling of how those Elite girls had treated her, I would have worried if I hadn't made sure she was safe. Also, it was four a.m. and I was really not looking forward to facing my grandfathers. Especially Abuelo.

"You were stupidly brave tonight." I told Cindy when we were at her door.

"Aww, you say the nicest things. I wuv you, too, Maria." She giggled and went inside.

I trudged home after that, wondering how long I'd be on restriction. Maybe I was already grounded. Probably had been for hours.

Easing open the front door, I tiptoed inside. Caught sight of Grandpa Holli and Toby facing away from the door, drinking tea at the dining room table. Out of real teacups. *Both* of them.

I crept toward the hallway, trying not to draw attention to myself. Sadly, like most things that happened tonight, it didn't go as planned. One of the floorboards creaked with a sound like an off-key accordion when I was barely halfway across the foyer.

Toby yipped and wagged his tail. I held my finger to my lips and tried to intimidate him into obeying me from across the room. He completely ignored both the sign and my attempt at intimidation, and yipped again.

Grandpa Holli spun around in his seat. "*Maria.*"

He jumped out of his chair and headed straight for me, his mouth compressed into a line. I'd never seen what he looked like when he was angry, but I was pretty sure this was it.

I held up my hands, took a small step back. "I know you're mad and I'm probably in big trouble, but I can explain. See, there was this—"

"Thank heavens you're safe." He pulled me into a hug as tight as the one I'd given Cindy after her run-in with the chimera. "I was worried sick."

The tension that had been thrumming through my muscles for hours slowly drained away, leaving exhaustion and soreness behind. "I'm okay, Grandpa. Are you and Toby having tea?"

"Oh, just a little chamomile-star-of-Bethlehem-cherry-plum mixture to keep us centered." Grandpa Holli held me at arm's length, his gaze scanning me as he looked for any sign of injury. When he found none, he exhaled with relief and put a hand over his heart. "Thank goodness you're all right."

"I'm sorry for making you worry."

Toby leaped off the dining room chair and trotted over to us. I apologized for worrying him by way of a scratch behind the ears.

"It's your abuelo to whom you should apologize. He's out there right now, looking for you." Grandpa Holli gestured toward the door. "Where were you?"

I thought about lying. Deception was never my first choice and it bothered me that it came to mind so easily now. I was *not* a liar.

"I went to a party."

"A party? You said you were 'hanging out with some friends.' You said nothing about a party."

"I know. It was wrong not to tell you. I'm sorry."

"What sort of party? Were there 'substances' there?"

I figured he meant booze and drugs. "Alcohol. But don't worry, I don't drink or do drugs. I can't."

"Can't? What do you mean?"

"With my ability … well, it's kind of dangerous. It's not good for me to lose control of myself."

"That certainly makes sense. Who was at the party?"

"A bunch of snooty Elites."

The front door slammed open behind me. I cringed.

"Emilio?" Grandpa Holli's eyes widened.

I looked over my shoulder to find my abuelo standing in the doorway. He was drenched. His expression hardened when he saw me, but he said nothing.

Grandpa Holli swiped a dishtowel off the dining table and dabbed at the water on his husband's face. "You're soaked to the bone. What happened?"

"Russ from the Fire Department had to douse some fires just outside town." He shrugged out of his coat and squelched across the room in his wet loafers to hang it over a dining room chair. Grandpa Holli intercepted the coat and ran it through the kitchen and into the laundry room. "His ability isn't exactly precise. The splash zone was bigger than anticipated."

"How did the fires start?" Grandpa Holli asked from the next room.

Abuelo's gaze slid to me. "Apparently somebody disturbed a mountain chimera."

"A chimera?" Grandpa Holli came back to the room carrying a laundry basket and a towel. He indicated that Abuelo should put his wet shoes in the basket. "They never come this close to town."

"They do if provoked." He put his shoes in the basket and accepted the towel. "Thank you, amor."

"You're welcome. Where is it now?"

"Back in the mountains. Apparently, someone performed one of the old rituals and the chimera agreed to leave."

"Really? I didn't think anyone remembered them."

"There are a few out there who make it a point to remember." He looked straight into my eyes, and I knew he knew Cindy had performed the ritual.

"Good thing, then." Grandpa Holli picked up the basket.

"Hollister, don't clean up after me. I can wash that stuff."

"I know you can, but I've already got a load ready to go in. It'll be no trouble. Come on, Toby. Time for a last trip outside." He took the clothing and my dog, and left the room without a backward glance.

If I were a betting woman, I'd have bet my last two bottles of prismatic nail polish he didn't have a load ready to go into the washer. Grandpa hated doing laundry and usually left it to Abuelo or me. He'd left the room on purpose so Abuelo and I could be alone.

How thoughtful of him.

When he was gone, Abuelo rounded on me. If flames had poured out of his mouth, he would not have looked any scarier than he did at that moment.

"What the devil were you thinking?"

26

NEITHER OF US SAID A WORD OR MOVED A MUSCLE.

I stood tall, preparing myself for whatever punishment he had for me. Coming home at four in the morning without so much as a phone call? I deserved it.

"*Tonta.*" Abuelo said.

Even though my knowledge of Spanish was beginner level compared to his, I knew what that meant. *Fool.*

I pressed my lips together to keep myself from speaking. *I deserve this.*

"What were you thinking, going to a chimera-watching party?"

Uh-oh. He knew about a lot more than Cindy performing rituals. "I was invited by some kids from school. I didn't know what would happen," I said, deciding that playing dumb would be my best bet.

It wasn't, if Abuelo's expression was any indication.

"You didn't know that a chimera would show up to a *chimera-watching* party? Dios mio, if you're going to lie to my face, at least do a better job than that."

"I thought it was just a prank. I didn't think one would actually show up."

"But one did."

I couldn't dispute that.

"The problem is, you don't seem to realize you aren't in the Other anymore." He pointed out the dining room window toward the Divide. "Things here have consequences. Grave consequences."

"That's true in my world, too."

"And do you have creatures like the chimera over there?"

"No." I stared at the teacups on the table and tried hard not to yawn. I was too tired for this conversation, but I didn't see any way of getting out of it. "On my side of the Divide, chimeras are myths, stories."

"Do you know why that is?"

I met his eyes, shook my head.

The creases around his eyes and mouth seemed to deepen as he spoke. "Because your world has very little magic. To support the life force of a chimera or any other creature in our Beyond, there must be magic."

"When you say magic, it sounds silly to me. Even magic is a myth."

"Here, we respect its power. Magic is a force as strong as gravity. It is in the air we breathe, in the soil beneath our feet, in the blood thrumming through our veins."

"That's why my ability is stronger here?"

He snapped a nod as he blotted his wet clothing with the towel Grandpa Holli had given him. "Speaking of your ability, your actions have put everyone in town at risk."

"*My* actions?" Was he really blaming me for unleashing the chimera on Dead End? I deserved to be punished for being late, but I was not taking the blame for that. "I didn't even get near the chimera, let alone upset her."

He seemed to give up on drying himself with the towel and flicked it over one of the wood dining chairs. "I'm not talking about the party, Maria."

"Then what are you talking about?"

Abuelo's tone went low. "I'm talking about the practice sessions you've been having with Samuel Bekker."

This again? Why was he so hung up on that? "What does that have to do with anything?"

"I told you that using your ability to try to stabilize a ripper was dangerous, but you thought you knew better than me. Now the chimera is hunting closer to town than it ever has before, and the limpid worms are appearing faster than we can get rid of them. Your reckless behavior is going to end up hurting someone."

Exhaustion pressed in from all angles. I gripped the chair nearest me, preparing to sit. "Why?"

"The vibrations draw them in. It's like a melody, playing especially for them. The beckoning call of a siren."

"Why didn't you tell me that before?" And why didn't Samuel mention it?

"I did. You didn't listen."

"No, you told me it was dangerous and that you wouldn't teach me how to stabilize a ripper." I released the back of the dining chair. There was no way I could sit now. I wanted to pace the room to work off some of my frustration, but I held myself still.

"It's the same thing."

"No, it's not." I fisted my hands, digging into my palms with my fingernails. "Do you even hear yourself?"

My grandfather's face flooded with color. He clamped his teeth together and forced the words out between them. "I am telling you now, Maria. Stop trying to stabilize the rippers. Not only are the rippers themselves exceedingly dangerous, but in doing so, you risk drawing more creatures out of the Beyond."

"I have to get to my dad." Heat suffused my cheeks, and I gritted my teeth. Could he not see how much saving Dad meant to me? Or maybe he did see and didn't care.

"You told us your father was a law enforcement officer. Would he want you to risk the lives of the people in this town to save his?"

No, he wouldn't, and I hated my grandfather for bringing that up.

"If you showed me how to stabilize one, I wouldn't need to practice so much. It would solve both our problems." My voice went soft and small. "I don't want to hurt anyone. I just need my dad. *Please.*"

Abuelo shook his head. "Rippers are dangerous, Maria. Don't go near them."

Desperation faded into resignation. He wasn't going to help me.

Not because he thought the rippers were dangerous, but because he didn't give a crap about me or my dad.

"I know the real reason you won't teach me."

"*Real* reason? I told you the real reason. It's dangerous."

"That's not it." I shook my head, shrugged. "Teaching me how to control my ability would require us to spend time together, and you've made it clear you don't want me here."

His forehead scrunched until I couldn't see where his eyebrows ended and his eyelashes began. "What are you talking about?"

"I'm talking about all those one-sided conversations through the pages of your newspaper. The looks of disappointment you give me when you think I'm not paying attention. You hate that it was me who twisted the lock on the café door. *I was the wrong Maria.*" I hit my chest with both hands as I sobbed out the words. My heart pounded my ribs sore, and the act of holding back my tears burned my throat.

He drew back as if I'd slapped him. "No."

"Admit it. You wish my mom had been at that café table. Not me."

"That is *not* true."

Tears streamed down my face now, and the emotion caught in my throat tapered my voice into a whisper. "Dios mio, if you're going to lie to my face, at least do a better job than that."

His lips tightened and he spun around, facing away from me.

"Tell me the truth." I swiped my hands over my face, wiped them on my jeans. "Admit you wish it had been her."

"Yes," he said.

Once, back when I was still allowed to go to school, I got accidentally kicked in the stomach while playing soccer during P.E. The feeling I had now was a lot like that. It was one thing to believe something awful was true, it was another thing to hear it from the source.

Abuelo didn't turn around, wouldn't look at me, as he spoke. "Do I wish that my daughter had been in the café that day? Do I wish she was still alive? Yes, I do. Every damn day."

I felt heavy. All noise, outside of his voice, had amplified to an abnormal level until his words were nothing but a distant echo. My chest hurt and my lungs had trouble drawing in deep breaths.

The floor rumbled beneath me.

More stupid tears welled up in my eyes and spilled down my cheeks. I missed Dad so much in that moment, I would have risked running through an unstable ripper for a hug from him.

The picture frames on the walls rattled. Abuelo turned to me, his brown eyes wide and alert.

"Maria, you need to calm down." He said this in the voice people use when they think they might be dealing with an unstable person. "Control it."

"The only thing I was taught about my ability was that it was something to hate and fear. That it was best kept hidden away, a shameful secret." I hugged myself since Dad wasn't there to do it. "One day the agency popped up on the road behind us. No warning, no hint that they'd been following us that closely. They tried to run us off the road. I reached for my ability and I used it to save us, but I couldn't control it. I'd never been taught." I stared down at my feet as shame poured over me. "I made this huge hole, this *chasm* in the highway, and the people chasing us drove straight into it. So did the people behind them. And the people behind them, and so on, until thirteen cars had crashed into the hole I made. Innocent people. Elderly people. Families. *Children.*"

Speaking softly, Abuelo said, "Take a breath, Maria. Cálmate."

But I couldn't calm myself. I was too angry and sad and frustrated.

"Cálmate," he said again, as if repeating it would help.

"The worst part was, we couldn't stop and help. We had to keep moving, had to use this terrible accident I had caused to get away. You know my father was a police officer. Do you know what it did to him, having to turn his back on all those hurt people?"

The rumbling intensified. The vibrations rattled my feet inside my shoes.

"He was ashamed of me. *I* was ashamed of me. He begged me to promise not to use my ability in that way again, and you know what? I couldn't even give him that, because I didn't know how I did it in the first place. What Samuel Bekker has taught me is the closest I've ever come to understanding how this all works." I sucked in a trembling breath. "And here you stand, with all the answers I need, and all you can do is tell me, 'Rippers are dangerous, Maria. Don't go near them.'"

The house creaked and moaned and popped. In the kitchen, dishes tumbled out of the cabinets and crashed onto the floor. Behind me, three framed photos shook off the wall. I glanced over to see what I'd done, and one of the photos caught my eye. It was a picture of my grandparents and my mother, when she was my age.

They all looked so happy.

The floor jerked and a wood-splintering *crack* came from somewhere in the house. The window in the dining room made a humming sound I'd never heard before. It was the glass. It was shivering like a leaf in a windstorm.

"Maria, you must calm yourself. That window is going to—"

"*Emilio? Maria?* Is everything—"

Abuelo swiveled toward the sound of his husband's voice. "Hollister, get out of—"

The window shattered. My grandpa hit the floor as bullet-sized shards of glass shot at him. The towel he'd been carrying fell into a pitiful pile beside his splayed-out body.

"*Grandpa Holli.*"

The rumbling stopped. I couldn't move. Couldn't speak beyond the whispered cry of his name.

Abuelo Emilio rushed to his side. "Amor? Mi amor, talk to me."

Grandpa Holli groaned, then said, "Ouch."

Swiping the towel from the floor, Abuelo gently dusted glass off his husband's head and helped him to his feet. Blood poured down the side of Grandpa Holli's face and drizzled to the floor below, reminding me of the water droplets dripping from Abuelo's coat earlier.

Grandpa Holli swiped at them with the towel. His gaze landed on me, then skittered away. For a split second, I saw fear in his eyes. My grandpa was afraid.

Of me.

My breathing burst out in harsh, fast puffs. Stars shimmered, then exploded in the corners of my vision.

"Maria, are you—"

Abuelo cut Grandpa Holli off. "*Look at what you've done.*"

"Emilio, I'm sure she didn't mean to—"

"I *told you* to calm yourself." His stony gaze locked with mine.

I backed away from them, shook my head. "I-I'm sorry."

Toby ran inside through the doggy door Grandpa Holli had installed the first week we arrived. He huddled under the table, ears back, tail between his legs. He looked more frightened than he had when the limpid worm had tried to eat him.

Frightened. Of *me*.

Glass crunched under my sneakers as I backed myself against the wall where the photo of my mom and her dads had once hung. A nail dug into my shoulder. I barely felt the sting.

I'd hurt Grandpa Holli and terrified Toby. Infuriated Abuelo Emilio. There was no place for me in Dead End. There never had been.

My thoughts spiraled like the whirlpool I'd created during swimming practice the day I'd hung on by my fingertips to escape death. I should have just let go that day. If I had, there never would have been a hole in the road and all those people wouldn't have gotten hurt. Dad wouldn't have a reason to be ashamed of me. Grandpa Holli wouldn't be bleeding. Both he and Abuelo would still believe Mom was alive. They would, in a way, still have their daughter.

No one would have been hurt if I had just *let go*.

"I'm so sorry."

I ran to the bathroom and threw up.

27

When I got out of the bathroom, my grandpas were gone.

Toby was outside the door, waiting for me. His scruffy ears were peaked, his short tail was wagging. I picked him up, hugged him to me.

"Sorry, Toby." I wiped my tears on his fur. "Sorry I scared you."

I carried him into my room, set him on the bed, and dug my backpack out of the closet. I wadded up the clothes I'd brought, less the jeans buried in the back yard, leaving the things my grandpas had bought for me.

"Don't be sad, okay? Remember how much I love you." I zipped up the stuffed backpack and grabbed the smaller one. Shoved my makeup into it, except for the prismatic black nail polish. That was going to Cindy. I'd leave a note and ask Grandpa Holli to make sure she got it. Surely he wasn't so angry with me that he'd take it out on her.

My dog sniffed my backpack and whined, and I picked him up again. "Crossing through a ripper is dangerous, Toby. Leaving you is the last thing I want to do." Dad's words on the other side of the One Way Café came back to haunt me. *It's the last thing I want to do, but it's the only way to keep you safe.*

After I packed, I cleaned. I'd just finished picking up the broken dishes in the kitchen, and was in the living room sweeping up window glass, when Aedan showed up.

"Whoa, what the hell happened here? Is that blood?"

"Go away."

"Are you bleeding?" He popped up in front of me, frowning. "Not you. One of your grandpas, then?"

Ignoring him, I swept the glass into the dustpan and carried it to the trash. Grabbed a cleaning rag and some herbal cleanser Grandpa Holli bought from Cindy's mom, and mopped up the blood. I set the photos on the table. Picked the broken glass from the frames.

When the room was as clean as I could get it, I tossed Toby one of the organic dog cookies Grandpa Holli had made him, and gave him a teary kiss on his head. Then I slung my backpack over my shoulder, wiped my face with the back of my hand, and walked out.

The air outside was that stagnant, gummy sort of hot only the desert can provide. It made me feel boxed in, for some reason. Trapped.

"Why won't you talk to me?" Aedan asked.

I slammed on my brakes, spun to face him. "How are you still here?"

"I'm attached to you. Anywhere you go, I can go, too."

"Could you make that sound any creepier?"

He grinned. "I could do it in a dirty-old-man voice if you think that might help."

"Not sure it would make a difference. Aedan, go away. I can't deal with you right now."

"Tell me what you're doing, and I will." His eyes narrowed. "You aren't moving in with that Samuel dude, are you? Because no. That's really not going to work for me."

I considered telling him yes, and that Samuel and I were sleeping together, but he'd only spin it as me trying to make him jealous ... and I'd never been good at mind games, anyway.

"No, I'm not moving in with Samuel. I'm leaving Dead End. I've been causing a lot of trouble around here."

"You? Hard to believe."

"I'd say sarcasm doesn't become you, Aedan, but it actually does. Your face was created to express irony and contempt."

"I love it when you insult me with your honors English vocabulary. Keep talking to me, Maria." He tilted his head and showed me that handsome, irresistible grin, and I did that stupid thing again. I started telling him everything.

"Aedan, I screwed up b-bad." My voice snagged on the last word. "I'm bad."

"I'm listening."

We plopped down—well, I plopped; he hovered—on the curb across from the fragrant green landscape of the sacred gardens that only those who had achieved internal peace and horticultural sanctification could enter, and I spilled my guts.

"You're really going to leave Dead End?"

I nodded.

"It was an accident. You're not bad." He leaned over and kissed me on the cheek. I wished I could feel it.

"I made my grandpa bleed, Aedan. Because of me, he's hurt. Does it matter that it was an accident?"

"Probably not to you."

"Exactly."

Aedan gestured toward a house across the street. If I had to guess, I would have said it was Mr. Martindale's house, since it was cally-corner from the sacred gardens, and also because there were plastic lawn flamingos and ceramic garden gnomes packed butts-to-guts, as Dad would say, inside the white picket fence.

Aedan pointed to the mailbox, underneath which five flamingos had cornered a cackling gnome. "Are the gnomes and flamingos fighting each other?"

"It's either a fight or a party," I said. "I'm thinking party, since I can smell the boysenberry syrup from here."

Aedan mouthed the word "boysenberry" and shook his head. "Are you sure you want to leave this place? It seems perfect for people as weird as we are."

I wasn't offended by the insult. I'd been weird all my life. *Weird, dork, creepy*. Some of the kids had hurled those insults at me from time to time. I hadn't liked being yelled at, but as insults went, I'd never been bothered by weird.

"I'm sure. I shouldn't be here."

"Why not?"

"Because I cause trouble." I stood, dusted off my pants. "As a thank you for listening, I'm going to offer you fair warning. Don't look for me on the other side, Aedan. Because the next time you Kilshaw a-holes show up, I won't hold back."

"Come on. You're still lumping me in with them?"

"Aren't you one of them?" I headed toward the ripper fields. It was going to be a long walk, so I figured I should get started.

"Not everyone is as lucky as you are."

Anxious, I ran my hand through my hair. My ponytail holder fell out, so I swiped it up and wrapped it around my wrist. "Lucky? Have you been listening to me at all?"

"Not everyone has a dad who would die to protect them. Not everyone has a *choice.*"

I halted. "You say that as if you know my dad." I squeezed my eyes shut and mentally kicked myself. "Wait a minute. You're part of Kilshaw. You'd know if they had him."

Why hadn't I thought to ask that before? I was so busy trying to use my ability to break through the Divide, I didn't consider that I had a spy in the organization standing, *floating,* right in front of me. For God's sake, how could I have missed such a simple thing?

"You can stop mentally punishing yourself now. Even if you had thought to ask, I wouldn't have had any answers for you." Aedan shrugged. "Since I 'lost' you at the café, no one trusts me with information about either your dad or you. After I project here, I report back to them, Maria, and I tell them things you're doing. Because if I don't, I'd never get to see you again. They wouldn't allow it."

I looked at him. Really looked. I'd been so caught up in my own problems, I hadn't considered Aedan might be having some too. His normally easy smile had faded, and he looked tired. The sort of tired that follows a long, losing fight with something awful.

"You have no idea why I work for a man like Kilshaw, so don't judge me, Maria Guadalupe."

He was right and it annoyed me, so I started walking again. "You don't want me to judge you? Tell me why you work for him."

"Someday I will."

"When?"

"Soon. Gotta go."

"I hate it when you do that," I muttered to empty air.

28

THE RIPPER FIELD WAS AS SCARY IN THE EARLY MORNING HOURS AS IT was in the afternoon. There were more picked-clean bones scattered beside the carnival mirror membrane that made up the Divide on this side, and I wondered how many were chupacabra, how many were cow, and how many were human.

It occurred to me that not bringing along some sort of weapon was a mistake I might not live long enough to regret.

I walked along the Divide, not too close, letting the vibrations flow through my body the way Samuel had showed me. When I got to the other side, I'd do everything I could to find his sister after I found Dad. If this worked, I might be able to send her home. That would be a good way to thank Samuel for the lessons.

Tears clouded my eyes as I thought about Cindy. She was the first best friend I'd ever had. We'd only known each other for a short time, but it didn't matter. Sometimes you clicked with someone and it felt as if you'd known them forever. I was going to miss her like crazy.

"Focus."

I shoved all the worries and regrets out of my head and, reaching out with my ability, tested the closest rippers. None of them felt right. I needed one that spoke to me, one with vibrations I resonated with, one that was begging me to fix it.

A half-mile walk later, I found the perfect ripper. It was partially underground and vibrating in a jarring rhythm I felt in my teeth. I could fix it. Make it hold steady.

I tightened the straps of my backpack. There would be no time to pick it up once I got the ripper stabilized, so I needed to wear it. Again, I wished I'd brought a weapon. It's not as if I had a clue where I'd end up on the other side. No one had told me how this worked. I could be halfway across the world, or right back in Arizona, near the diner. The possibilities were endlessly frightening, so I decided not to think too hard about them.

The vibrations from the ripper seeped into me. I welcomed them, let them boil my blood and rattle my bones. I drizzled my ability into the ground until the tremors I created blended with the chaos of the pulsations and beat like a drum into my heart. Together we created a melody so instinctive and ancient that it must have been around when the world was born.

The ripper settled, and as though through the surface of a calm lake, I was able to see right through it. Desert scrub and a dusty highway. Tumbleweeds. Cactus. In the distance, I spotted the abandoned café. Still in Arizona, then. Maybe Dad was close by, watching for me.

In my excitement, I dropped a few notes of the melody, but I picked it up again and refocused. The ground shook, but it wasn't as frightening as it had been yesterday in my grandfathers' house. I'd learned something from digging holes with Samuel. My ability wasn't static and unchangeable. It was flexible and elastic, and capable of more than just making holes in the ground and destroying things. It could fix things, too.

The edges of the ripper peeled back, revealing more of the desert and café and road. A large black SUV sped up to the café and slammed on its brakes.

I recognized that SUV.

"So *that's* what he meant by soon. I should have known."

The passenger door opened, and Aedan climbed out. His long silver hair was pulled into a braid and he was wearing jeans and a black T-shirt instead of his Kilshaw uniform, but it was him.

My stomach rolled over. *Of course*, it was him. Who else could betray me so perfectly? The guy I was stupid enough to trust after he'd screwed me over.

The driver's door opened and a man whose face I knew as well as my own, even though I'd only seen it in nightmares and blurry photographs, exited the vehicle.

Tristan Kilshaw.

His hair was black and threaded with silver that perfectly matched the color of his business suit. His skin was brown and lined with age. He was tall, and though I wasn't a great judge of height, I estimated he was two or three inches over six foot. Aedan was an inch or two shorter, closer to my dad's height.

"You did it."

I backed up a step as Kilshaw strode toward me, toward the ripper. He could just walk right through. Or I could. Did I want that? This was everything I'd hoped for, and nothing I'd hoped for, at the same time.

"Did it?" I knew what he meant, so I don't know why I said that. Probably because I was scared half out of my mind and not making any sense.

"You've learned to stabilize a ripper. Good job, Maria."

Aedan trailed behind him, his chin on his chest, eyes on the rubber toe of his sneakers.

"This is tremendous news for you. Because now I won't have to kill him." He whistled then, loud and sharp and long, and two men stumbled out of the SUV.

One was short, red-haired, with milk-white skin. The other had the same skin tone, but he was tanned from outdoor work and had golden brown hair. His clothes were ripped and dirty, and his hands were tied behind his back. He shuffled in my direction as if his feet were chained together.

"Loops?" His voice was faint, but I had been listening for it.

"Dad?"

The red-headed man shoved him, causing him to trip and fall to his knees.

"Let my dad go." I lost control of the ripper for a second as fury boiled through me.

"Oh, I will, I will." Kilshaw's voice was like a razor blade dipped in honey. "After you bring me through."

"No." My dad struggled to his feet and the short guy punched him in the back.

This time my fury didn't boil, it froze. I stared at Aedan's downcast face. "You told me you didn't know anything. Did you do this?"

He lifted his head and gave me a miserable look. "None of this was my idea."

"Of course it wasn't. It was a *good* idea," Kilshaw said. "Maria, you really—"

"Don't touch him again or you'll regret it." I caught the redheaded man's gaze. "You have no idea what I'm capable of."

"Loops, I'm okay," my dad said. "Don't do anything." He'd stumbled up to Kilshaw by then. The four males stood in a semi-circle around the ripper.

For no reason I could see, the short guy gripped the back of my dad's neck and forced him to his knees. More than anything else, it was that stupid, senseless violence that made me do what I did next.

The ground in both places trembled. Samuel had never told me my ability would work on the opposite side of a ripper, but then, maybe it would have been news to him, too.

I took a step closer to the Divide. It felt as if I were slogging through wet sand.

"Think, my dear little Maria." Kilshaw's expression was the dictionary definition of condescending. "It's a good deal. We both get what we want. You get your father and I get into Sanctum." He edged toward the tear on his side and I pulled my ability back. The ripper shrunk by half. He stopped, cursed. "Grady, Maria needs a little convincing."

"This isn't necessary." Aedan's gaze went from me to my father. "She'll let you through."

Kilshaw ignored him. "Now."

Grady kicked Dad in the ribs. His breath huffed out, along with a groan of pain.

"Stop it!" Energy filled my entire body. It was a little like I imagined sticking my head in an oven would feel. Painful, but mostly suffocatingly hot and terrifying.

"That wasn't even hard." Grady spat on the ground by Dad's head. "Wuss."

"You should run away now." My anger was a big thing. Too big for my mind and body. "I'm warning you."

"Loops," my dad gasped, "don't."

"No, Maria," Aedan shook his head. "Don't use your ability over here."

"Shut up, Aedan. Again, Grady." Kilshaw was watching me, and I was watching for an opportunity.

This time, the short man took six steps back. He wanted a running start, I guess. It gave me room. Just enough.

I thrust my ability into the sand under his feet.

"*No*," Dad rasped, but it was too late.

Grady was sucked beneath the surface of the ground so fast he didn't have time to scream. The only evidence he had been there at all was a shock of red hair sticking out of the sand.

"Damn it, it's not enough! If you want something done right, you have to do it yourself," Kilshaw bellowed, red-faced with fury. He stomped to where Dad lay and yanked him to his feet. Pulled out one of those weird guns—it looked like the one the man working with Aedan had fired at me—and jammed it against my dad's head.

"Don't," Aedan said. "She'll do what you want. No one has to get hurt." He glanced at where Grady used to be. "Well, you know, no one *else*."

Kilshaw lifted his chin. "She attacked my associate."

"You hated Grady. You brought him out here to kill him yourself, remember?"

"He was mine to kill." Kilshaw pointed the gun at me.

"He's not dead. Yet," I said. "You can still save him—if he's good at holding his breath."

My father gaped at me. Kilshaw looked interested.

One side of Aedan's mouth lifted into a grin.

"No." Dad shook his head in what looked like a mixture of disbelief and disappointment. "This isn't you. Loops. Set him free."

"Why?" Aedan's brow scrunched into a frown. "He wouldn't think twice about killing you."

"She knows why," Dad said.

I did, but I also didn't care. "No."

"This isn't you." Dad shook his head sadly. "This isn't my little girl."

"He hurt you."

"I can take the pain. What I can't take is you letting Kilshaw turn you into a monster."

Aedan's puzzled frown turned into an angry one. "Don't call her that."

"You think I'm a *monster*?" I'd suspected Dad saw me that way since the accident on the highway, but he'd never said it aloud. It felt like a knife to the heart.

"You know that's not what I meant, sweetheart."

Did I? Because it sure didn't feel like it.

"Don't kill this man and allow him to turn you into something you aren't. *This isn't you.*"

Maybe he was right. Maybe this wasn't me.

"Don't listen to him, Maria," Aedan said, "Using your ability to protect someone you love doesn't make you a monster."

"No, it makes me a murderer." And a disappointment to my dad.

I sent a small ripple through the sand, freeing Grady's head. When I heard him gasp for air, I knew he was alive, but what I didn't know was how I felt about that.

Kilshaw didn't even glance in Grady's direction. "Walk through the ripper, Maria. Prove it's safe."

My dad lifted his bruised face. Not to me, but to my lying, astral not-boyfriend, Aedan. "Please. Don't let Maria do this," he begged.

Aedan's shoulders drooped. "I can't help her, Mr. Thompson."

Dad's jaw tightened and he got that hard, stubborn look in his eyes I knew so well.

"Yes, you can. In fact, I think you're the *only* one who can."

29

NONE OF MY URBAN FANTASY STORIES HAD PREPARED ME FOR THIS. NOT even the Patricia Briggs or the Ilona Andrews books. Nothing in fiction, in Dead End, or in any other part of my life up to this point, had prepared me for this.

I forced myself to take a step.

And another. And another. Until I stood directly in front of the ripper. Once there, I discovered it wasn't only difficult to put one foot in front of the other, it was also difficult to breathe. The vibrations amplified the closer I got, and they repelled me. My vision doubled. Tripled. A warning?

Don't do it.

The music the ripper and I made together formed lyrics. There was no audible voice. The words were the music, and the music was the words.

Don't do it.

"Please." I heard my dad beg Aedan. "She'll die."

"Hurry up, girl." Kilshaw's gaze swept over the ripper. "It's starting to collapse."

Dad lunged at Aedan, grabbed his shirt, and shook him. "*Do it now!*"

Kilshaw reached over and backhanded my dad like an

afterthought. As if he were a black ant on the tip of his finger to be flicked away.

Teeth gritted, I lifted my foot to step over the threshold. My legs were cement, my lungs filled with sand. Every inch I moved was a battle won.

"That's right. Come across and I'll let you and your daddy go home. Wouldn't that be nice? Wouldn't you like to go home?"

Yes. I would like to be home right now, surrounded by my books, safe with my dad. How things were before we started running. Things would be normal, if not perfect, and safe.

I thought of Cindy and Toby and wondered if it really would be all that good without my best friends. And did I really want to return to normal, hiding away for the rest of my life?

There was one last sorrowful, "Please," from Dad as I broke through the resistance and reached the other side.

The second my shoes touched warm Arizona dirt, something slammed into my chest, sending me back through the ripper, breaking my concentration and knocking the wind out of my lungs as I hit the hardpacked sand with an enormous *whomp*.

Gasping for breath, I climbed to my knees, dug my fingers into the dirt, and spider-crawled to the ripper.

It was gone.

"Dad." I thought I'd screamed it, but all I'd managed was a whisper.

"Maria." Aedan sat a few feet away, silver eyes wary.

"You," I gasped, tried to catch my breath. "What have you done?"

"Saved your life. Ended mine."

"You've ruined everything. Kilshaw is going to kill my dad and there's nothing I can do." The words caught in my throat.

Aedan looked at me. "At least this way he won't kill you, too."

Once my lungs had recovered, I pushed to my feet and ran along the Divide. I was desperate. My body was working overtime just to keep me conscious, but I pushed it harder, making my feet move, forcing my eyes to focus.

"Ripper." My voice returned, though it was deeper now, as if I had a cold. "I need another one. I have to get back to him."

"You can't. We lucked out finding each other this time."

"*He's going to kill my dad,*" I shrieked. "I have to get to Kilshaw."

"And do what?" Aedan stomped through the sand behind me. "Were you planning on sinking him in quicksand like you did Grady? Do you really think your little parlor trick back there would work on Tristan Kilshaw?"

"It works on everyone."

"Not him."

"Everyone."

"That only goes to show you have no idea who you're dealing with. He'd let you try, laugh at your weak attempt, and shoot your dad in front of you."

"Why?"

"Because it would break you, and then you'd do whatever he wanted." Aedan's eyes were flat, emotionless. "I've seen him do it dozens of times before."

"If you knew he was doing it, why didn't you stop him?"

"Because I'm not strong enough." The way he said it made it seem as if voicing the words caused him physical pain. "I tried and I tried, Maria, and after he'd had his fun teasing me, letting me believe I had the upper hand, he'd crush me. Humiliate me. Over and over again."

It was the truth. I read it in his eyes. Tristan Kilshaw was even more evil than I'd thought.

And he still had Dad.

I found a ripper. It was too small, and the wrong rhythm, but I poured my ability into it anyway. The tear widened until I saw through to the other side. A city, crowded with people and tall buildings, but I wasn't sure where. Pedestrians bustled past the ripper, never seeing it.

"That's Tokyo," Aedan said. "Close it."

Another ripper opened to the right of Tokyo. Another wrong one. Again, I gave it what I had.

"Looks like Cape Town. I was in South Africa once when I was twelve. The agency was tracking a kid with an oceanic ability. His family hid him so well we never found him. Kilshaw had his family murdered." His eyes went cold. "Close it."

I opened another tear. This one I recognized by the wrought iron lattice tower in the distance. "He's not in Paris, Maria."

My ability powered through me. I felt lightheaded and out of control, but I wasn't going to stop until I found what I was looking for. Another tear opened and I widened it. Desert, but it looked more Sahara than Arizona.

I worked fast, opening another ripper, then another, until I'd opened so many that the Divide looked like the television section of an electronics store.

"Close that one, Maria." Aedan leapt to his feet. He'd collapsed into a seated position behind me and had gone quiet for the last ten minutes, which had to be some kind of record for him.

"Which one?" There were hundreds open now, so many it was getting hard to see where one began and another ended.

"The one with a bunch of nothing in it. That's a black hole, Maria. Close it."

"No time. I have to find him." Desperation clawed through me. I had to get to my dad, had to save him.

Aedan gripped me by the waist, spun me around. "If you don't close that thing now, you won't have to worry about saving your dad because we'll be dead."

I jerked away from him and stared into the nothingness that was the ripper. I wasn't sure it was a black hole, but it didn't look inviting. I pulled instead of pushed, manipulated my ability out of that ripper and into another. It closed with an audible pop and my stomach turned inside out. I ignored it and peered into the new ripper.

"That's Mexico City. At least you're on the right continent now."

Closer was good. I opened another.

"I don't know. Looks like Alaska. Maria, stop this."

"Would you stop if you were me?"

Aedan shrugged. "If Kilshaw wants your dad dead, he's already dead."

"Shut your mouth."

"There won't be a damn thing you can do about it except get yourself, and possibly me, killed too."

"I said, shut up."

"It's no use. You can't find the right ripper and if Kilshaw—*umph*."

I launched myself at Aedan. Knocked him to the dirt, straddled his waist, and wrapped my hands around his throat. "This is your fault. If you hadn't distracted me..."

"You mean, the way your dad *asked* me to?" Aedan lurched up, tossed me to the ground, and pinned my flailing arms over my head.

"Get off me."

"He begged me, Maria. What was I supposed to do?"

"Help him!"

"If I'd had any power in the situation I would have. Do you have any idea what I risked by disobeying orders? I have *nothing*." He tightened his grip on my wrists and pressed his forehead against mine. He felt hot to the touch and smelled like the tip of a blown-out match. "And it's *your* fault. But you don't see me throwing a tantrum like a kid. *I'm* dealing."

"*Your* dad isn't in danger."

"And neither is yours. He's dead or safe. There's no other option."

"Stop saying that, you ass." I bucked beneath him, tried to free my arms.

"Why?" He pulled his head up. "You'd rather have me lie to you?"

"Yeah. Lie to me. You're such an expert at it, why aren't you doing it now?"

His eyes softened. "Because I hated lying to you and I don't intend to ever do it again."

"More lies." I got one leg free and kicked him.

"I'm not lying." He deflected the wimpy blow, rolled off me, and sat up in the dirt. "This time. For what it's worth, I don't think he's dead."

"Why not?" I sat up, chest heaving, heart hammering.

"Simple math. Kilshaw needs you plus Kilshaw doesn't have you equals Kilshaw still needs leverage. That would be your dad."

The ass did make a certain kind of sense. "You really think he's alive?"

He shrugged. "I'd give him a good ninety percent chance, which is more than I'd give Grady."

"You are the least comforting person I have ever met," I said, "and I still hate you."

"Still or again? I felt like we got over the first time you hated me." He got to his feet and held out a hand. "Come on. You need to close these things before someone gets hurt."

With great reluctance, I let him pull me to my feet. I was suddenly nose-to-nose with him, and it was very different from being astrally nose-to-nose with him or choke-him-out-in-the-sand nose-to-nose with him.

"You're valuable," Aedan said, his voice little more than a murmur. He stroked my chin with one finger, and I felt that touch to my toes. "And Kilshaw isn't stupid. He knows he has nothing without your father. He won't kill him."

"You seem to know him well," I said in the same soft tone.

"You have no idea."

Our conversation was interrupted by what sounded like a throttled scream. "Maria? *Dios*, what have you done?"

30

"Is Grandpa Holli okay?" I was almost afraid of his answer, but I had to know.

"He's all right. Resting at home. He'll be better when we get these rippers closed. We all will."

"You can't close them. I haven't found my dad yet," I said.

"Listen to your grandpa," Aedan said.

I glared at my astral not-boyfriend. He tucked his hands into his jeans pockets and backed away, putting some distance between us. Smart guy.

Abuelo didn't respond to either of us. Instead, he lowered himself to his knees and dug his fingers into the dirt. Energy flowed through him the way electrical current travels on a wire. His power rattled my teeth as he sent shockwaves of his own energy into the rippers, closing them one by one.

When we were down to the last few, he gazed up at me. "You opened all of these?"

Although I didn't regret it, I wasn't exactly proud of myself, either. "I know what you're going to say. It was dangerous and stupid."

He nodded, not as if he agreed with my statement but as if he were answering some question he'd asked himself. "You were right earlier, but you were also wrong. Just like your mother. Always jumping to conclusions."

Sweat beaded on my forehead as I stared into a ripper that looked out onto a date farm. Swollen fruit clumps swayed as the palm trees tried to grasp the desert wind with spiny green fingers.

I concentrated on the tear, closed it. "About what?"

"Perhaps I did wish Maria could have been there that day at the diner. But that doesn't mean I wasn't happy to see you, granddaughter. It was simply a shock. I'm not good with those—ask your grandfather."

"You were disappointed."

"I was sad. For reasons that had nothing to do with you."

Sad. I could understand that. I'd woken up sad every morning since my mom died. A little less so as time wore on, but the sadness was easy to bring back to mind. Like a rabbit waiting for a magician to pull it out of a hat, it was always crouched in the felted darkness of my mind, ready to bounce out with a flourish. *Tada! Remember how much this hurts? No? Here you go.*

I reached for a ripper that revealed nothing but ocean. Closed it. "She used to make the best cookies."

Abuelo smiled. "Chocolate chip. Your grandfather taught her. That man makes a mean chocolate chip. But I taught her how to make albondigas." He closed another ripper. "My secret ingredient is—"

"—fresh mint," I finished.

"She taught you." He nodded. "That must mean she forgave me."

Forgave him? "She loved you and Grandpa Holli. Said she had the best childhood and wished I could meet you both. I'd always wished it, too."

He closed a small ripper. "And then I made you feel unwelcome. I'm sorry for that."

There were only six rippers left, but two of them were enormous. I shoved my ability at the largest one. "So, you said I was right and wrong. What was I right about?"

"Our ability isn't something to be ashamed of. It must be respected and even feared. You come from ten generations of earthmovers. Our ancestors would be furious with me for denying you and your mother proper training. I had my reasons, but they seem inadequate now. Foolish."

The largest ripper resisted me, opened wider. "I can't do this one."

"Focus on the upper right. Match the ripper's vibrations with your own, then ease the corner down until it reaches the center."

I did, though I struggled to hold it in place. "O-Okay."

"Now reach for the lower left. Once you have that one pinned into place, go for the upper left. Your problem is you're trying to cinch it shut like a drawstring bag. With the small ones that works, but the larger ones require finesse."

Matching the uneven rhythms of the ripper was no easy task, but I managed. The tear closed with a sound like a gunshot.

"Good, good." Abuelo smiled. While I was struggling with the big ripper, he'd closed three others. "Now for the last ones."

With gentle encouragement, Abuelo guided me in closing the final two. I liked working alongside him. For the first time since discovering I had this ability, I felt good about using it, though my satisfaction was overshadowed by my fear of whatever Kilshaw was doing to Dad.

"Make sure they're all closed. It's very important that we don't leave even one open."

"Abuelo, there's a dangerous man on my side of the Divide. He has my dad," I said. "The man's name is Tristan Kilshaw and his agency has been chasing me for two years. I have to—"

"Kilshaw?" Abuelo looked like someone had slapped him. "*That's* who's been chasing you?"

"*Tristan* Kilshaw." Aedan said this with a strange edge that snagged my attention. "But here in Sanctum he's known as— "

"Kilshaw Sterling. *Dios.*"

"Sterling?" I stomped to where Aedan stood, the strange edge in his voice joined by a strange look in his eyes. "Then you're—"

"Aedan *Kilshaw* Sterling." If Abuelo looked slapped and sick, Aedan looked gut-punched and anemic. "Tristan Kilshaw is my father."

I backed away. Gaze locked with mine, Aedan followed me. "I'm not like him, Maria."

"How could you do this? How?"

192

"They were watching me. Watching, listening... Maria, my life has never been mine. Not in nineteen years have I owned a single second of my life. Every thought, every action was governed by my father and the agency until ... I met you."

"Don't." There wasn't a single thing about me that wasn't shaking. My hands, my knees, my voice... "I liked you, Aedan, so much."

"You still do. I know, because I feel the same way. Nothing has changed—"

"*Everything* has changed. Until now, I never truly saw you as an enemy. But you are. You're the reason I had to leave my life and go on the run, you're the reason I got sent to Dead End. You're the reason my dad is dying or dead."

"Don't confuse me with my father," Aedan said coldly. "But yes. I am the reason you're here. I'll give you that." His beautiful mouth twisted into a snarl. "I herded you to that damn café. I knew what it was from the stories I'd heard, and I also knew that my father would never leave you alone until he got what he wanted. And then he'd dispose of you the way he'd done the others." He dragged a hand through his hair, mussing the shiny silver strands. "Maybe I couldn't stop him from hunting you, but I could do one thing right: I could send you to a place where he'd never be able to hurt you."

I hated that he was making sense, hated that everything he said had the ring of truth. Hated that the whole time I was fighting him, he was protecting me.

"You probably don't believe me."

Had he really saved me? I wanted to believe it so badly. "Aedan, I—"

"Did you close them all, Maria?" Abuelo demanded. "Every single one?"

"I think so. There were so many, and I spread them out..." I trailed off as I scanned the Divide for rippers I might have missed. I found one right away and concentrated on closing it.

"Sterling cannot be allowed to get through. The consequences would be catastrophic." Abuelo dropped to his knees, dug his fingers into the sand again.

"Why?"

"He is a poison to the people of Sanctum. An odorless, tasteless, undetectable toxin that will slide into their bloodstream and contaminate their minds. There will be war again."

My gaze flicked to Aedan, who nodded. "It's true. His endgame is war in Sanctum, leading to a new world order that encompasses this world and ours."

Thud.

Abuelo, Aedan, and I swiveled to face the origin of the sound. Twenty feet away, a human body lay face down in the sand, unmoving. As we watched in horror, a single leg burst through the Divide next to the body. A ripper we'd somehow missed.

"No." Aedan's face lost all color. "There's no way."

Abuelo's power infused the soil beneath our feet, but he was too far away to close it. I shoved my ability into the ripper, tried to shut it the way he'd shown me, but I needed to get closer. I used up so much energy closing the others I was too weak to do it from this distance.

I ran as fast as I could, but I knew I wouldn't make it in time.

The other leg, then the rest of the man, slid through the ripper seconds before I snapped it shut. My abuelo crouched behind me, panting. My pulse was doing triple time. Closing that ripper had taken a lot out of both of us, and it hadn't even been worth the effort.

Tristan Kilshaw, Sterling, or whatever the bastard's name was, stood tall and strong and here. The monster was *here*. In Dead End.

In Sanctum.

Kilshaw sucked in a huge lungful of air and blew it out. Twisted his head around and stared straight at my grandfather.

"Long time no see, Emilio."

31

"IT FEELS GOOD TO BE HOME AGAIN."

Kilshaw lifted his hands. A peculiar, inert energy built up in the space around him. The energy wasn't dead, and it wasn't alive. It was as if it were waiting for something.

"*Dad*." I slid to my knees and rolled him onto his back. He winced and choked out a pained cough, his face bruised and swollen. His wrists and ankles weren't bound anymore, but his right leg and arm were twisted unnaturally, and blood dripped from a cut on his head.

Fury rocketed through me. "*Monster*."

"We're all monsters, aren't we?" Kilshaw gave me an insouciant shrug. "Had you done what I asked, this all could have been avoided." He smoothed out his suit, straightened his cuffs, flicked something off his sleeve. "He could've had a quick, clean death instead of soiling my suit with his mid-caste blood."

I lunged at him. Aedan grabbed me, his arms twining with mine, locking me in place against him.

"Let go." I lifted my legs and made myself dead weight, but Aedan simply readjusted his grip.

"He'll kill you if I do."

"Didn't you see what your trash father did to my dad?"

"Keep pissing him off and he'll finish the job," Aedan said. "You can't win this battle by charging in blindly. There's more at work here. If you attack him, he can—"

"Quiet now, Aedan. You wouldn't want to spill any family secrets while I've got Maria's poor papa at my mercy, would you?"

"No, sir." Aedan shivered as if he were cold, but I knew he wasn't. He was terrified. That made me stop fighting him and start paying attention, because something was going on, and Aedan wasn't going to be able to tell me anything.

I glanced at my dad. His breathing was labored, his face screwed up in pain. I couldn't do anything to jeopardize his safety. If it cost me some pride to keep him alive, well, so be it. Pride was cheap.

Kilshaw regarded me with a glint in his eye and a half-curve to his mouth. "That look. I've seen it before."

"Tristan." My abuelo raised one eyebrow and pursed his lips. He did not look happy.

"Ah, that's where I've seen it." Kilshaw's mouth finished the curve, arching into an oily grin. "Emilio. You got old."

"Been a few years."

"Fifty." The grin dropped off Kilshaw's lips and he snarled, "Fifty *goddamned* years since I was cast out of my own home." He jabbed his index finger at Abuelo. "By you, Emilio."

"You gave me no choice."

"There is *always* a choice." Kilshaw drew his strange weapon, pointed it at Abuelo. "You betrayed me because you were too weak to stand up to a bunch of lessers."

"I wasn't too weak to take a stand against your totalitarian Elites. Since you're all so powerful, that should have been a tougher fight."

Kilshaw's jaw hardened. "I am going to kill you."

The ground beneath me rumbled as my anxiety rose. My body was worn out from opening and closing the rippers, but as the ground began to shake, I realized that not only did I still have power, I was stronger than I'd ever thought possible.

I could end Kilshaw right here, right now.

"*Maria, stop*," Aedan and Abuelo yelled.

Kilshaw knelt to the ground and drove his free hand into the sand. "Thank you, earthmover."

The rumbling bounced from Kilshaw to me. Back and forth, like a game. Every time it returned to me, the vibrations felt less my own. They were warped and discordant, like a song played on an out-of-tune piano. Then my grip on my ability was slapped away, the force of it knocking me back a step.

I blinked at him. "What did you do?"

"Your granddaughter is something." Kilshaw smiled at Abuelo. "She doesn't even need to touch the earth to affect it, does she? Amazing. I've never felt an earthmover so deliciously powerful." Kilshaw closed his eyes and the ground rumbled more intensely than before, a familiar energy thrumming beneath us.

"Oh no." I heard Aedan say from behind me.

Sand curled around my ankles like hands, and yanked me hip-deep into the ground. From the grunts behind me, I figured the same had happened to the others.

"You used my ability. How?" I was in shock, but more than that, I was sickened by what he'd done. It was a violation.

"By using *his* ability." Aedan jerked his body to the side so he could see me from his sand-hole. "He can exploit any attack from an ability. Why do you think I haven't electrocuted him?"

I glanced at Abuelo, who nodded. That's what Kilshaw had meant on the other side of the ripper when he'd said it wasn't enough. When I sank his henchman into the sand, I hadn't used enough power for him to steal it from me.

"Did it occur to either of you that I might have needed to know this information?"

"I tried to tell you." Aedan gave me a pained look.

"You told me not to use my ability on that side." Which was all he *could* say at the time. I let my head drop. "I should have listened."

"Ooo, I'm much more powerful here. Don't you feel the difference in the air, kids? On the other side I was so … *limited*." Kilshaw shivered, but it was the sort of shiver where the person seemed to enjoy doing it. Eww.

It was my fault we were in these holes. If I hadn't acted impulsively, he wouldn't have been able to use me. If I'd relied on my brains instead of my power, I'd be on solid ground now. We all would.

My gaze shifted to the others. Abuelo was still, his body relaxed. Aedan had sunk in farther than the rest of us, and was trying to keep himself above the surface. Dad was slumped forward and breathing heavily. He had to be in agony, but he didn't cry out, only hung there like a wilted flower, waist-deep in the sand.

Kilshaw crouched beside Abuelo Emilio, who crossed his arms, set his jaw, and looked away.

"I've imagined this moment many times, old friend."

Abuelo said nothing. His lack of response seemed to annoy Kilshaw. He slapped Abuelo so hard across the face I felt the whoosh of air from where I was. My grandfather took the blow without so much as a whimper. He didn't even uncross his arms. Just eyed Kilshaw as he licked his busted lip, turned his head, and spat blood out of his mouth.

Whoa. Abuelo was a badass. Chuck Norris and The Rock combined.

I caught his eye, wordlessly asking if I should do something to help.

He snap-shook his head. There was nothing I could do to help. If I attacked, I'd only make things worse.

"Haven't you done enough, father? We're at your mercy here." Aedan sounded bored.

"Don't antagonize him," I snapped.

Aedan winked at me.

"Betrayer." The hate in Kilshaw's eyes was a cold, miserable thing. The frost in his voice froze me from the inside out.

"I am," he replied. For all his flippancy, Aedan was afraid. Terror radiated from him in icy waves. Despite his fear, or perhaps because of it, he snarled, "If your plan of revenge requires you to lash out like a child, Father, lash out at me. *I* betrayed you. *I* deserve it."

Was he trying to drag Kilshaw's attention away from Abuelo? Guessing that might be the case, I dug into the sand around me, tried to pull myself free. The sand loosened, then sucked me down deeper. Now my arms were trapped too.

Kilshaw chuckled. "You know better than that, earthmover. Quicksand doesn't forgive escape attempts. The more you move, the deeper down it pulls you."

I set aside my personal anger and appealed to Kilshaw's flawed sense of compassion. "You wouldn't hurt your own son, would you?"

"No." He retrieved the gun, then turned and pointed it at me. I froze. "But I'd hurt you."

"*Me*, damn it." Aedan struggled to free himself from the sand. "*I'm* the one who betrayed you."

"Better stop me, son. You know what this gun is capable of." Kilshaw slid his finger onto the trigger.

"Don't." Aedan's entire posture changed. The lightness in his tone went heavy and dark. "Don't hurt her."

"You care about this girl? Funny. You had no problem spying on her, ratting her out. He told me everything." This last he directed to me.

"I didn't, Maria. I only told him enough to keep him off my back. It isn't like he's saying." Aedan looked so distressed that I'd believe his father's words, I felt compelled to comfort him.

"I understand," I said. "You had no choice."

"There's always a choice." Kilshaw smiled like a hungry shark, all teeth and mindless violence. "Like now, for instance. See, I'm *choosing* to kill you, earthmover, to repay my son for his betrayal and he's *choosing* to let me."

32

ELECTRICITY STREAKED FROM AEDAN TO KILSHAW, ENVELOPING THE other man's body in a flashing, silver fire. The gun dropped out of his hand.

"You got him," I said.

Aedan's eyes were sad. "No. I didn't."

Kilshaw braced himself as Aedan's power swarmed around him. The silver fire crackled and popped, but Kilshaw never flinched. Instead, he drew in a deep breath and held out his arms as if welcoming the electricity into his body.

Oh no.

"You've been holding out on me." Kilshaw tsked, waving his finger back and forth. "I thought you were like your mother. A weak mid-caste. But you're much more. Yet another betrayal?"

"What makes you think Mom was a mid-caste? Because she told you she was?" Aedan's voice whisper-trembled with rage. "Mom knew what you were. She told me to keep quiet. She said if you ever figured out what we could really do, you'd lock us up. She feared you. Hated you."

"She loved me."

"You killed her love. And then you killed her."

Kilshaw scowled at Aedan. "Lies. I didn't kill Maggie."

"The sad thing is, I think you've convinced yourself that's the truth. But it's a lie. I know. I was in the training facility the day you did it. I saw her yelling at you, saying she wouldn't let you hurt me anymore," Aedan snarled. "She lunged at you and you pushed her into the wall. She hit her head and there was so much blood … I saw what you did. I saw it all."

"I didn't kill her. I tried to help her." For a moment, pain flashed in Kilshaw's eyes. "I tried to help…"

"She wouldn't have needed help if you hadn't hurt her."

"Shut up. Shut your mouth." Silver electricity flowed down Kilshaw's arm and enveloped his son.

Aedan's body jerked. A blip of a sound escaped him, but nothing more. Apparently, that wasn't good enough for Kilshaw, because he did it again, for longer this time.

"*Aedan.*" I looked to Abuelo, racking my brain for something, anything, we could do. "How can I fight a man who uses my attacks against me?" I whispered.

Abuelo whispered back, "Attacks, Maria. He uses *attacks.*"

But what else could I *do* but attack him?

Aedan's breath whooshed out as another zap of his own power jolted through him. He was slumped over, his entire body trembling. It was a faint tremble, not a full shake, and as he moved, I noticed something. The sand holding him prisoner was loosening, and it wasn't pulling him down.

And it was alive with electricity.

Continuing our whispered conversation, I asked, "Why is the sand around Aedan crackling like that?"

"My guess is there's water nearby. Sand isn't a good conductor unless it's wet."

"Why aren't we being electrocuted, too?"

"Looks like your young man is keeping that from happening."

He wasn't *my* young man, but now wasn't the time to argue about it.

"I have an idea," I mouthed. Abuelo Emilio nodded.

I really hoped this worked, because if it didn't, we were all toast. Then again, if I did nothing, we were just as toasted, so…

Please work, please work, please work.

With the lessons I'd learned from Samuel—and today, with Abuelo —in mind, I eased my ability into the ground beneath me. It took all my concentration to keep the brakes on, but I knew that if I didn't, I'd end up literally digging my own grave.

Using slow, circular movements, I weakened the sand's hold on my limbs, using the gentle pulsations of my ability to assist. There *was* water nearby. I felt the difference in the way the vibrations soaked into the layers of wet sand as opposed to the way they powered through the dry. I'd never noticed the difference before because I'd been too busy sledgehammering my way into the ground.

I drew the moisture toward me, working it into the sand around my arms and hands, all the while keeping my eye on Kilshaw—and Aedan, whose head was drooped forward, chin on chest. Panic shot through me, but I took a couple of calming breaths and concentrated on the task at hand. Aedan's life might depend on my control, so I couldn't allow myself to give in to emotion right now. Later, I'd fall apart. But right now, Abuelo, Dad, and Aedan needed me to keep my focus.

I let my body fall back as if I was floating in the ocean, and freed my hands. My lower body was still beneath the sand, but I wasn't trapped. I could climb out. However, if I did it without first figuring out a way to take care of Kilshaw, I'd find myself right back in it, or worse, toasted like a marshmallow at a campfire.

Abuelo gave me a quick smile. Nodded again. I was doing it. Everything was going to be—

Aedan screamed, and my heart stumbled in my chest.

"You are killing your own child," Abuelo said to Kilshaw, fury deepening his already low voice. "Is that what you've been reduced to, Tristan? You tell me I was wrong to cast you out of Sanctum, but you prove my actions correct with everything you do."

Kilshaw snapped his head to Abuelo, then back to Aedan. Blinked as if waking from a dream. For a second, his face registered worry, brows pulled into a vee above his nose, forehead crinkled, mouth drawn down.

Then the second passed. His brows shot up, forehead smoothed, mouth curled into a wicked smile. "I'm seventy years old, Emilio. What makes you think this is the first time I've killed one of my children? Like this one, they've all been such ... disappointments."

He hit Aedan with another jolt, and sent one in Abuelo's direction, too.

Both men grunted. Aedan's sounded hoarse and weak. He wouldn't last much longer. I wasn't even sure he was conscious.

Fear gripped me, held me as immobile as the sand had. Who did I think I was, thinking I could pull this off? Just a seventeen-year-old girl with an ability I didn't even know how to use, going up against a man who'd *led a revolution against an entire world* a half-century ago. A man ruthless enough to murder his own wife and child.

There was no way out of this. No way we were going to win. No way I could outsmart Tristan Kilshaw.

"Tú puedes hacer esto, María," Abuelo whispered.

Although I wasn't fluent in Spanish, my mother had spoken both English and Spanish to me as a child, and I understood him. *You can do this, Maria.* I wondered if he'd ever said those exact words to my mother.

"Fuerza," he said.

I knew that word, too. It meant strength, but it also meant force. Power.

Fuerza was something I had, but I couldn't use my power to attack Kilshaw or he'd turn it back on me and everyone else.

Unless I didn't attack him.

Abuelo's words from earlier returned to me. "He uses attacks."

And suddenly I knew what I was going to do.

If Kilshaw was only able to use attacks, all I had to do was *not attack him.*

I fought panic with slow breaths and pure concentration, the same way I'd fought the sand holding me tight. Set my focus on a patch of ground directly behind Kilshaw and poured my ability into it. The sand in that spot loosened, then began to rotate inward like an ocean whirlpool.

I waded to the hard bank of sand surrounding me, lay as flat as I could manage, and shimmied out of the hole. Wet sand clung to my legs and seeped through my clothes. I was tired and cold, but I was free.

Kilshaw stopped his assault on his son and whipped his head in my direction. Aedan flopped over. He was conscious, that much I could see.

"Damn you, girl. This is your fault." Kilshaw shot a bolt of electricity at me. I threw myself to one side and the bolt struck the sand, the energy harmlessly dissipating.

"Perhaps you need bifocals, Tristan," Abuelo said.

Kilshaw's response was a furious shriek and a bolt of electricity. This bolt seemed weaker, though. Abuelo flinched, but he didn't grunt or cry out.

"I can't help you yet," Aedan whispered to me. His face was gray, his eyes bloodshot, his nose bleeding. "He short-circuited my ability."

"It's okay. I have a plan." Oh God, I hoped this worked.

Aedan's bloodless lips curved into a grin. "I knew you'd think of something."

"*You.*" Kilshaw stalked toward me, and away from the trap I'd set.

"*You,*" I echoed, planting my feet in the sand in front of Aedan. "You won't hurt him again."

He looked amused. "How do you plan to stop me?"

Keeping my gaze on Kilshaw, I set my focus on the sand trap, pulled it closer.

"By sinking you into the sand up to your neck and covering your head with honey." That last part wasn't true, even if it sounded good. I didn't have any honey on me.

"You can't use your ability against me, and without that, you're nothing. Face it, there isn't a thing you can do to stop me." He shook his head in Abuelo's direction. "I lament the youth of today, Emilio. They've got more power than we had, but they don't use it properly."

"Shame," Abuelo said, winking at me.

The trap swirled behind Kilshaw.

"Actually, there is one thing I can do," I said.

"Is that right?" Kilshaw held out his arms and closed his eyes. Laughed arrogantly. "By all means, let me have it."

I ran as fast as I could straight at him, ducking low as I rammed into his gut with my shoulder. He was a foot taller, and much stronger than me, but he hadn't anticipated a plain old physical attack. His eyes flew open as my momentum made him stumble, arms windmilling, two steps backward. It was enough. He dropped into the sand trap, immediately sinking up to his neck.

I released my hold on the whirlpool and the surface sealed, holding him captive.

"Does anyone have honey?" I asked.

Kilshaw screamed with fury.

Aedan smiled. "You're the best girlfriend ever."

I SPENT the next few minutes helping the others free themselves. One by one, they crawled out of the holes. It took all three of us to free Dad, who hadn't yet regained consciousness.

I was pretty sure I was in shock. My legs felt like noodles and I could barely stand, so I plopped down beside Aedan to rest. He was cross-legged on the ground, hunched over, and still sizzling.

"Hey, babe."

"To be clear, I am not your girlfriend."

"I know," he said. "But I have high hopes for the future."

Sighing, I wrapped my arms around my legs. "Guess you're okay, then, since your sarcasm is back."

"Yeah, I'm good. Not like this is my first round of shock therapy. Father routinely tested me against my own powers when I first began manifesting, which was when I was a toddler. Why do you think my mother taught me to hide the extent of them?"

He winced once, before covering it with his usual ironic grin. His hair stuck straight up from all the electricity, and his face was splotched with pink and red blisters.

Strangely, he'd never looked better. I liked this look more than the smooth, hot guy at the abandoned diner, and I really liked it more than his astral projection image, which turned out to be an idealized version of him, sanitized of the white burn scars on his arms and neck that I could see clearly now in the glaring desert sunlight.

He caught me staring and pointed at his hair. "Checking out my hot new look? I call it 'fork in the outlet.' You'll be seeing it on all the Paris runways this fall."

"You could have shown me these." I reached out, stroked my fingertips over the healed wounds on his throat.

His grin faded. He caught my wrist and held it. "I don't like them."

I stared straight into his eyes. "You're very strong. I had no idea how strong."

"Because of some ugly scars?"

"Because, after all you've been through, you're still … you. Your mom must have been an amazing person." After all, someone had instilled a sense of decency in him. I was betting it was her.

"She was." I caught the glint of tears in his eyes before he turned his head and released me. "Your dad is waking up. You should check on him. I'll watch mine."

"Okay, Aedan." I smiled, and this time when he smiled back, it wasn't ironic or sarcastic. It was shy and sweet, and real. Maybe the first real smile he'd ever given me.

"Take it slow." Abuelo was on one knee beside my dad. "Help is on the way. Lie still."

Despite the fact that his arm and leg were very clearly broken, Dad kept trying to stand up. His clothes were covered in dirt and blood, his face was puffy and bruised, and he seemed dazed.

"Loops," he murmured.

"Dad, I'm fine. Please stop moving." As if my voice had broken some sort of magic spell around him, he fell back and closed his eyes.

"Is he okay?" I asked.

"With rest and medical attention, he will be fine." Abuelo cocked his head so he could look me in the eye. "You saved him. You saved us all."

"We saved us all. I couldn't have done it without you."

Abuelo wrapped an arm around my shoulder, hugged me. I hadn't realized that the tears were coming until the first drop rolled down my cheek. After that, it was as if the floodgates opened wide. All the fear, the anger, and even the relief, hit me.

A hand settled on my knee. "Loops?"

"Right here, Dad." I took his hand, threaded my fingers through his. The weather was on the warm side of sunny, but he was shivering.

"M-missed you."

"I missed you, too, Dad. I tried so hard to find you."

"I'm s-sorry. Thought I w-was doing the right th-thing, s-sending you here."

Even though it had worked out in the end, I was still angry with him for not being honest with me. Maybe I'd always be angry, but this wasn't the time to discuss it. I was controlling myself better, but I wasn't perfect, and I couldn't risk getting upset and triggering my ability with what amounted to a power vampire buried to his neck in sand only a short distance away.

"We're going to get you to a hospital. Just hang on," I said.

His hand tightened on mine. "Kilshaw?"

I knew what he meant, even without him saying it. With a lightness I didn't feel, I said, "Alive. I didn't kill anyone, don't worry."

Relief settled into Dad's face and he closed his eyes. Obviously, the news that I hadn't murdered anyone had reassured him that I wasn't an even bigger monster than he'd already assumed I was. I wiped away my tears and slipped my hand out of his.

Abuelo and I stood together. He slung my two backpacks over his shoulders and patted my head. "My car is parked just beyond that dune." He shaded his eyes and pointed south, to a spot where the ripper field and the outskirts of Dead End converged. "I'll drive back into town for help. We can't handle Kilshaw by ourselves, mija. We need backup."

I smiled at the endearment, but my smile faded when I caught sight of Kilshaw. His gaze followed me, a predator stalking its prey. How a guy buried to his chin in dirt could look threatening, I didn't know, but he managed it.

"Did you like what I did to your father, earthmover?"

I stopped dead in my tracks.

"It's a shame I wasn't able to finish the job. Maybe I should have blinded him. Made his worthless mid-caste powers disappear altogether."

The ground rumbled.

Aedan shook his head. "Don't do it, Maria."

"I'm going to kill him, and then I'm going to kill you." He stared straight into his son's eyes. "While *you* watch, betrayer."

I hunkered down a couple of feet away from Kilshaw's head. "Be careful. If I wanted to, I could take down the entire Divide and you with it."

"Maria." Aedan pushed to his feet, started toward me.

"Prove it," Kilshaw said, emphasizing the "t" sound. He was trying hard not to look excited, but his flaring nostrils, sweating temples, and wide eyes gave him away.

"No, thanks. I've got nothing to prove to you."

Aedan stopped. Let out a loud sigh.

"You really thought I was going to use my ability?" I rolled my eyes at him. "How stupid do you think I am?"

"Stupid is not a word I'd ever use to describe you, Maria Guadalupe. Short-tempered, stubborn, gorgeous…" Aedan said.

"You're lucky you added that last one."

"*Silence.*" Kilshaw's face was so twisted with rage he looked years older than seventy. "Do either of you have any idea what's going to happen now that I'm back home?"

"You'll be tried for your crimes by a jury of your peers?" Aedan took a step away from his father as he said it. Ingrained fear was hard to fight, even if you were as brave as Aedan Sterling was.

"Peers?" Kilshaw laughed. "My family ruled Sanctum for hundreds of years. We have no peers."

"Then I guess a jury of the descendants of your victims," Aedan muttered. "Should be a quick trial, then."

"Wait. You ruled Sanctum?" I asked.

"My father and I did, yes." Kilshaw sneezed. It made him seem almost human.

"So, one might say you were once 'the head' of Sanctum?"

"That was awful." Aedan said, but he snickered.

"Earthmover, you speak as if you think you've won." Kilshaw's satisfied expression worried me, because *he* was speaking as if he thought *he'd* won and, even though he was buried in the sand, I was terrified he was somehow right.

The ground rumbled beneath us.

"Maria, you can't do that around him," Aedan said.

"It's not me."

"Well, it's not him. He can only use what someone gives him."

Kilshaw narrowed his eyes at his son, but said nothing.

I shrugged. "Well, if it's not me and it's not him, then who is it?"

33

ABUELO REAPPEARED ON TOP OF THE DUNE HE'D CLIMBED OVER TO GET his car, and half-ran, half-slid down the sloping hill, a duffel bag clutched in his hands. A blonde head popped up on the dune directly after he hit bottom, and the person it was attached to also slip-slid down, landing on her butt.

"Cindy?"

She got up, dusted herself off, and ran to me. "Sorry I'm late, but I walked all the way over here as soon as I could—so basically, as soon as my parents' backs were turned." She pulled me into a fierce hug. "When your grandpas came home and found you gone, they called me because they figured I might know where you were. Of course, I did." She hugged me even tighter. "Don't ever do that again, Maria. Best friends don't abandon each other."

"I needed to find my dad."

"No, you were running away."

She knew me too well. "I won't do it again."

"Good." I knew the second her attention snagged on Aedan. It was as if a flashbulb went off behind her eyes. "Who is *this*?"

"I'm Maria's boyfriend," he said.

"Really? I'm Maria's best friend. Nice to meet you, boyfriend."

"Nice to meet you, best friend."

Oh no, they were bonding.

"He is *not* my boyfriend," I mumbled, as I watched my grandfather dig in the sand around Kilshaw. "Abuelo, what are you doing?"

"Spinning my wheels, it seems." He sat back in the sand. "We need to get to town, and we can't leave him here. If the Beyond beasts don't kill him, the scavengers will."

"Scavengers?"

Cindy nodded. "A group of lessers and mid-caste talents that eschew society. They live in a caravan town west of here. They scavenge anything that might be of value, and human life is pretty low on that list."

"This place just gets weirder and weirder," I said.

"Not to interrupt, but does anyone have anything to eat?" Aedan wrapped his hands around his middle. "I'm starving."

"That's right. You crossed through the Divide. Wait. Does that mean he's going to conk out on us?" I asked.

Aedan ignored me and focused on Cindy. "Do you have a crushed granola bar at the bottom of your purse? A box of raisins? I'll take stale ones. I've never been this hungry in my life. At this point, I'd gladly eat an entire bowl of kale."

"Oh wow. He *is* hungry," Cindy said.

"Yeah." I didn't like the way Aedan was eyeing the animal bones a few feet away.

"I have something that might help. You're probably not going to like it." Cindy dug in her shoulder bag, producing a baggie filled with brown chunks that looked like some sort of root. "It's called gin—"

"Ginger root? I like ginger. Not usually in this quantity, but I don't care at this point." Aedan swiped the bag from her and popped one of the pieces into his mouth.

"Ginger *pepper*. It's one hundred times hotter than a jalapeño pepper. Do you have jalapeños in your part of the world? Mom said you don't have ginger peppers, so I—"

"*Fire*. Mouth. *Fire*. Help." Tears streamed out of Aedan's eyes. "You … carry this … stuff around … with you?" He gagged.

"Cindy is resourceful like that. You're lucky she didn't feed you limpid worm larvae instead." I peered at him, wrinkled my nose.

"Good news is, the color has come back to your face. Bad news is, that color is purple."

He opened his mouth wide and huffed out a breath. "Mean. This stuff is… meaner to me … than you are when … I make you mad." He huffed again. "Pepper. Hot, hot … my esophagus is ashes … burned away…"

"Toughen up, kid. The heat wears off soon enough." Abuelo unzipped the duffel he carried down the dune and took out a thick blue, black, and white woven blanket. It reminded me of a Mexican blanket I had back home. He snapped the folds out of it and draped it over Dad.

"This thing is really hot," Aedan said.

Abuelo shook his head. "This is your boyfriend, nieta? He seems a little whiny."

"Nieta?" Cindy asked.

"Granddaughter," I translated.

"Umm, yeah, I was totally kidding." Aedan puffed out his chest, sucked in several deep breaths. "It's no big deal." Sweat drooled down the sides of his face and coated his neck. "I'm cool."

Cindy said, "If you let the heat dissipate on its own, it takes care of the worst symptoms from coming through the Divide. Not forever, but it should buy you half a day or so."

"When I came across, I ate a lumberjack breakfast and then passed out for fifty-two hours," I said.

"That sounds amazing." Aedan coughed, then glanced at Abuelo and thrust his hands on his hips and his shoulders back. "So, what's this about Scavengers, sir?"

"No time to worry about them now. We have to get him out." Abuelo grunted as he worked one hand into the sand.

"Why? What's the rush?" I asked, as another rumble shook the earth from below. "I swear that's not me."

"I know it isn't. You're smarter than that."

My dad coughed and slowly raised his head. "There's an enormous dust cloud about eighteen to twenty miles away. East. Rising like smoke in the sky."

"I don't see it," Aedan whisper-wheezed. "I don't see anything but sand. Mountains of sand. Hills of sand. Sand, sand, sand. I thought I'd ended up in the Sahara when I first got here."

"The town is over there." I pointed east. "You have to climb the dune to see it."

"Then how is your dad seeing the smoke?" Aedan asked.

"It's his ability. In ideal conditions, he can see up to thirty miles away."

"Fifty," my dad croaked, "if conditions are ideal."

"Something that would have been valuable to know months ago," Kilshaw snapped the words at his son.

"That explains how you were able to stay ahead of us for so long. Cool." Aedan coughed a little, then frowned. "Why didn't you tell me?"

Abuelo paced in front of Kilshaw's head, either not realizing, or not caring, that he was kicking up dirt in the man's face. For that matter, Kilshaw suddenly didn't seem to care, either.

"You there, lesser girl. Give me some of that ginger pepper," he said. "The hunger is upon me."

Cindy frowned at him and shook her head.

"Don't call her that." Abuelo eyed my dad. "Cindy, we might need some of your ginger pepper over here."

"I'm on it." She knelt beside my dad and handed him a piece of ginger pepper. It was half the size of the one Aedan had eaten. "Chew it fast, Mr. Thompson. It'll be easier."

"Well?" Aedan asked. "Why didn't you tell me?"

"Dad always hid his ability and told me to hide mine," I said. "I didn't feel comfortable talking about his without his permission. I still can't believe I told you about mine."

Aedan grinned. "I'm incredibly persuasive."

"You're incredibly arrogant."

"That, too." He blinked. "Hey. The burning is gone. The weird hunger, too."

"For now," Cindy said, a little mysteriously, in my opinion.

My dad held the bite of ginger pepper between the fingers of his non-broken hand. "I was only trying to keep you safe. You make it sound as if I'm ashamed of your ability."

"Aren't you?" I asked, a bit more sharply than I intended.

"No. I'm not ashamed of you in any way." He popped the pepper into his mouth.

Maybe it was wrong of me to doubt my own dad's word, but I did.

Abuelo stopped pacing, scratched his head, talked to himself, shook his head, and then started pacing again.

"Whew, this is one hot pepper." Dad puffed out his cheeks, but he didn't seem as affected as Aedan had been. He wasn't even sweating, but that could be because he was still shivering.

"The sand is like cement." Abuelo stood with his hands on his hips.

"Good. That way we don't have to worry about him getting away," I said.

"Besides, he'll be passed out before long," Cindy said. "I'm not sharing my ginger pepper with a bigot who tried to hurt my friend."

Kilshaw cleared his throat. "You can't leave me here."

Abuelo sighed. "Unfortunately, he's right."

"Do you want me to help him out? The way I helped you all?"

Abuelo shook his head. "It's too risky. That's why I haven't tried it myself. If you hurt him in any way, it would be considered an attack, even if it was an accident."

"The dust cloud is closer now. I'd estimate ten miles away." Dad tried to lift himself into a seated position using his good arm, but dropped back down. "It looks like a sandstorm, but there's no wind."

"Fire?" I asked.

Dad shook his head. "Not like any fire I've ever seen."

"It couldn't be the chimera, could it?" I asked Cindy.

"No. She accepted the offering."

"Offering? Ridiculous," Kilshaw said, and spat. "Only lessers bother with the old ways. Such an embarrassment."

Why did the man make it so easy to hate him?

"It wasn't embarrassing when she singlehandedly took on a mountain chimera and saved the town. Something an entire group of Elites couldn't do. Most ran off with their tails between their legs."

"Lies." Kilshaw blew dust from his mouth. "No lesser could take on a mountain or any other chimera."

"And yet she did," I said.

Cindy sent me a quiet smile. "It's probably limpid worms."

"Makes sense." Abuelo nodded his agreement. "The vibrations coming from the rippers draw them in. And with us disturbing the vibrations…"

"Limpid worms? They're coming here?" My voice cracked. I was glad I'd forgotten about those things when I was trapped underground, or I really would have panicked. "What the heck? I thought the town was deworming or something."

"Only the worms who nest within city limits." Abuelo said. "We have to cull those or they'll eat everything in sight. Mostly we try to redirect them, but they aren't the sharpest creatures and sometimes return."

"How many are there within the city limits now?" I paced in front of Kilshaw's face. He blinked as sand flew into his eyes. Or was he getting tired? I hoped it was the latter. I'd be happy to see him take a fifty-two-hour nap about now.

"According to my father, the deworming has been pretty success-ful, so I'd think not many." Cindy held up two, then five fingers. "My guess is more than twenty, less than fifty."

"*Fifty*? You can't hold up five fingers and say fifty. Five fingers is five."

"Oh. Sorry." Cindy stared at her fingers. "I'm not sure anyway. Samuel would know better, since he can hear them."

Samuel. That's who I needed.

"Where is he?"

"Knowing him, I'd say somewhere between the worm horde and the city."

34

CINDY, AEDAN, AND I RAN UNTIL WE SPOTTED A RUSTY, NOT-QUITE-classic-Chevy truck trundling down the road. It stopped when Aedan waved it down, and an elderly man in overalls and a dirty ball cap told us he'd take us the rest of the way into town. I was leery of accepting a ride from him, but Cindy hopped right in. Apparently, the guy was a member of her mother's gardening club.

"Took you long enough." We met up with Samuel on the edge of town. He leaned against his ATV, arms folded across his chest, watching the worm cloud.

"We had to stop and tell my dad what was going on so he could alert the city council." Cindy's tone could have cut glass. "Then we had to find you. It's not like you left a note telling us where you were."

Aedan gave me a wide-eyed look. I nodded. Yep, my friend had claws. It was one of my favorite things about her.

"I didn't mean anything by it," Samuel grumbled. He glanced at Cindy's mutinous expression, then away.

"It's okay. I missed you too, sweetie." I winked.

Aedan laughed. Of course, he thought it was funny. Sarcasm was his native language.

Samuel did not wink back at me. He was too busy staring at the massive dust cloud bearing down on us. "They're coming from the mountains."

"To attack the town?" I asked.

"Limpid worms are all instinct and drive. They aren't capable of a coordinated attack based on any sort of logic. For some reason, they think there's food nearby and they want it."

"I opened some rippers today. A lot of rippers."

"I heard," Samuel said. Had he actually heard, or had he heard someone talking about it? Either choice was a possibility.

"Abuelo thinks that's what's drawing them."

"Probably," Samuel said. There was no blame in his tone, only interest.

"So, these are the worms you told me about?" Aedan asked. "The giant, dog-eating, exploding ones?"

"Yes."

He glanced down at his T-shirt, jeans, and black Converse sneakers. "I really hope they haven't eaten. This is my only set of clothes."

"At least your T-shirt is black. It won't show stains," I said. It wouldn't matter, of course. It would have to be burned if limpid larvae exploded on it.

Samuel took me by the elbow, pulled me to one side. "Were you able to get across?"

"Not exactly."

"Did you see anyone on the other side? A woman?"

The hope in his eyes made me wish I had better news for him. "No. I'm sorry, Samuel. I didn't see Mica."

A muscle twitched in his jaw. It was the only sign of emotion he showed, but it was telling. We rejoined the others.

"You guys okay?" Cindy asked.

"Yeah, we're okay." I glanced at Samuel, who probably was not okay but was putting up a brave front.

"Where's the prisoner?" he asked.

"You know about Kilshaw already?" How was that possible?

"The capture of Tristan Kilshaw Sterling, the biggest war criminal in the last century, is big news. The minute the council knew about it, so did everyone else. The editor of the local paper is a telepath and a gossip."

"Telepath?"

Samuel wrinkled his nose. "A low-grade telepath. He can only catch very strong emotions. No one in Dead End worries much about him reading their mind—it's his gossiping that really pisses them off."

Maybe the town didn't worry about the man's telepathy, but it sure made me uneasy. I'd have to figure out who the editor was and steer clear of him.

"The city council deployed a security team. Also, someone with a backhoe," Cindy said.

Samuel's brows dipped low. "Backhoe?"

"Maria buried Kilshaw to his neck in the sand."

That netted me a rare, and precious, Samuel grin. "Nice work."

"I had help. Abuelo Emilio stayed behind to make sure no one did anything dumb like use their abilities around him. He's also waiting for the medics to arrive for my dad." I'd hated leaving him so soon after getting him back, but there had been no other option. If I'd caused the worms to come to Dead End, I had to help fight them.

Aedan touched my hand. A gentle brush of his fingers, letting me know he understood. I wished he'd stop it. When he did things like that, it made it hard to forget I wasn't really his girlfriend.

Samuel said, "They'll encase him in a stasis container. Possibly induce a light coma. With medication, not magic."

Aedan's expression didn't change, but I felt his discomfort. "If they know what's good for them, they'll put him in a deep coma. He has plans for Sanctum and they aren't good ones—except for Elites." He eyed Samuel, who had his head cocked at a forty-five-degree angle, obviously trying to listen to the approaching worm storm.

"Samuel isn't like the others," I said. "He's seventy-five percent less of an a-hole than your average Elite."

"Thanks," he grumbled.

"Don't get mad. You can be a little judgmental sometimes, is all. Though you'd better get over that fast if you ever want to date Cindy."

A deep red flush worked its way from Samuel's neck to his scalp, but he didn't deny it. Cindy's face was pink around the edges. Neither of them looked at the other.

"Who's this?" Samuel demanded.

"Are you seriously just noticing him?" I asked.

"No. I was preoccupied a minute ago, so I'm asking now. Who is he?"

Aedan held out his hand. "Aedan Sterling."

Samuel shook it, then seemed to realize what he was doing and stopped. "Tell me you aren't…"

"The war criminal's son? The one and only. But I'm at least seventy-five percent less of an a-hole than he is, so no worries, pal."

The earth rumbled, this time so hard it sent Cindy flying against Samuel's ATV. I went to check on her, but Samuel was already there. "You okay?"

She righted herself. Straightened her shoulders. "I'm fine, thank you."

"Whoa, that's a lot of worms." Aedan shielded his eyes with his hand. Stared at the oncoming duststorm. "It's like Wormageddon up in here."

Cindy and Samuel appeared confused by his joke.

"Definitely," I replied. "So, what are we going to do to prevent it?"

Samuel spoke up. "I have a plan."

"So do I," Cindy said.

We all looked at Samuel. He'd spoken first, so I figured he got to lay out his plan first. It seemed fair.

But Samuel didn't. Instead, he nodded to Cindy. "Not making that mistake again. Let's hear yours first."

"That's a terrible plan," I said.

"Horrible," Samuel said.

"The worst," Aedan said.

The three of us stood in a huddle around Cindy, giving her the same 'are you kidding me' look.

"Maybe I didn't explain it right. Here, I'll show you." She dug into her pants pocket and pulled out a test tube filled with green liquid. She uncorked it, and we all retched. "This is the crushed malodorous root."

"Oh God, I'm going to barf up my ginger pepper," Aedan said.

Samuel's eyes were watering. "Where'd you get it?"

"My mom grows it in her garden." Cindy popped the cork back into the tube and tapped it with her prismatic black-painted fingernail. "As I said, a quarter of a cup of this stuff could spread through the entire town in minutes."

"Would the town stink like that forever?" I dry-heaved. The smell was so putrid I could taste it in the air.

"No, it dissipates after a while. A couple of hours, I guess."

"Hours?" Aedan coughed.

"To be honest, I'm not entirely sure about the time, but I know it disperses. My mom mixes it with specialized herbs and alkaline dirt to make it less potent, and uses it as fertilizer. The limpid worms are drawn to the smell the way garden gnomes are drawn to boysenberry syrup, but they eventually go away." She pursed her lips and placed a finger over them. "I'm thinking that if I douse myself with this stuff and start running, I can lead the worms away from town without any issue at all."

I held up a hand. "Uh, I have an issue. I don't particularly like the idea of my best friend risking her life on an insanely reckless plan."

"I second that." Samuel said, and Aedan held up three fingers.

Cindy blinked at us in disbelief. "What? I'll be fine."

Samuel eyed her. "Do you know that for sure?"

She held his gaze for a second, then looked away, murmuring. "I'm 95% sure."

"Then tell me how you plan on escaping once you've led the worms out of town."

"Okay, 85% sure," she said.

I put my hands on her shoulders. "Cindy, we aren't trying to come down on you. We just don't want to risk your safety."

She looked at me as though she wasn't sure I meant it. I could hardly blame her. Her relatives had been persecuted for centuries by

Elites. It was hard for her to tell the difference between someone worrying about her and someone disregarding her.

"We care about you," Samuel said softly. He seemed embarrassed by the admission, as if he'd blurted out "I love you, Cindy," instead.

Finally, she nodded. "Okay. What's your plan, Samuel?"

I hugged her.

"I'll tell you, but first I have a question." He regarded Cindy. "Could we put the malodorous root on, say, a car? Or some sort of tank? If we could do that—"

"No. It has to be mixed with an organic substance. Steel won't work." Cindy smiled. "Thanks for taking my idea seriously, Samuel. Not many Elites would."

"No problem." Samuel's complexion darkened. He cleared his throat, smiled a little, cleared it again.

"Your plan?" I prompted.

"Yeah." He motioned for us to kneel. He drew a cloud shape in the sand with his finger, then added a big circle about three inches below it with D.E. in the center.

"Okay, this is the worm horde," he pointed to the cloud, "and this is the town." He pointed to the circle.

"We're with you," I said.

He drew four stick figures, two between the cloud and circle, and two inside the circle.

"We need two people to be on the front lines, running interference against the oncoming horde, while the other two are in the town, helping people get to the bunkers and taking out any straggler worms. Once the people are safe, the two in town send out a signal to the others, then retreat to the bunker and wait out the worms until they pass through."

"But won't they destroy the town?" I asked.

"Damage can be repaired," Samuel said. "The people here have lived through a lot worse and landed on their feet."

Cindy acknowledged this with a nod, and they shared a smile. It was the knowing look of someone who had grown up in this odd town, in this strange world. I hadn't lived here long, but in the short time that I had, I'd learned to like it. The people in it, at least. The giant worms I could do without.

"Look, we can have our kumbaya moment later. Right now, we need to deal with the problem at hand. Problems, actually," Aedan said.

"What's *kumbaya*?" Cindy asked him.

"I'll explain later if neither of us is digested by a mutant worm." He clapped his hands. "So, how are we deciding who goes where? Do we get to choose our partners?" Aedan slung his arm around my shoulders and pulled me to his side. "I pick Maria because she's strong and mean and can protect me. Also, I like her."

I pinched his arm, making him yank it back. "Aedan and Samuel can be on the front lines while Cindy and I round up the town. Sound good?"

Samuel and Aedan sized each other up.

"Why do I have to go with him?" they said simultaneously as they frowned and crossed their arms.

And people think teenage *girls* are dramatic?

I spoke to each male in turn. "Because Aedan can shoot electricity out of his body, and because Samuel has more experience fighting these things. Also, if we signal from town, Samuel will be able to hear it with his ability, since there are no cell phones here."

"What?" Aedan went a pale shade of green. "*What?*"

"You get used to it," I said.

"Wait. You're an elemental Elite?" Samuel looked down his nose at Aedan. "I've never met one before."

Aedan flicked a piece of imaginary lint off his shirt. "I'm signing autographs later."

"Thought you'd be taller," Samuel drawled.

"I am taller," Aedan replied, then glared at me. "Wait a damn minute. You're sending me to fight a stampede of carnivorous worms with a dude who can hear really good? Do you know how crazy that is?"

"I also have an ax." Samuel took it from his back sling and held it up.

"Oh good." Aedan swiped the ax, swung it around. "If I get cold, you can build a fire."

"Mine." Samuel snagged his weapon back without any effort whatsoever. One second it was in Aedan's grip, the next it wasn't.

That scored him a grin from Aedan. "How did you do that?"

"I listened for the sound of your grip shifting."

"Holy crap, that's awesome." Aedan motioned toward the oncoming worms. "You know what? We're good. Lead the way, Batman."

Samuel eyed him speculatively. No doubt the reference had soared right over his head and he was trying to decide if Aedan had insulted him again.

"It's a compliment," I said.

"Yeah, it's a compliment." A look of pure panic came over Aedan's face. "Are you telling me they don't have the DC Universe here?"

I shook my head.

"I'm going to die."

"Come on." With one last look at Cindy, Samuel took off toward the impending horde, Aedan jogging behind him.

35

As I expected, the park was filled with people. Kids swarmed the playground equipment like bees on a hive while their parents chatted on benches. Joggers jogged, picnickers picnicked, and practitioners of Tai Chi Tai Chi'd.

Cindy and I stopped at the entrance and surveyed the scene. There was no way we could get everyone out by yelling.

Still, I tried. "Limpid worms are coming. Everyone get to the bunkers. *Hurry!*" I yelled this as loud as I could. A few people looked over, then immediately returned to what they were doing.

"It's no good. We need a bull's horn," Cindy said. I was nearly positive she meant the actual horn of a bull, not the voice amplifying device, and likely not the sort of bull I was thinking of, either.

"*Worms are coming!*" I yelled again. A little boy on the slide stuck his tongue out at me.

"You're really bad at that."

Cindy and I turned to find Gilda standing behind us. She was dressed in yoga pants and a tank top, and her hair was tied up into a bun and accented with three blue butterflies. I don't know how she did it, but she managed to look just as stunning in workout clothes as she had in a designer dress.

"How do you get those things to stay in your hair?" I asked.

"These?" She lifted a delicate hand to the butterflies. One alighted on the tip of her finger. "They're family pets. Why are you yelling at everyone in the park?"

"What are you even doing here?" I asked.

She gestured to Tamara and Ava, formerly Thing One and Thing Two. They were dressed similarly. "We run here on Sundays. Answer my question."

I did, explaining the situation to her, leaving out the parts about Kilshaw. If what he'd said was true and he was leader of the Elites way back then, I wasn't sure it was a good idea to mention it to an Elite like her. She'd find out soon enough, anyway.

"Limpid worms, huh?" She peered at the dust cloud outside of town. It was larger, which meant the worms were getting closer.

"Where's Samuel? Is he—?"

"In the thick of it, yep. He and a friend of mine are buying us some time by distracting and, hopefully, thinning out the herd."

"So, we need these people to evacuate? Head to the bunkers?"

"Yes. Quickly, please," Cindy said.

"Okay." Gilda bounced around and cleared her throat.

I slapped my hands over my ears. Cindy, Tamara, and Ava did the same.

"*Dead Enders. There is a worm horde headed straight for town. Elites, please stand by for instructions. The rest of you, head to the bunkers and wait for the all-clear. Go now.*"

With a rehearsed fluidity, everyone in the park went into action. Parents grabbed children, picknickers put out BBQ fires and gathered up food, joggers jogged in the direction of the bunkers, and the tai chi practitioners tai chi'd the heck out of there.

This definitely wasn't their first rodeo. The majority of the town headed toward the bunkers while the Elites formed a crowd near the jungle gym. I saw some familiar faces from the party last night and the town meeting.

Gilda approached the group with the air of a natural born leader, and I motioned for Cindy to follow her. She seemed hesitant, but did as I asked. When we came to a halt in the circle of Elites, I felt the unfriendly stares and knew they weren't aimed at me.

"What is *she* doing here?" the pyrokinetic guy that had burned the sleeves off my dress last night asked.

Cindy took a step back, shoulders bowing. I could tell it was a conditioned response, and I hated that it was. Glaring at the punk, I grabbed Cindy's hand and yanked her to my side. I'd taken a neutral stance when dealing with this issue before, and I wouldn't make that mistake again.

"Shut it, pal." I guess I could have been more diplomatic, but I wasn't feeling it. "She's with me."

"Her kind doesn't belong here. She should run and hide with the rest of the sheep."

"The way all of you big brave Elites ran when the chimera attacked?" I jabbed my finger into his chest, looked him dead in the eyes. "*You're* in charge? Wow, I feel safer already."

The parents of the Elite teens looked at their children with confusion. The pyrokinetic frowned hard, and a patch of grass near my feet caught on fire. "Watch it, earthmover."

"God, you're annoying." I stomped out the flames. "Exactly who do you think stopped that chimera when you were all at home, hiding in your mom's basements? I'll give you a hint."

I pulled Cindy closer. Some of the Elites looked interested, some surprised, but most glared at us and began whispering amongst themselves.

"All right, enough." Gilda moved between the pyro and me. "Max, take a walk."

He huffed, then spun on his heel and disappeared into the crowd.

"Why are you in charge?" one of the older Elites asked. She appeared to be around twenty, though it was hard to judge the age of what I'd call an "opposite-Sphynx." Instead of possessing a human head and a lion body, her body was human, and her head had the mane, nose, and teeth of a lion.

"Gilda is the Elite-appointed Jr. Evacuation Director," Tamara replied coldly. "If you'd attended the training sessions, Mara, you'd know that."

"Thank you, Tamara," Gilda said loftily.

"Whatever." Mara crossed her arms over her chest and rolled her eyes.

Gilda gave Cindy a brisk nod. "Regardless of your lucky break during the chimera incident, Max is right. You should evacuate with the others. You'll only be a burden in a fight."

"She'll be the exact opposite, actually." I was getting really tired of repeating myself. "I need her help. She stays. End of story."

"Fine. Have it your way." Gilda spun on her heel and faced the crowd.

"You okay?" I asked Cindy.

She nodded. "Not like it's the first time I've heard that."

Gilda's siren voice rang out over the park. "*Elites, we've done this as a drill many times, so you know what to do. Evacuate the town to the bunkers and eliminate any worms that cross your path. Stay in groups of three. Go.*"

I tried to unplug my ears with my fingers. "A warning would be nice."

Cindy grimaced. "You know, I'm really starting to dislike that particular Elite."

"So, it's true that Kilshaw Sterling is back in Dead End?" Gilda asked as we ran through town in search of other townspeople.

I cursed under my breath. Damn telepathic editor.

"Because I'd heard he was, but there are always rumors about him floating around Elite circles, so I didn't pay any attention. It is true?"

I nodded. "My fault. I opened a ripper and let him in."

"You seem upset about it." Clearly, she wasn't.

"The guy is a murderer. Yeah, I'm upset about it."

Gilda pursed her lips, side-eyed Cindy. "In some circles, you'd be hailed a hero."

"Those are not the kinds of circles I want to belong to." I watched as Cindy grabbed the hand of a crying little girl and led her across the street to her frantic parents.

"There are circles you belong to, whether you want to or not."

There was wistfulness in Gilda that made me think she wasn't only talking about me.

"Not me. I don't buy into the whole 'Elites are the best' thing. My grandfathers don't believe that garbage, either."

"You may not like it, but it's the truth. It's not only about being superior, you know. It's the duty of Elites to stand between danger and the lessers, because they're simple people who need protection."

"Hate to break it to you, but you're still being superior. The sad thing is that you Elites have all this power, but you're limited by your own small minds."

Gilda lifted her chin. "That's ridiculous. There are no limits for an Elite."

"Your belief in that only makes it truer. Trust me. I read dystopian fiction on the regular. First sign in a book that a person or organization is going down? An unshaking belief that it will never happen to them because they're too powerful. *Classic.*"

Her perfect forehead crinkled into a frown. Guess they didn't have dystopian books in Dead End. Good thing I'd brought a couple with me.

I turned away from her and pointed to a mountain of soil erupting through the asphalt in the street outside the sacred gardens. "What the heck is that?"

Cindy replied, "Limpid worms."

"But they didn't make those mountain things before. The one that attacked Toby and me only made a little sort of volcano-looking thing, but nothing like that. And the ones that went after those kids didn't, either."

"The ones near the school erupted on the outside of town. You just didn't see the exit mound. And one worm makes a little hill, but something this big indicates a lot of worms."

"Like how many?"

She frowned in concentration for a moment, then gave me a proud grin. "A *shit ton.*"

"I have got to stop teaching you slang words," I muttered.

"Either that or one really, really big worm."

The mountain kept growing. Soon, it had grown taller than the house next to it, and still the worm, or worms, had not emerged. Thankfully, the house and the surrounding neighborhood had been cleared of all residents. Only the unwelcome visitors remained.

"Hey. Do you still have that malodorous root?"

"Of course." Cindy pulled the test tube filled with green stuff out of her pocket, handed it to me. "Careful. Even a few drops of this will bring whatever is about to jump out of that mountain of dirt right to you."

A red-hatted garden gnome opened Danford Martindale's white picket fence and chucked a screeching plastic flamingo into the street. The bird landed on its back, kicking its metal rod legs in the air. One rod fell off and landed with a clang on the asphalt, then rolled into the rain gutter. The gnome cackled.

"I'm counting on it," I said.

Chirping what I was sure were obscenities, the lawn flamingo popped up on its single leg and bounced back through the gate. A second later, the red-hatted gnome went flying over the fence, landing on the sidewalk with an audible crack.

"Cindy, we're going to need a lot of boysenberries."

36

Cindy coordinated the boysenberry-gathering efforts. It turned out that several of her mom's gardening club friends lived near the park. Many of them grew boysenberries for the sacred garden altar.

In a surprising turn of events, the Elites began taking orders from Cindy as she pointed out where the berries grew and told them how to pick them so that the gnomes would eat them.

"Honestly, gnomes aren't that picky. They'll eat the berries any way if they're hungry. But if you twist them off like this, they'll eat them even if they're full." Cindy found an atomizer in one of the gardener's sheds to spritz the boysenberries with malodorous root. "Even if they *stink*."

The strange mountain in the street was now two stories high and slowing. "Hurry," I said. "I think that thing is about to burst."

"Only if they smell us. Otherwise they'll go somewhere else." Cindy crossed her arms and cocked her head to the side. "Still, they should have busted through by now. I wonder why they haven't." She inspected the two wheelbarrows filled with berries. "This is good enough. Let's do this."

Gilda ran over, towing a young boy with black hair and a wide smile behind her. "This is my cousin Jeremy. He'll push the wheel-barrow to the gnomes for us."

I frowned. "Gilda, he's a child. I can't let him—"

"Go ahead, Jeremy."

The wheelbarrow shuddered, once, twice, then shot off toward Danford Martindale's front yard. A second later, it was back.

"Whoa," I said.

"My cousin is only six, but he's a fifth generation telekinetic Elite." Gilda's smile was smug. "The strongest in his family."

"Are you ready, Jeremy?" Cindy asked. "Because once I spray this, we have to move fast."

Jeremy nodded. "Say when."

Cindy sprayed the first wheelbarrow. "Now."

While the first batch rolled up through the front gate of Mr. Martindale's house, Cindy spritzed the second batch. "Now."

Gilda put her hand on her cousin's small shoulder. "You're doing great, Jeremy. Push it right up through the gate."

He did, and the gnomes attacked the berries in a frenzied mob, like a school of piranhas on a hunk of dead meat. The flamingos hung back after sniffing the fruit. Cindy had said they might detect the malodorous root, as their taste buds tended to be more refined, but she was certain the gnomes wouldn't.

"They're eating the berries." Gilda sounded surprised.

"Lawn gnomes are pure id," Cindy said. "They're only interested in what feels good to them—often to their own detriment."

Javier Rivas, the older Elite teenager from the chimera incident, cleared his throat. I hadn't even realized he was in our group, which was a good indication of my level of distraction, since he was pretty noticeable.

"You're smart about creatures, Cindy. We're lucky to have you here." Javier shot Gilda an approving look. "Good call putting her in charge."

Gilda said nothing. I said nothing. Cindy said nothing. There was a lot of saying nothing going on with a background of obnoxious eating noises from the gnomes a block down.

"Something is happening with the worm mountain." Javier's face reddened and sweat dripped down the sides of his face.

"Can't you petrify it?" Gilda asked.

"What do you think I'm trying to do?" Javier snapped. "If it weren't for me, that thing would have burst open by now. But there are too many of them and I can't hold them back much longer."

"There's more than one?" I asked. "That's a relief."

"*How is that a relief?*" The veins stood out on Javier's temples.

"Can you imagine the size of the worm if it was only one?"

"She has a point," Gilda said.

"Is that Samuel and Aedan?" Cindy pointed toward the other side of the sacred gardens, opposite Worm Mountain.

"What are you doing here?" I asked as they approached. "You're supposed to be on the front lines."

"This *is* the new front line," Samuel said.

"The worms changed direction," Aedan replied. "Fast. It was weird. Sam turned on his robo-ears and we followed them here."

I'd had a back of my mind suspicion that was the case when the mountain appeared. Were the nasty things learning how to cooperate? That couldn't be good.

"Gross." Aedan grimaced at the monstrosity in the middle of the street. "That thing looks like a giant zit."

"Uh-oh." Samuel took a step back.

Javier shuddered with effort. Aedan wrinkled his nose, and Cindy's eyes flew wide open.

"The worms are coming too fast. I can't petrify this many," Javier said.

"Let's hope this plan of yours works," Gilda said to me.

"Plan of ours," I corrected, with a nod at Cindy, who gave me a nervous smile.

"Plan to run the hell out of here, now!" The words burst out of Javier as the worms burst free of the dirt mountain.

"No worries, bruh. I'm already gone—" *Thunk.* Aedan's eyes rolled back in his head and he dropped to the grass in a crumpled heap.

I knelt beside him, pried open one of his eyelids. "Aedan?"

"Huh. The ginger pepper didn't last as long as I thought it would," Cindy said.

"He's fine." Samuel picked up Aedan like he weighed nothing, and flung him over his shoulder.

"But we aren't. Let's *move!*" Javier yelled.

As one, we spun. Gilda held tight to Jeremy's hand while Javier grabbed mine and Cindy's. Samuel, with Aedan's limp form slung over his shoulder, scowled at Javier. We ran like our lives depended on it—which they did.

Mom and Dad had made me attend Sunday School as a child, and though I hadn't been in years, I'd never forgotten the story of Lot's wife. While Lot and his family fled the burning cities of Sodom and Gomorrah, Lot's wife turned back for one last look and turned into a pillar of salt.

I knew this story, and yet I couldn't help it. I had to know.

A quick glance over my shoulder showed me five truck-sized worms poking through the stiffened translucent bodies of the worms Javier had petrified. At first, they headed in our direction—five, no, ten, *twenty*, oozing, grotesque, eyeless tubes writhing toward us.

The worm in front halted. Then the next.

And the next.

The entire group flopped their big bodies around, knocking over garbage cans, trampling trees and bushes, basically destroying every-thing in their path, and headed in the opposite direction.

"It's working," I said, and dropped Javier's hand.

Cindy did the same, turned around. Neither of us was a pillar of salt or a worm snack, so I figured it was okay to keep watching.

"What are they doing?" Samuel asked. He and Javier had stopped to look, too. Gilda and Jeremy had already turned the corner and disappeared.

"Oh, wow. That's unfortunate," Javier winced.

"Depends how you look at it," I said. "Mr. Martindale will be happy."

The first few gnomes were unfortunately—or fortunately, depending on your point of view—slurped up by the giant worms. After that, the little creatures began scampering for their lives, their ceramic boots making a hollow, stampeding sound as they sped away from the worms. The worms chased the gnomes, which headed straight toward the mountains bordering the Beyond.

Without speaking a word, we took off after them. We had to see for ourselves that the worms were gone.

Other Elites joined us as we ran toward the outskirts of Dead End, the worms a mile or so ahead of us, the gnomes tiny red and blue blurs beyond them. When they reached the mountains, there was a rumbling sound and a mighty screech.

I stumbled, nearly fell. "Is that the—"

"*Chimera*," Cindy said. "She's back. And look! She brought her family. *Aww*."

The chimera sat up tall, her eyes glowing with excitement. Around her, three smaller chimeras had popped out of the earth, their serpent tails wagging, and then two older chimeras, and finally, what I was going to call the daddy chimera, since he was as big as the female, but with a thicker body and mane.

The chimeras squeaked and screeched and sang with delight as they snatched the limpid worms out of the ground and gobbled them up.

Their appetites were unending. I counted twenty-three worms guzzled down by one chimera alone. They ate until the limpid worms stopped coming, then lounged on their backs in the rocks and basked in the noonday sunshine.

37

"YOU DIDN'T HURT ANYONE DID YOU, LOOPS?"

Dad was staring at me from my grandpas' living room sofa with worried eyes. Abuelo Emilio had set him up with a pillow and blanket, so he was as comfortable as he was going to get. Since the medical clinic had been evacuated with the rest of the town, my grandfather had tended to Dad's wounds himself.

"Some lawn gnomes. A bunch of worms," I replied, my tone dull and flat. I glared at Abuelo. "How is he awake? Aedan dropped like a stone a couple of hours ago."

Abuelo was in the chair beside the sofa. He lowered his newspaper so I could see his face. "I've been dosing him with ginger pepper since we got home. We had some here. Your grandfather uses it in his chicken marsala." He held up a hand. "It's perfectly safe. Once you've fully acclimated to Sanctum, it has no effect except to spice up your food and settle your stomach, in small doses."

"Why did you keep him awake? He should be resting."

"He demanded to stay awake until he knew you were safe. His next dose is in fifteen minutes, but now that we know you're safe, I won't be giving him anymore." He raised the newspaper again.

I'd headed straight home after the chimeras returned to the mountains with full bellies and sunshine-warmed bodies. Cindy had gone home too. Samuel had agreed to put Aedan up for now, though with Aedan's mouth and Samuel's grumpiness, that might not last long. Good thing he was still passed out.

My dad frowned. "Worms and gnomes? What?"

"Never mind. Just know that your daughter wasn't a murderous monster today. Of course, there's always tomorrow." I looked around the room. "Where's Grandpa Holli?"

"Loops, that's not what I meant. Why do you say things like that?"

"She said it because that *is* what you meant." Abuelo folded his newspaper and set it aside. "You question her the way you'd interrogate one of your criminals. You tell her you don't think she's a monster, yet you treat her as though she is one. And then, when she brings attention to your attitude, you push the blame on her for mentioning it."

It made me sad that Dad was so transparent even Abuelo saw through him, but it also comforted me. I wasn't crazy or wrong. Dad did hate my ability, and he was terrified I'd end up a monster.

"I'm sorry if I—"

"*That*, not if. You are sorry *that* you made her feel like a monster," Abuelo corrected. "You are sorry *that* you made her feel guilty for saving your life. You are sorry *that* you made her feel bad for something outside of her control."

Dad went silent for a long minute, but he was thinking. I could practically hear the thoughts racing through his mind.

"How did Hollister get hurt?" Dad didn't look at me when he asked the question, but I knew he was talking to me. "Why does he have stitches?"

"It was my fault. I lost control," I whispered.

"See? That's what I'm talking about." His handsome face fell. "I know you'd never intentionally hurt your grandfather, but you did it because you were using your ability. You have to stop. Your mother told me that the ability you both have is dangerous, and that I should never encourage you to use it."

Low. I felt low and terrible. Not only had I disappointed Dad, but I'd also somehow managed to disappoint Mom.

"I told my daughter those things." A long, loud sigh escaped from

Abuelo. "Years ago, I used my ability to open a tear in the membrane between our worlds, in order to banish Kilshaw Sterling to your side of the Divide. In doing so, I weakened it and left the citizens here open to dangerous things. My guilt caused me to raise my daughter to fear her ability the way I feared mine."

Dad nodded. "That's what she told me."

"I was wrong to teach her that."

"Abuelo?" I lifted my head.

"Instead of teaching her to control her ability, I taught her to run from it. That didn't work very well, did it, Maria? Because you were never taught how to handle your ability, you didn't know how to stop it and your grandfather was hurt. But that isn't your fault. It is not your mother's fault, either. It is mine."

The bedroom door down the hall creaked open and Toby shot out. He bounded into my arms and licked my face.

When Toby finished with me, he leapt onto the sofa with Dad and gave him the same treatment. "Hey boy. I'm happy to see you, too." Slowly, gingerly, Dad reached into his back pocket. "Brought you something, pup."

It was a slightly gnawed and dusty dog chew. Toby's favorite. His furry ears perked up and his tail wagged.

I grinned. "You had that in your pocket? Why?"

"I wanted to have it with me for when I found you two again," Dad said.

"You were looking for us?"

"Of course I was looking for you, Loops. How do you think Kilshaw found me? He went back to the abandoned café where I was camped out, trying to figure out a way to get you back home."

The idea that he'd worked so hard to keep his promise warmed my heart. "I still can't believe you kept that old piece of rawhide."

"It's not rawhide. It's made with this special stuff that's healthier for dogs."

"Elfin leather?" Abuelo asked.

"What is that?" Dad asked.

I closed my eyes and crossed my fingers. "Please don't tell me it's made from real elf skin."

Dad's face lost color.

"*Real* elves?" Abuelo chuckled. "Listen to yourself, Maria. There's no such thing as a real elf."

"Thank goodness." Dad's face regained some of its lost color. "What is Elfin leather made of, then?"

"The bark of the Elfin tree."

Relief swept through me. "Tree bark. Okay, yes. That sounds much less awful."

"Indeed." He picked up a different newspaper, this time it was the *Arcadia Valley Press*, and flipped it over in his hands. "Though the trees do scream when they're being de-barked. They volunteer for it because they're compensated well, and because it's against the law to harvest the bark, fruit, or branches of any tree in Sanctum without said tree's consent. But it's a painful process."

I faced my dad. "This is why you don't ask questions here."

Abuelo shrugged and stared down at his paper.

"Why are you always reading a newspaper?" I asked. "Every time I see you, you've got a different newspaper in your hands."

Abuelo pointed at a news story buried on the next-to-last page of the paper, sandwiched between a recipe for chupacabra meat chili and an article on how to summon garden spirits to chase away tomato hornworms.

"*Sisters of the Sanctum Originals meeting. Bring your genetic ID and your best ideas to the Good Eastern Inn, six p.m., September 30th.*" I frowned. "Sounds like a boring meeting."

"It's anything but boring, Maria. It's the most dangerous news in this paper." He flipped to the front page where the headline described a bus overturning and injuring sixteen people in Sanctum City. "Far more dangerous than this."

"I don't understand."

"Supposedly disenfranchised Elites have been gathering. Smaller meetings for now, but that's where it starts."

"Where what starts?" Dad asked.

"Revolution." Abuelo resumed reading his paper.

None of us spoke for a while. Toby snatched the chewy from my dad and trotted to one of his many beds to give it his full attention.

"Maria. Thank the gods." Grandpa Holli shuffled down the hallway. His face was already starting to bruise. "After we saw your note, we worried ourselves sick."

I stood, hurried over to his side, helped him walk into the room. "I'm sorry, Grandpa. I was ashamed of myself for hurting you."

"Well, it seems to me that the window hurt me, not my grand-daughter."

"I made the window break."

"Did you?" He glanced at his husband. "There was more than one earthmover in that room. Also, I'm smart enough to know not to step in between two Elites when they're in high spirits. We all own a small portion of blame. You no more than your abuelo and me."

"Thank you for saying that." I blinked back tears.

"It's the truth." He gripped the back of a dining room chair with one hand and held out the other. "I'm glad you're back home, Maria."

I let out an embarrassing sob-gasp and hugged him tight. "I love you, Grandpa."

He kissed the top of my head. "I love you too. No more running away. Your abuelo, Toby, and I were absolutely distraught."

When I'd first got to Dead End, I'd wanted nothing more than to return to my world. It was all I thought about, my entire focus. Then I met Cindy. And Samuel. I saw ceramic gnomes and lawn flamingos take over a man's yard. I met a dentist who was also a merman, and I fought a giant worm for my dog—and a whole bunch more for my town.

I now realized that my old world, where I had to hide who and what I was, wasn't home to me the way this world was. Sure, Dead End was weird and dangerous, but this place didn't ask me to hide. It accepted me … for me.

I loved my dad, but he was comfortable in the other world. He wouldn't want to stay in Dead End. He wouldn't be happy here the way I was. Part of me wanted to hold onto him, to hold onto my old life. To go home.

But the bigger part of me? It knew I was already there.

38

After our family discussion, the healer from the medical clinic was finally able to come and see to everyone's injuries, so Abuelo went ahead and dosed my dad one more time to keep him awake for the examination.

Abuelo warned me about what to expect so I wouldn't stare, but when a hyper-articulate grizzly bear humanoid figure wearing dark blue scrubs, reading glasses, and carrying a battered black medical bag strolls through the front door, it's hard to resist a lingering look or two.

After the healer finished her work on both grandpas, she went to work on Dad. I sat on the couch by Abuelo's chair and watched.

"So, what's happening with Kilsh—"

Abuelo shot me a silencing look over his newspaper, glanced at the healer, and shook his head. Apparently, he didn't want me bringing up Kilshaw in front of her. I guess that made sense, considering the rumors of impending revolution and the way some Dead Enders seemed to be way too pleased by his appearance.

I nodded and lowered my voice. "Did you dig up that *poisonous root* in the garden yet?" Not exactly one of my most subtle moments, although I did stop myself from using quotation fingers, so I considered it a victory.

Abuelo lowered his newspaper to his lap. "Yes."

"And?"

"It's locked up in a glass box. But..."

"But?"

Abuelo ran a hand through his hair, squeezed the base of his neck. "I fear its presence has caused such a disruption that it may interfere with the... *flower bed.* I was advised to keep it in perfect condition until the gardening club can decide what to do with it."

I swallowed hard. Kilshaw was locked up, but if his detainment was dependent on the sympathies of the people of Sanctum, I worried how long he'd stay in custody. The way Samuel, Cindy, and my grandfathers made it sound, there were a lot of residents who still believed that only Elites should run Sanctum.

Abuelo patted my knee. "Don't worry. Nobody knows how to open that box but me. The root isn't going anywhere any time soon." He smiled and returned to his newspaper.

Dismissed, I went to see what the healer was doing to Dad. Mostly she was massaging herbs into his skin. With only a few herbs and a little magic, the healer was able to turn my dad's injuries from deep lacerations and broken ribs to minor scrapes and bruises. She'd set the broken bones in his arm and leg, and splinted them. Without pain, and without an X-ray.

"That's amazing," I said.

"Just a little magic and medicine," Dr. Behr replied in a musical voice that reminded me of a mom from an old TV sitcom. "Mr. Thompson, you'll need to apply this ointment for the next few days to avoid infection."

My dad tentatively accepted the tube of ointment from her paw-like hands. "Thank you."

He'd looked awed and fearful the moment she'd come in, walking and talking like a human being, and had kept that same expression throughout the procedure.

"The injection I gave you should take care of some of the aftereffects of traveling through the Divide, too. You should be feeling much better soon. Perhaps a little hungry. The broken bones might take another day or so to knit together. Call me if they aren't fully healed by the end of the week."

"A *day* or so?" Dad frowned in obvious confusion.

Grandpa Holli patted the healer on her shoulder. "Thank you so much for coming on short notice, Beatrice. We know how busy you are."

"Yes, thank you." Abuelo's injuries appeared to be gone. He wasn't moving stiffly anymore, and his face wasn't swollen, either.

"Of course, Holli. Emilio. Anytime." Beatrice collected her things before turning to face them again. "Now, if I could just collect my payment for services, I'll be on my way."

"Of course." Grandpa Holli hurried to the kitchen, returning a minute later with a lunch sack clutched in his hands.

"Payment in full, plus a little extra for you to share with Virgil." He handed it to her. "Prepared it just before you got here."

Beatrice lifted the bag up and sniffed it once, her natural smile widening. "Wonderful. Gentlemen, if you'll excuse me."

With a nod, she stomped out the front door, then stuck both her medical and the lunch bags between her teeth and barreled down the street on all fours.

I stared after her until she was no longer in view. "What exactly was in that bag, Grandpa Holli?"

"Smoked salmon pâté. Beatrice is independently wealthy, so money doesn't interest her, but she is quite the foodie. It was her favorite from my restaurant, so I trade it for medical services."

"LET'S GET SOME AIR, DAD."

He'd slept for nearly twenty-four hours, which wasn't bad. If I ever had to go through the Divide again, I was getting one of those shots from the healer. Not only that, but his broken arm and leg were mostly healed. He still had a slight limp and his shoulder was sore, but overall, he was much better.

After a breakfast of crepes and fresh blueberries, prepared by Abuelo, Dad showered and changed into some of Grandpa Holli's clothes while his own were being washed. He looked clean and healthy, if still a little confused.

"Some air? Out there?"

"A quick stroll around the block, if you're up to it. We'll take Toby." I smiled in a way that I hoped reassured him.

"All right. Let's go for a walk."

Toby took point, sniffing every flower, gate, and mailbox we passed as Dad and I walked quietly alongside each other. We walked up the street to Dan Martindale's house, which I recognized immediately by its proximity to the mountain of soil, asphalt, sidewalk, and grass, the petrified worm carcasses, and, of course, the subdued cluster of lawn flamingos.

Smarter than the gnomes, they hadn't taken the bait of the malodorous boysenberries during the worm horde, but they had witnessed the gnome carnage. The entire group was huddled under Dan's purple bougainvillea bushes. They didn't seem fearful so much as thoughtful—and sneaky.

City workers in hazmat-like gear swept plaster red hats and black boots into dustpans and sprayed squished boysenberries and slimy worm guts into a dirty pile, from where they were shoveled into the back of one of several dump trucks.

Just another day in Dead End.

"This is quite a scene." Dad shoved his hands into the front pockets of his trousers.

"Yeah."

"Were you scared to face those things?"

"Big time. But people were in danger. I couldn't just walk away knowing I might be able to help."

"You're a natural white hat cowboy."

"Like my dad," I said.

We shared a smile and continued walking, avoiding eye contact with the flamingos, who turned as one as we passed by, tracking us with their beady black eyes. I made a note to never, ever disturb the altar in the sacred gardens.

Teams of Dead Enders—non-humans and humans, all shapes and sizes and species—worked together to chop up petrified worm carcasses and push dirt back into the volcano-shaped mountain. Some used tools. Some used abilities.

"I wonder where they're taking all this stuff," I said.

"About forty miles northwest of here. They're burning it." He gestured to a funnel-shaped cloud of black smoke I hadn't noticed.

"Eagle eyes."

"We all have our abilities," he said.

City Councilmembers Bert, Mr. Gale, and Mrs. Beeson were directing workers to the center of town, where there had also been damage. Mrs. Beeson had a thick sheaf of papers pinched into a large clipboard, and seemed to be doing most of the actual directing—being a high school secretary probably gave her an organizational edge over the others.

Dad and I weaved through town, finally ending up at the park where Cindy and I had yelled ineffective warnings about the worms. We rested on a bench while Toby nosed around in the grass. The park was empty except for the Tai Chi group that always seemed to be around. I was starting to think they weren't doing Tai Chi at all, but something scarier, like conjuring a magical ward to protect us from something horrible I didn't want to know about.

Dad sat up taller on the bench. "I can't stay here, Loops."

"I know."

He clasped his hands together. "With Kilshaw in custody, we don't have to worry about the agency anymore. No more running for our lives, no more cheap motels, no more day jobs. I could get my old job back. We could be a normal family again."

"We were never normal, Dad."

"Sure we were, Loops."

"No, we weren't." I stared down at my clenched hands.

"Fine. Maybe we weren't perfect, but we do love each other."

Mom's face popped into my head, as clear as the last time I saw her. Over the years, I'd lost her by increments. She'd become more ephemeral to me than even Aedan at his most ghostly. But today she returned. I saw her soft smile, heard the gentle music of her voice, smelled her chocolate chip cookies, felt the warmth of the last hug she gave me.

"Yes, we love each other."

"Come home with me, Loops."

Disappointing Dad was the last thing I wanted to do, but there was no way around it. It was time for him to accept that I was old enough to know what was best for me, even if he didn't agree. I only hoped he didn't hate me for it.

"I can't. I have an ability—a strong one—and there are going to be times when I get angry or sad, or scared, and my earthmoving ability is going to rear up. If I keep it bottled like I always have, and don't learn how to control it properly, I'm going to do something I'll regret. Maybe I'll hurt someone again." I stared out at the Tai Chi group, which was now burning some sort of grass torch and chanting rhythmically. "I'll truly be the monster you see every time you look at me."

"I don't see you as a monster. I admit, you scared me that day on the highway, but I never saw you as anything but my sweet girl. I was trying to follow your mom's last wishes, is all."

I blinked back tears. "You hid me away in motel rooms and kept me caged in shame and fear, with an ability that feeds on those emotions. I could never win."

"Sweetheart." He sounded so defeated I nearly stopped talking, but I had to get it out, had to make him understand why I couldn't return home with him.

My voice was small and clogged with tears. "You don't cage a person, Dad. You cage a monster."

Revulsion, self-directed, twisted his face. "*Loops.* I never meant to do that to you."

"But you did, Dad."

He lowered his head, dropping his face into his hands.

"I understand now why you did it and I love you, but I can't go back to that life. I was scared all the time. And so lonely."

"I'm sorry, honey."

Toby brought me a tennis ball he'd unearthed from somewhere in the park.

"I know." I picked up the ball, examined it to be sure it was safe for my dog to play with, then threw it. Toby took off after it like a bullet. "You have a life there, a job, friends. I don't have any of those things.

But here in Dead End, I go to school, I have friends, and people don't see me as a freak or a threat because they're all different, like me."

"You've been going to school?" He seemed surprised, but interested.

"Yeah. My grandpas take me. I like my classes and I've made some friends."

"You have a life here. People love you." He stood, extended a hand to me. "Of course, they do. You're just like your mother was. Smart and funny."

I let him pull me to my feet. "Don't forget amazing."

"How could I?"

"And gorgeous."

He chuckled. "Smart-ass."

"Takes one to know one, as my dad always says."

"Throwing my own words back at me. Can you believe the nerve of this girl, Toby?"

My dog trotted proudly to Dad with the bright yellow tennis ball clutched between his jaws, tail wagging.

My dad gave me a sideways grin. "Yorkshire terrier."

I shook my head. "Norfolk terrier."

"*Bull* terrier."

This time I laughed. "In spirit maybe, but this guy is Cairn terrier through and through. I bet he'd even answer to 'Toto' and let me carry him in a picnic basket."

"Did Dorothy actually carry Toto in a picnic basket, though?"

I shrugged. "Come to think of it, maybe not. I was bluffing anyway. Toby wouldn't get into a picnic basket unless the inside was slathered with peanut butter."

Dad knelt to scratch under my dog's chin, his face turned away from me. "You're turning eighteen in a couple of months, Loops."

"I know."

"Practically an adult." He raked a hand through his hair. "Old enough to make your own decisions about your future."

Was I? Eighteen seemed like this massive turning point, yet I couldn't imagine feeling much differently about my life than I do now. In a way, it was like I had just started my life—as if the day my dad sent me through the portal into the One Way Café was my real birthday.

"I'm going to miss you."

This was it. He'd accepted it. He was letting me go. Why did that make me feel so awful, and so happy at the same time?

"I'm going to miss you too. You can come visit, you know. All you need is a café card." I smiled through a mist of tears.

He stood, opened his arms. I dove into them. I might be mature enough to make my own decisions about my life, but I was always going to need my dad.

"Take care of my books." I sniffed. "If I come visit, I'll be looking for them."

"I will."

"And make sure you cook for yourself. Eating out all the time isn't good for you."

"Got it."

"Also, don't take too much overtime, make sure you get plenty of rest. Oh, and—"

"Loops." He squeezed me a little tighter. "I'll be fine. Just like you will."

A group of people dressed in gardening gear filed into the park. One of them towed a large wagon crowded with plastic pots containing leafy plants and colorful flowers. The flowers had yellow and orange petals like a sunflower, and a dark brown center. Within the center of each one, was a tiny face. It looked a little like a baby— and sounded like an angry one.

The gardeners picked up the flowerpots and cradled them. Some sang lullabies.

"You absolutely sure you want to stay in this strange place?" Dad stared hard at the gardeners. "Squalling sunflowers, bear healers, giant worms, and all?"

Cindy and her mother rushed into the park. They were dressed similarly to the other gardeners, and were dragging another wagon crammed with gardening tools, a pile of dark brown soil, and four watering cans with large spouts.

"Here, Cindy. Hurry, please." Mrs. Gale pointed to a patch of dirt.

"Got it, Mom."

Once she'd dug a hole big enough, Mrs. Gale handed her one of the sobbing flowers. Cindy cooed at it as she gently cut away the plastic pot. She then set the flower into the ground, covered it with fresh soil, and showered it with water from one of the watering cans. The flower immediately stopped crying.

I had to learn more about those flowers.

Cindy looked over at me and waved. I waved back.

"I'm sure." I took out the café card Laverne had given to me. Handed it to him.

"What's this?"

"Just in case you decide you miss me too much and need to get back here. You remember the way to the One Way Café, right?"

"Yes, I do." He tucked it into his shirt pocket. Right next to his heart. "Thanks, Loops."

39

"So, the flamingos have settled down?"

Cindy, Toby, and I were sharing a booth and a plate of French fries at the One Way Café. Aside from Laverne and the two guys who just stomped in, we were the only customers in the place. The jukebox was rolling through the nineties. There was a mix of songs I recognized from the oldies station back home and some, including *Smells Like Exploded Limpid Larvae*, that I was sure had never been released on the other side of the Divide.

"That's what I heard. Mr. Martindale told my dad that the flamingos are being a lot nicer to him since the worms ate all the gnomes," Cindy replied. "They've been trimming his hedges, and yesterday they brought his mail right to the—"

"You're *still* upset? I apologized for burning the chair. How long are you going to give me the silent treatment?"

Aedan slid into the seat Toby and I were sharing. Samuel scooted in next to Cindy, crossed his arms over his chest, and glared at Aedan. After a moment, his gaze shifted to Toby, who blinked back at him.

"No bacon?" Samuel asked.

Toby's ears peaked at the word. He yipped twice.

"Coming right up," Laverne called out from the kitchen.

"Thanks a lot," I said, to Samuel. "He's supposed to be starting his diet today."

"You owe me for having to put up with this one."

Aedan helped himself to a few of our fries. "I'm no trouble. You're exaggerating."

"What did you do?" I stared hard at him.

"Nothing. Samuel's making it sound worse than it is."

"What's this about a burned chair?" Cindy asked.

Aedan grabbed a few more fries. "Nothing. It wasn't that big a deal."

"*What did you do?*" I repeated.

"Do you have a few hours?" Samuel grumbled.

"Look, I'll pay you back for everything. You have my word."

"With what money?"

Aedan's brows drew together, his expression thoughtful. "Oh yeah, I'm broke. That's going to make paying you back a bit more challenging."

"A *bit*?" Samuel ground out the words. "I'm one more singed lampshade away from kicking your ass, Sterling."

"Come on, you know it wasn't intentional."

"Enough." I slapped Aedan's hand when he tried to sneak another fry. "I know he can be a handful, but there's no need for violence. Besides, if we discuss every one of his recent screw-ups, we'll be here all day."

"Not cool." Aedan scowled. I shot him a look and he piped down, shoved another fry into his mouth.

"Heard you told your dad you're staying in Dead End." Samuel said. I nodded. "He understands."

"Sounds like you don't need to work on stabilizing the rippers anymore." He pulled a paper napkin out of the aluminum holder at the head of the table and began folding it into symmetrical squares. I didn't think it was for any purpose other than to keep his hands busy.

"I promised I'd help you get to the Other to find your sister." I put my palm on top of his and he stopped folding. "I meant it."

He pulled away, continued with his napkin. "We made a mutually beneficial deal. There's no benefit to you now. You have everything you want."

"But my friend doesn't."

He blinked at me. "Your friend?"

"Maria, the rippers are still dangerous," Cindy said, "and you saw what happened with the worms when you stabilized them."

"She's right."

"The rippers are dangerous, true. And they can bring dangerous things to town, also true. But as long as there are doorways to other universes, like this place—" I swept my hand around in a small circle to indicate the café. "—there are possibilities. And I'm going to help you find them."

"Thanks." Samuel's mouth remained a straight line, but his eyes smiled at me.

"Well, I want to hear about the chair." Cindy angled her head so she could peek around Samuel's arm to see his face. "Tell me about it?"

Samuel relaxed a little. "Sparky here should tell it."

"*Sparky*? Not cool, Sam," Aedan said. "It's not that big of a deal."

My eyes narrowed. "I'll ask you one last time. What did you do?"

Aedan rubbed his side. "You have bony elbows. They hurt." He glanced at Samuel, then at me. "Fine. I accidentally zapped one of Samuel's dining room chairs this morning."

"Zapped?" Cindy asked.

"Like static electricity," Aedan said. "A tiny zap."

"Tiny?" Samuel jabbed a finger at Aedan. "This wasn't one of those walk-across-the-living-room-rug-and-touch-a-light-switch sort of zaps. You set the chair on fire."

"It wasn't that bad."

"Really? If I hadn't walked in when I did, who knows what might have happened. You could've burned down my house!"

Aedan cringed. "I'm sorry about that. Really I am."

A *but* was coming. I was as sure about that as I was that Aedan would be standing on my grandfathers' porch tonight, begging for a place to stay.

"*But* you were kind of asking for it with that weird rug in the living room."

"Here we go again." I lowered my face into my hands.

"I could've powered the whole town with the static electricity I picked up from that thing," Aedan continued, apparently enjoying the taste of his own foot.

"I want to hit you in the face." Samuel closed his fist tightly for emphasis.

With a loud clatter, a plate of bacon was set on the table and we looked up to see Laverne standing there, arms crossed and brow lowered. She didn't speak, but the effect was a lot scarier than if she'd started yelling.

Cindy, Samuel, and I sat up straight, flashing our best-behavior smiles. I kicked Aedan under the table, and he sat up, too.

"Sorry, Laverne," Samuel said.

"You know the café rules."

"Yes, ma'am. No violence allowed in the One Way Café. Won't happen again."

Laverne gave us a final, suspicious look before turning and heading back into the kitchen.

We let out a collective sigh of relief, except for Aedan, who clearly didn't see he was the one at fault in all this.

"Well," Samuel said, "on that note, I better go. I need to see if I can salvage what's left of my chair."

"What's the chair made of?" Cindy asked.

"Oakenwood," Samuel replied.

"Oak?" Aedan asked.

"*Oakenwood* from an oakentree." Cindy sat up in her seat as she spoke. "It's a tree grown in sustainable forests at the base of the Beyond Mountains between Dead End and Track's End."

"Please tell me it doesn't scream," I said.

"Scream?" Aedan leaned back in the booth as Toby stomped across his lap and leapt off the bench seat. "Ouch. Trim that dog's nails, would you?"

"Don't bother Laverne," I warned Toby.

"He's fine," Laverne responded.

"Harvesting oakenwood isn't painful for either the trees or the harvesters," Cindy said, leaving me to wonder if there *were* trees that caused pain to the people who cut them down. I decided to ask later. "The trees barter their branches for water and fertilizer to wood harvesters for industrial use. Some oakentrees are quite highbrow, and will sell only to artisans who pass a series of tests."

A huge grin spread across Aedan's face. "I can already tell I'm really going to like living here."

40

"SEE YOU GUYS AROUND." SAMUEL STOOD.

"Wait. I just thought of something that might help you." Cindy rummaged in the bag she'd brought with her. I'd convinced her to stop carrying odd creatures and stinky liquid from her mom's garden in her sweatshirt pockets, so she'd taken to carting them around in one of her dad's old satchels.

Samuel slowly sat down again. He stared at Cindy when she was turned away, and lowered his eyes to his hands when she glanced up.

Aedan and I exchanged a look. He waggled his brows, and I stifled a laugh.

"What's funny?" Cindy pulled a pad of paper and a pencil out of the bag and began sketching.

"Maria burped. What are you drawing?" Aedan asked, as I kicked him under the table.

"Instaurabo. It's a plant my mom grows. If you prepare it with alcohol and the crushed leaf of a meridian tree, you can use the tincture to repair any oakenwood surface. My mom uses it all the time on our furniture. Dad gets clumsy when he's focused on work."

"You're really good at things like that." Aedan tapped the edge of the paper with a French fry. "You were amazing with those worms."

"Thanks." Cindy's cheeks pinked. "I learned it from my mom and grandmother."

I didn't even have to look to know that Samuel was frowning big time at this exchange. I was also sure that was part of the reason Aedan was doing it. Samuel was an easy target when it came to Cindy.

"Do you think the tincture will work on Samuel's chair?" I asked.

"I'd have to see how severe the damage is."

"Then it's settled. You go with Samuel to see the chair and help him put the Insta-whatchamacallit stuff on it," Aedan announced.

Samuel's head whipped around. "Huh?"

"Insta*urabo*." Cindy turned to Samuel, tucked her hair behind her ear. "Would you like me to? Come over, I mean."

Samuel opened his mouth, then closed it again.

Cindy cleared her throat. "If it's too much trouble, I can just—"

"Yes-I-want-you-to-come-over," he blurted. Was he sweating? The café had to be sixty-eight degrees inside.

"Okay." Cindy smiled. "I have to stop by my house first. I can meet you in an hour."

"I'll walk you home and we'll go to my place together." Samuel made it sound like a command. He seemed to realize this, because he added, "If that's okay with you."

Cindy nodded, and they slid out of the booth together. Samuel tossed his café card down on the table.

"Use this for the bill. And *only* the bill, Sterling."

Aedan winked. "Love you too, bro. You kids have fun."

Samuel gave him a seething stare as he ushered Cindy out of the café.

"Why do you insist on antagonizing him? You know he could very easily kick you to the curb," I said.

"Nah," Aedan swiped the last fry from my plate and tossed it into his mouth. "Sam's cool. He yells and threatens to beat me to a pulp, but at the end of the day, he won't do it."

"I don't have your confidence, so I'd suggest you don't push him," I said. "Also, behave yourself. He's doing a nice thing letting you live with him."

"I know, I know. I'm still getting used to everything here. It's a lot to process." He sat back in his seat and exhaled, his shoulders relaxing. I hadn't noticed it before, but he'd been tense the entire time the others were around. He knew what people thought about him when they heard his name, and he hated it.

I rested my hand on his forearm. The muscle tightened beneath my fingers. "You aren't your father. None of us think that."

His silver gaze slid over me. Apprehensive, at first, but it soon softened.

Aedan picked up my hand and slipped it into his, intertwining our fingers. We sat in the booth in comfortable silence, absorbing everything. I knew without a doubt that I would recall this moment later in my life whenever I heard dishes rattling, smelled French fries cooking, and tasted soda that was close to, but not quite, Dr. Pepper.

It took me back to the days before Dead End, when I only knew Aedan as a ghost. Before everything flipped upside down in both our worlds. The hours spent in cramped motel bathrooms, communicating through fogged mirrors, sharing our deepest secrets. Hours falling slowly in love.

It felt like so long ago.

Abruptly, Aedan slipped his hand from mine and slid from the booth, grabbed Samuel's card and took it to Laverne.

"Table's already been taken care of," Laverne called. Aedan stopped short, pocketed the card, and headed for the exit.

"Aedan?"

He ignored me and walked out.

I sat in stunned silence. This was exactly like what he used to do when he was an astral projection. Disappear on me with no notice, no explanation, no apologies. I'd almost forgotten that.

A moment later, Aedan knocked on the window beside me.

Startled, I jumped away from the glass and scowled at him. "What are you doing?"

He breathed onto the window, fogging it up. When it was opaque, he began writing on it with his index finger.

"Aedan?"

He wrote: *What's shaking?* It was backwards, but I could read it just fine.

"You are such a weirdo." I laughed.

His eyes crinkled at the corners as he shot that smug Aedan Sterling grin back at me. My heart skipped a beat.

Sliding close to the window, I waited till his message disappeared, then fogged it up from my side. My stomach was fluttery, and my heart beat a little faster. I couldn't wait to see his expression when he saw what I wrote, but I also dreaded it. What if he didn't feel the same? What if he couldn't read backwards? What if he could?

I mustered up all my courage and wrote on the fogged glass with my pinky finger so I could fit it all in.

My ♥. When u r near.

The smug grin slid off his face. He ran back into the diner, pulled me out of my seat, and dragged me outside. Toby followed, bounding down the steps behind us. Silver eyes glowing with something other than electricity, Aedan took both my hands in his.

"Do you mean that, Maria? Really?"

You've already risked most of your pride. Might as well toss in the rest. I took a deep breath. In a clumsy rush, I closed the distance between us, wrapped my arms around his neck. His lips brushed my forehead.

"Yes, I mean it." I took another deep breath, leaned back, and looked him straight in the eye. "Every word. I like you, Aedan. I like you a lot."

For once, the guy had nothing to say. He blinked rapidly, cleared his throat six times in a row, shifted from foot to foot.

Unbelievable. He was speechless. I hadn't been sure it was possible, until now.

I laid my head against his chest. "Do you like me?"

"Yes, Maria," he said hoarsely, "I like you."

"A lot?" My heart was beating so hard I was sure he could hear it.

"Yeah, a lot. I walked through a ripper for you, remember?"

"I remember."

My breath caught as he slid his arms around my waist. Holding my gaze with his, he ducked his head and brushed his mouth over mine. Slowly. Achingly slowly.

My body felt light and heavy at the same time. My pulse was speeding, my head was spinning, and I couldn't stop trembling. He pressed his lips against mine, a little harder, but still going slow, as if he were waiting for me to catch up. I didn't have experience, but I did have instincts and I knew what I liked.

I parted my lips, leaned into the kiss, and followed his lead.

My second first kiss.

It was everything I'd wanted it to be. I sensed Aedan's excitement in the way he held me, our hearts beating in time with each other, and knew he felt the same way.

When we finally broke apart, he gave me one of those genuine, crinkly eyed smiles that made my heart beat like crazy in my chest.

"Why do you like me, Aedan?" I was truly curious, and I wanted to hear it from him while he was being as sincere as he ever got.

"I told you why that night in the motel bathroom. No one sees me the way you do." He reached over and brushed my hair out of my eyes, tucked it behind my ears. "As someone separate from my father, from his cause. Being with you makes me feel stronger, like I'm … I don't know, a braver person when you're around."

It was the most romantic thing I'd ever heard in my life. I went up on my toes and kissed him again. And once more after that, just because it made me happy.

Then I threaded my fingers through his and the three of us walked home.

ALSO BY C.P. RIDER

SPIKED

SUMMONED

EARP & CHANDRA (novella)

SABOTAGED

SHATTERED

EXPIRED

SHIFTED (July 2021)

DEAD END with Alex Pitones

Thanks for reading *Dead End*!

If you liked this book, please consider leaving a review on the retailer site where you found it. It helps a lot.

For a FREE audio recording and updates on new releases, sign up for our mailing list at www.1waycafepodcast.com

Thanks again for picking up *Dead End*.

ACKNOWLEDGMENTS

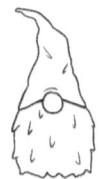

Special thanks to:

Mona Enderli, ReAnne Martin, Wendi Sotis, Shannon Gallagher, and Coralie Tate. We're so grateful for your ideas and guidance.

JeriAnn Stoklas for always being there.

Our families for your unwavering support and unending love.

ABOUT THE AUTHORS

Alex Pitones is a paranormal and urban fantasy writer and podcaster. Her podcast, *The One Way Cafe*, based on the cafe in *Dead End* releases in 2021. You can find her at www.1waycafepodcast.com or on Instagram.

C. P. Rider writes paranormal and urban fantasy romance. You can find her at www.cprider.com or on Facebook.

instagram.com/1_way_cafe
facebook.com/urbanfantasyromance